UNDER ITALIAN STARS

The Abruzzo Series

Barry Lillie

Barry Lillie

Copyright © Barry Lillie 2024

Cover design © Flatfield Books

The moral right of Barry Lillie to be identified as the author of this work has been asserted in accordance with the Copyright, Designs and Patents Act of 1988.

All rights reserved. No part of this publication may be reproduced, stored in a retrieval system, or transmitted in any form or by any means, electronic, mechanical, photocopying, recording, or otherwise, without the prior permission of the copyright owner of this book.

This novel is entirely a work of fiction. The names, characters and incidents portrayed within are the product of the author's imagination. Any resemblance to actual people living or dead is entirely coincidental.

For news about new releases and free content sign up for Barry's Book Club at:

www.barrylillie.com

Barry Lillie

For Susie

Travelling is the ruin of all happiness!
There's no looking at a building after seeing Italy.

Fanny Burney (1752-1840)
English novelist and playwright

Barry Lillie

Aldo I

Sitting opposite his uncle's bed, Aldo watched as Giacomo instinctively reached up and rubbed at the scar above his right eye socket.

Just muscle memory, he thought. Knowing the old man had no recollection of how he'd sustained the injury that had left the groove in his skull.

Giacomo's memory or lack of it had been a big part of his family's life and as the months since the injury had slid into years, their frustration had sunk beneath acceptance.

The orange glow from the streetlights outside bled into the room casting a jaundiced hue across the old man's face as he lifted his shoulders off the pillow to sit up. Aldo followed Giacomo's eyes across the room towards the photograph hanging on the wall. A woman smiled out from behind the glass. A woman who for decades had been a stranger to the family, and a woman Giacomo couldn't remember.

The ceiling fan spun but did little to prevent the dusty heat of the Naples evening from filling the tiny room. Outside the sound of mandolins and accordions drifted upwards from the pizzeria below at odds with the American rock music from the bar next door.

Aldo rose from his seat and closed the balcony doors that did little to shut out the noise, he poured a glass of tepid water from a flask and held it to his uncle's lips. As he sipped the excess spilled down his chin.

After drying the old man's face Aldo eased Giacomo back into a sleeping position and as his rheumy eyes looked up at the ceiling, he wondered what thoughts were passing through his uncle's mind.

Sitting back in the old chair Aldo waited until sleep came to Giacomo. He refreshed the water flask beside his bed and tucked in the bedclothes to keep the old man secure.

Sitting at the kitchen table Aldo poured himself a glass of grappa, his attention was briefly taken by the wailing sound of an ambulance outside and picking up the newspaper he settled himself into another night of waiting for the hours between evening and morning to pass.

Chapter One

Rachel squeezed her eyes hard together to prevent the tears from forming and removed the shirt from the wardrobe took a deep breath and slid it from its hanger. After folding it she placed it on top of the chest of drawers under the open window. Outside the May sun was high in the sky and the scent of lilacs drifted inside, the comforting spring air was at cross purposes with the miserable atmosphere inside the bedroom.

Rachel repeated the process until the last of Marco's work shirts were ready to be placed neatly inside one of the black plastic bags that she'd bought especially for this purpose. This was a job she'd been putting off for weeks – it seemed so final – but now, every time she saw his clothes, she saw him. And the hurt inside her was fed again.

The questions she had been left with since her husband's death continued to resurface, How could he suddenly die? She knew most of the answers, the doctors' had explained everything to her several times, but still, she couldn't believe that Marco, a fit and active man of thirty-three had had a fatal heart attack. He'd complained of heartburn a few times but he'd never suspected anything serious. None of it seemed fair, they had so much to live for and now all she had was a wardrobe filled with his clothes and memories.

After carrying the bags downstairs and placing them in the hall she walked into the kitchen, took a bottle of wine from the rack and a glass from the draining board and returned to the bedroom.

Rachel looked at the cardboard tube holding her husband's ashes and said, "I've finally got around to sorting out your clothes." She couldn't remember when she had first started talking to his ashes, but now she moved him from room to room to keep him with her. She gave him a rundown of her day as she cooked dinner and wished him a 'good morning' as she woke each day.

Getting back to the job in hand she decided to tackle the drawers containing her husband's socks and underwear. Removing socks, balled up into pairs she was dropping them inside a plastic bag when she picked up a ball that was his festive pair. Unfolding them to reveal a Christmas tree and the word 'Noël' knitted into the ankle she felt a new batch of tears rising. "No you don't," she told herself as she re-balled the socks and dropped them inside the bag.

Picking up the wine, she unscrewed the cap and poured herself a generous measure, telling Marco she had every right to drink at this time of the day. "That's one of the benefits of being married to an Italian," she said, raising her glass to his cardboard tube. "A more relaxed attitude to wine drinking during the day."

Marco, although British born had inherited his parents' attitude to alcohol and frowned upon public displays of drunkenness. Rachel had once questioned him about why it appeared that the Italians drank more than the Brits but were never seen stumbling around drunk. "It's not what you drink, but how much you drink," he had said, "and importantly when you drink."

Without taking a sip of her wine she placed the glass back on the windowsill and went back to the chest of drawers and began to remove the T-shirts neatly folded inside. As she reached in, her fingers brushed over a cardboard folder. Pushing the T-shirt aside she removed it and looking inside saw it contained a handful of photocopied pages written in Italian. "I can't deal with this now," she said. She dropped it onto the bed and went back to packing away her husband's clothes.

By early evening she'd almost finished. All that remained was the casual shirts. Marco's favourites that she had purposely saved until the end. She removed a black shirt with olive-coloured palm leaves covering the shoulders, as she folded it, she remembered him wearing it on a day trip to Herculaneum. An orange one that she had always disliked reminded her of a beach barbecue in the Maldives and the one with pink flamingos that he'd worn to a street market in Mallorca tugged at the corners of her mouth, forcing a smile. She checked the sleeve for the stain left by the fresh tomato a street vendor had handed him. Her mind replayed the memory, of Marco biting into the red fruit and the juice running down his wrist and onto the cuff.

She drank the remaining wine in her glass and then removed a Dolce and Gabbana grey print from its hanger. Marco's favourite shirt, holding it against her cheek recreating the last time he'd worn it when she'd rested her head on his shoulder. She picked up another shirt and buried her nose into it, hoping to find his smell still there. It wasn't. Every shirt had been laundered; his fragrance removed. Rachel searched for it, sniffing at one, then another, grabbing at them frantically and inhaling the fabrics, until she collapsed sobbing and exhausted sleep took over.

Later when she woke up, she looked at herself in the mirrored wardrobe and said, "Rachel, You look like shit." The shadowy circles under her eyes matched the dark stripe of roots showing through the red-coloured hair that hung lank and lifeless around her shoulders that seemed to be permanently sagging. She wondered when she had started to look so old and scraping her hair back, she rose from the bed, picked up the wine bottle and took a mouthful before walking into the en-suite and splashing her face with cold water.

Returning to the bedroom, she drank the remainder of the wine in her glass and lifting the duvet, she slid beneath it and shivered as her skin came into contact with the cool cotton. Rachel knew her skin's reaction had less to do with the temperature of the mattress and more to do with the loneliness of the space she had shared with Marco. As she lay looking up through the blackness her mind replayed the events of the day and sleep didn't come. Rachel was used to passing the seemingly endless hours of darkness looking up at the ceiling as questions careered around inside her head. Facts collided with anger and memories became wishes.

Getting up again, she poured herself another glass of wine before taking the folder she'd found earlier and opening it. Sat with her legs under the duvet and the glass of wine on her bedside table, she ran her hands over the buff-coloured cardboard surface wondering why Marco had hidden it away.

Inside were cadastral copies relating to property and although Marco had taught her enough of the language to be confidently fluent, parts of the document's contents went over her head. What she did understand was that she was looking at a recently drafted *rogito notarile* that stated that her husband was the new owner of a hotel.

The last document in the folder was an invoice from a solicitor with a small envelope stapled to it. She lifted the flap and removed a plastic card: A bank card. An Italian bank card and turning it over in her hand, she saw Marco's signature.

"How does Marco own a hotel?" she said aloud, "More importantly, why does Marco own a hotel? Where did the money come from and when, if he did, go to Italy?" Opening another envelope, she saw airline tickets for flights to Rome in both his name and hers. She looked at the flight date and it stabbed at her. The flights had been booked for the day after he had died.

She let the papers slide across the duvet and looked for her phone. She scrolled through the contacts and just before pressing the connect button she stopped herself. "I can't go back to calling Louise in the early hours again," she said and swapped the phone for her wine, lay against the pillows as the thoughts in her head became crowded with more questions, and sleep moved further away.

Chapter Two

Rachel moved Marco's ashes into the kitchen as she prepared a green salad and popped a homemade lasagne into the oven. "Louise is coming over for dinner," she told him, "so before she arrives, I'll have to move you into the sitting room, she won't want to be eating with you watching her." She allowed herself a small laugh, knowing anyone on the outside might find her conversations with a cardboard tube odd, but it helped her to make sense of his passing and her feelings of loss.

She was grating a garlic clove over slices of ciabatta when the doorbell rang. Wiping her hands on a tea towel she opened the front door.

"Ta-Dah," Louise said holding up two bottles of prosecco. "I've brought the lady petrol." She stepped into the hallway and seeing the black bags nodded towards them, "You have been busy. I'm proud of you."

"Thanks for saying you would take Marco's things to the charity shop for me. I've bagged it all up. The bin men took the bag of underwear this morning so I'm guessing that's heading off to landfill. I'd do it myself but I can't face it."

"It's no problem," said Louise.

I won't hug you yet, I'm covered in garlic."

"Probably best not to. I'll put the bags in the car while the door is open." Rachel returned to garlic grating and parsley chopping while trying to ignore the sound of the bags moving from the hall into the back of Louise's Hyundai.

Louise heeled the door closed, kicked off her shoes and padded into the kitchen. "What's going on?" Rachel looked up at her confused. "The prosecco isn't open."

A cork was popped and as their dinner heated through the friends retired into the sitting room and sat together on the sofa. Louise leaned over and kissed Rachel on the cheek, she turned, her eyes questioning. "That's from Ben."

"Tell him thanks, I appreciate it."

For several minutes they sat in companionable silence. They'd been friends for so long they could just appreciate being in a room together and saying nothing. Rachel remembered them both meeting at sixth-form college and how they'd originally been love rivals, both vying for Marco's attention. Louise had conceded defeat and afterwards, the two of them had called a truce and formed an unbreakable bond and had been inseparable ever since.

The timer on the oven pinged and Rachel jumped to her feet, "Garlic bread's ready, can you light the candles for me?"

When Rachel returned with the bowl of salad and the aromatic ciabatta slices Louise was already sitting at the dining table, the candles bathed the room in a soft glow. The warmed plates were followed by the lasagne and Rachel stood up serving as Louise watched her closely. "What?" she said cutting into the pasta.

"You. You're a natural at looking after people." Louise offered her plate.

"Maybe that'll be my next job, a hostess."

"Isn't that just a fancy title for an escort?"

"Cheeky bitch."

The ladies talked shop as they ate their dinner, the conversation starting with a whey-faced temp who was working in sales. "Honestly, she gave him a three and a nine," Louise said before stuffing the last of her bread into her mouth.

"Martin from accounts?" Rachel said, her voice rising a semitone." Louise still chewing nodded her head. "How can she give him three for looks, but nine for shag-ability?"

"I know it's insane."

"I can't see how he can score so low in looks but so high in shag-ability. Surely the two must be close score-wise?"

"Well," Louise said leaning forward, conspiratorially before removing her phone from her handbag. "Not at all. Okay, Martin isn't the best-looking bloke in the office, but he does have a… well take a look."

Rachel took the offered phone and looked at the screen. "Ouch, that's huge. Is it real?"

"Apparently so. He had a thing with a girl in dispatch they sent each other sexts regularly."

Rachel said, "That's not normal" and handed back the phone before bursting into laughter.

"It's good to see you laugh, it's been ages," Louise said reaching over and squeezing Rachel's hand.

Rachel nodded gently, her head barely moving. "I was worried about all of this," she indicated towards the table. "The lasagne was one Marco had made and stored in the freezer. I thought I'd break down eating it, but I've surprised myself." Louise didn't reply, allowing Rachel to say everything she wanted, and needed to say. "This is the first dinner I've eaten at this table since…"

Louise reached over and placed her hand on Rachel's.

"He usually sits where you're sitting, but tonight I've left him in the bedroom."

"Best place for a man," Louise joked.

"I'd give anything…"

"Well, if you want my opinion, for what it's worth," Louise said, "I don't think you've fully got used to Marco being gone yet."

"I never want to get used to him being gone." Rachel stared straight ahead, and her vision began to blur. The pricking that had become familiar to her began stabbing at her eyes.

I'm sorry, I didn't mean to…"

"It's okay. You'd think I'd be over the tears and snot stage by now."

Once dinner was finished, Rachel stacked the dishwasher as Louise made a pot of coffee and the ladies retired to the sofa again. Pressing a remote, music played at a discrete volume and Louise poured the coffees. "There was something I wanted to talk to you about," Rachel said. "As I was clearing out Marco's drawers, I found a folder full of Italian paperwork." Louise nodded, listening. "Before Marco's accident, he'd been to Italy to see a lawyer."

"Was he in trouble?"

"No. Turns out he owned a hotel."

"What, he bought a hotel?"

"I'm not sure, it's all a mystery. I've looked at the notary papers and checked them out online and it all appears legal. But how and why, I haven't a clue."

"So, what will you do?"

"I'm not sure. I've booked an appointment with Marco's lawyer for next week."

"Video call or in-person?"

"In Italy. I fly into Rome, hire a car and drive to Lanciano." Rachel opened a box of chocolate truffles and placed it in front of Louise.

"How long will you stay?"

"I'm not sure, maybe a week or two. I'll have to stay for as long as it takes to sort it all out."

Louise dropped a chocolate into her mouth and then said, "So, when are you leaving?"

"Tomorrow. I've booked my flight online."

"Bloody hell, tomorrow. That's a bit sudden, isn't it?"

"It is, but the sooner I get there the quicker I can find out what this hotel nonsense is all about."

"Mind you, I do think a short break in Italy will do you the power of good. Do you need me to look after the house?"

"Oli is coming to stay for a while."

"How is your brother?"

"Lurching from one crisis to another as usual. He was supposed to arrive tonight but there's been no word."

***

Later as Rachel was about to go to bed there was a knock at her front door, pulling her dressing gown around herself she opened the door on the chain and peered around it to find Oli standing there grinning. "What time do you call this?"

"I was delayed. Are you going to let me in or what?" Rachel closed the door, undid the chain and opened the front door. "Here." Oli thrust a box towards her. "It's fragile," he said as he bent down to pick up the supermarket carrier bags overflowing with the clothes stuffed into them.

Within minutes of her brother being in her home, it looked like a riot had taken place. The sofa and chairs in the sitting room were covered with clothes and shoes. Boxes littered the floor, most with gaming cables snaking out of them. Rachel left Oli to sort himself out and went into the kitchen to reheat some of the leftover lasagne in the microwave.

As he ate his dinner Rachel began to lay down the ground rules for his stay at the house. "You cannot use my bedroom. Don't forget to mow the lawn. I'd prefer it if you have a friend to stay over that it's someone you know and not some random you've picked up off Grindr."

"What do you take me for?" Oli asked, trying his best to look suitably offended.

"Oli. You forget I know you better than you know yourself. There are boxes of beers in the garage, Marco's stash, feel free to drink them or they'll just sit there going to waste."

"I appreciate you putting me up," Oli said.

"You'll be doing me a favour too. I'm not sure how long I'll be away for."

"I hope this hotel business turns out okay for you. Do you think you'll sell it?"

"I think so, I can't see I'll have a use for it. Saying that it could just be a pile of old stones, habitable means different things to the Italians."

"Would you like me to drive you to the airport?"

"Thanks, but I've booked an Uber. You'll need to stay home and sort out all of your stuff that's cluttering up my sitting room." Oli went to reply but Rachel's raised eyebrow prevented him, "And don't think I won't be asking Louise to drop by to check that everything is neat and tidy."

"I'll be on my best behaviour," Oli held up crossed fingers and smiled, "and I'll take care of Marco, although the conversation will be one-sided."

"There's no need," Rachel replied. "I'm taking him with me." Oli's face said it all as his mouth fell open. "I have travel documents from the undertaker and crematorium and my lawyer has emailed me the permission from Italy."

"Right then," Oli said, "Looks like it's just me, Billy no mates."

"You'll cope." Rachel placed a kiss on her brother's cheek and after saying goodnight she made her way upstairs.

That night as she slid beneath the duvet, she looked across the room to where her packed suitcase stood. Her passport, tickets and hotel confirmation were double-checked into her flight bag and after saying 'goodnight' to Marco she turned over, knowing that this time tomorrow she'd be slipping between the sheets of a hotel bed in Abruzzo.

Aldo II

Aldo placed his coffee cup down gently, hoping the clack of the cup against the saucer wouldn't disturb Giacomo, who was sleeping through the noise of Naples that clambered in through the open window. Sirens and car horns. Raised voices and barking dogs. Noises that Giacomo had spent his life sleeping through and yet his nephew worried about the chink of china upon china.

Giacomo stirred with a cough, a phlegmy hack. Aldo picked up the jug of water and poured some into a glass in readiness, his uncle would be thirsty.

With eyes as watery as the contents of his glass, Giacomo looked across the room, his eyes falling upon the photograph which held no recognition. Hanging there it had become a part of the furniture, established and unimportant, overlooked by its normalcy.

Giacomo's trembling hand caused the emerald ring he wore to knock against the glass and Aldo reached out and retrieved it. With the glass back on the bedside table, Giacomo beckoned his nephew closer and with his mouth touching his nephew's ear he whispered, "Yesterday the priest came, I told him I don't think I have long left." Aldo moved his head away and shook it, but Giacomo's raised finger prevented him from disagreeing. "Listen, Aldo, I have been seeing visions in my sleep, maybe they're memories, maybe they're secrets that I have carried with me for too long now."

The old man began coughing and allowed himself to be aided in sipping at the glass of water and after Aldo had settled him back against his pillow, he said. "Sleep now uncle, we shall talk in the morning."

Aldo rose from the chair beside the bed and walked towards the door, he turned to see Giacomo. The man looked small against his pillow. He touched his lip and then threw the kiss across the room to the ancient man and before he closed the door Giacomo said, "*Aldo. Non dimenticare é molto importante.*"

"*Dormi zio. possiamo parlare domani.*" After telling Giacomo they could talk the next day he closed the bedroom door quietly.

Chapter Three

Rachel watched as her lawyer; Dario Bianchi read the documents that she had brought from England. She looked at the patch of hair thinning at his crown and wondered if he knew he was going bald. He looked up and smiled, his dark eyes were comforting and his slight lisp when he spoke made her feel at ease.

She had been surprised to discover that Marco had not purchased the hotel but had inherited it. *Another secret to unravel*, she thought. "I just assumed he had bought the hotel."

Dario had confirmed that the hotel had belonged to Marco's great aunt, and he had been the last surviving relative. "It took quite a while to find him. I believe his mother and aunt had lost contact many years before." Dario looked back at the papers in front of him, "Marco had said it was to be a surprise for you. He was planning to bring you over to explain everything. It's unfortunate that he never got to do this with you."

Unfortunate, she thought, *there's a word I've not heard yet*.

"When you emailed me, I was to receive the news, saddened."

It was obvious that English was not Dario's first language, but she liked his disjointed phrasing. "It was all very sudden. He had a problem with his heart that he didn't know about."

"And so young still."

"Yes, he was only thirty-three and I didn't expect to be a widow at thirty-two."

"*Certamente*. And now you must your life pick up again."

Rachel nodded and smiled at Dario's attempt to be benevolent albeit in mangled English.

Dario opened another folder and took out more papers and a brown envelope. "The transfer of the deeds will take a few weeks, but I'm happy to give you the keys that Marco left with me. I have spoken with the manager at the bank, and he has confirmed that Marco opened an account, but until the inheritance is finalised, he told me that he's not at liberty to say how much money there is."

"I wasn't expecting there to be any money."

Dario nodded to confirm that there was a sum of money and he held up the copy of the will Marco had made with him.

"As you may know, In Italy the law is different," he said as he played with the slender gold ring on his wedding finger. "Under Italian law, we have what is called, *legittima*, which means other relatives can inherit. You as the wife come under, *successione necessaria*, this means you are automatically entitled to your share."

"But Marco wasn't an Italian citizen, he was English."

"Yes, signora this is true, but his money is Italian." Rachel was about to speak again when he cut in. "I'm certain there will be nothing to worry about. This is Italy and here things take time." he handed her the brown envelope. "Here is a photocopy of the hotel's cadastral and the keys, also I have enclosed a letter from my practice confirming everything. You may need this if the *Carabiniere* come to visit."

"Thank you."

"I have arranged for you to obtain a fiscal code; you will need this for the bank account, but as I have already said, I can't see there being any problems. Your husband's will is very specific."

Rachel thanked Dario and shook his hand before leaving the office. Despite having many questions answered her mind was now filled with many more new ones. She stepped out onto the street and squinting in the midday sunshine she looked inside her handbag for her sunglasses and collided with someone.

"*Mi scusi*," the man said.

"I'm so sorry."

"*Niente*," he responded, his smile revealing perfect white teeth. He turned the corner and she watched him as he walked away, taking in his slender hips, his defiantly horizontal shoulders and the mess of dark curls touching his shirt collar.

***

Rachel had enjoyed her afternoon in Lanciano. She'd had lunch at a small family-run trattoria in a small piazza she'd discovered just a few minutes' walk from the main street. She walked off lunch, strolling through the narrow side streets taking respite from the afternoon sun before chancing upon a communal garden, where she spent an hour sitting on a bench beside a fountain, allowing the cool air and sound of water to relax her, letting her process the meeting with Dario earlier.

As the evening crept in and the sun sank behind the cathedral on *Piazza del Plebiscito* she took a seat at a bar and ordered herself a spritzer. The shops were reopening for the evening trade and as she sipped her drink she watched as the quiet streets began to fill again for *passagiatta.* She marvelled at the couples who walked together seeing and more importantly being seen as they strolled up and down the *Corso*.

Engrossed in her people watching she was startled when the man from earlier stopped to speak with her. "Hello again. You have had a good day in town?" he opened his arms as he spoke indicating towards the buildings around them."

"Oh, hello," she said. "Yes, thank you I've had a relaxing day after my drive from Rome yesterday."

"You drove from *Roma*, was it your first time?"

"Yes, but I'm not sure I'd like to navigate my way around the giro again." She gave a small laugh and he reciprocated. "The journey was thankfully quiet after I'd left the city."

"There's very little traffic coming into Abruzzo," he shrugged and added, "But that is how we like it."

"I'm guessing this isn't a busy tourist area then?"

"Oh yes, the tourists that come here love it. The Germans and British come to enjoy our hospitality and coastline. Are you here on holiday?" He pulled out the seat opposite her and raised his eyes asking permission to sit.

"I came here on business, but it looks like I might be staying a little longer than anticipated, so I'm hoping to do some sightseeing."

"You must see the *Chiesa di Santa Maria Maggiore*, it is very beautiful."

"I'll put it on my list of places to visit."

"I hope you don't mind me saying. Your Italian is good." Rachel thanked him and told him that her husband was Italian, and he'd taught her. "Ah, and your husband is here in Lanciano with you?"

"No," she picked up her glass took a larger than intended mouthful of spritzer and started to cough. He handed her a napkin and she apologised before telling him that she had been recently widowed.

"I'm sorry," he said, and the conversation dried up with them sitting in silence until a waiter dropped a menu on the table between them. "Would you like to eat with me?"

"I'm sorry but I'm not –"

"It's just dinner."

"Very well…" Realising they hadn't been introduced she offered him her hand and said, "I'm Rachel."

He shook her hand and added, "My name is Luca." Beckoning over the waiter he ordered two glasses of Aperol. "Have you had *aperitivo* before?" Rachel shook her head as the orange-coloured drinks arrived. "You cannot enjoy dinner without one, it is the law." He winked, making sure she knew he was joking and she picked up the glass and sucked the bittersweet drink up the straw. "*Buono?*"

"*Si, buono,*" she replied.

"Do you mind if we speak in English?" he asked and she agreed, thankful as her day speaking Italian had become mentally tiring.

Over a complimentary platter of olives and bruschetta, she told Luca about the hotel that Marco had inherited and how she was hoping to visit it.

"I'm not sure of the address. My lawyer gave me some paperwork earlier, maybe I'll find it written there when I look later."

They ordered sea bass and when the waiter arrived with their dinner Rachel was surprised to see the whole fish. She watched as Luca deftly sliced off the top fillet and then removed the skeleton from his fish in one piece. His hands were slim, almost feminine with long slender fingers and well-manicured nails. She wondered what it was he did for a living, dressed in a blue linen suit she guessed he was an office worker. He noticed she was watching him he looked up and she looked away.

She began hacking at her fish, telling him that in England they'd probably be served just the fillets. "Let me help," he said, and leaning over he removed the skeleton for her.

After their plates had been cleared away the waiter brought out two small glasses of *limoncello* and Rachel felt for the first time that she was experiencing life like an Italian. The air was still and warm and the sound of humanity spilled out from the open doors on the balconies of the palazzo opposite. Televisions mingled with the rattle of saucepans and laughter blended with the chastising of children as families prepared for dinner.

Rachel refused a second glass of limoncello as Luca accepted his. She watched as he sipped at the yellow drink, his full bottom lip pressed against the small glass taking her attention away from their conversation.

"So?" he asked bringing her back from her thoughts.

"Sorry?" she shook her head.

"So, what do you know about this mysterious hotel?"

Rachel removed the folder from her bag and placed it on the table. She removed the cadastral and handed it to Luca, he studied the plan of the property and then looking closely at something handwritten in the corner he said. "It's in *Sant'Andrea*," he said, "it's at a place good... for..." He stumbled over his words for the first time, "*Come si dice...* how you say... *qui vicino*?"

"Nearby?"

"Yes, nearby. I think it is nearby a place good for the holiday people." Rachel smiled; like Dario's, Luca's sentence structure was becoming more appealing with every word he spoke. "I have an idea of the general area, a few questions for the local people and we should find it."

Luca insisted on paying the bill and they left the bar, with Luca walking her back to her hotel. Rachel felt at ease beneath the apricot-coloured glow of the streetlights. It's surprising what a change of scenery can do, she thought as they stopped outside the hotel.

"Thank you for a lovely evening," she said shaking the hand he offered her.

"I too have had a lovely evening. I hope we can see each other soon again, to look for your hotel."

"I'd like that." Rachel turned and began walking through the hotel entrance when Luca called out.

"I am free tomorrow after 11.00. Maybe I can take you to show you where the hotel, I think it is?"

Realising it was out of character and before she had time to think about it, she found herself saying yes.

Chapter Four

Rachel had woken feeling awkward about having had dinner with Luca the night before. Nothing had happened, it had just been dinner *and* he had said he could maybe help her to locate the hotel. But still, she felt uncomfortable having done something so out of character and so soon after Marco's death. There seemed to be only one solution to assuage her feelings of guilt, so she took the tube containing Marco's ashes out of their box and sitting on the bed, she told him everything about the previous day. "If anyone could see me, they'd think I was certifiable," she joked as she ran her fingers down the smooth surface of the cardboard tube.

Having spoken with Marco she felt better, purged of any guilt and picking up the ashes she slid them back inside their box and after choosing her outfit she went to shower.

Dressing in a simple white T-shirt beneath a green see-through blouse with small golden roses embroidered in panels and three-quarter green trousers Rachel went downstairs for breakfast.

The dining room looked welcoming, tables were laid with crisp white linen and rose-coloured napkins complimented the blush-coloured walls. It was already quite warm outside and the doors leading onto the terrace were open the sheer carmine voile hung at the windows, and moved lazily in the breeze.

She chose a table overlooking the garden and was watching the hotel gardener as he went about his duties when a waitress spoke to her. *"Buongiorno signora."* The girl placed a tiny bottle of pear juice onto her table, *"Caffe?"*

"Yes please." Before her coffee arrived, Rachel returned her attention to the garden and as she watched the man trimming the borders beneath an oleander hedge, she wondered if her hotel had a garden. Spotting her, the old man tipped his hat and smiled as the waitress appeared again.

"Do you have plans for today *signora*?"

"Yes, a friend is coming over and we're going to drive along the coast."

"It is nice weather for a drive, not too hot. I hope you enjoy it."

Stirring a sweetener into her coffee Rachel breathed in the heady aroma of fresh coffee and the sweet smell of warm pastries that blanketed the room. Over at the far end of the room, a table was laid with cornetti and she took her time selecting one with an apricot jam filling. Beside it was a toasting machine and she watched as a man slid two slices of bread inside the silver box. She smiled knowing that after they'd been swallowed by the machine and transported beneath the grill, they'd be returned just warm and in need of a second trip inside the toaster to gain any colour.

After breakfast, she collected her sunglasses and hat from her room and as he arrived in the lobby she found Luca was already waiting for her. He leaned in with a traditional kiss on both cheeks and asked if she'd slept well.

"I did, I fell asleep almost at once."

"It's the Abruzzese air, it must agree with you."

It took just minutes to leave the town behind and Rachel looked out of the window as the Alfa Romeo snaked along the coast road with Luca pointing out points of interest. He slowed down so that she could get a better view of a trabocco and as he explained how the wooden fishing structure worked, she stared out at the greenish blue of the Adriatic. Looking up the coast she saw other fishing platforms stretching out seawards, and said, "I can see now why it's called the trabocchi coast."

The car swept around a series of bends until the beaches started to give way to houses, each one in an enviable spot overlooking the sea. They drove through the centre of a small town where tables lined the pavements. "This is San Vito," Luca said, "very busy in the summer." He pointed to a table where four people were sitting in the sun, each one with an enormous cone of ice cream in their hand. "In the summer every one of these restaurants is filled each day, people come for the seafood and ice-creams. I think your hotel is very close, which would make it good to catch the tourists." Rachel laughed and he glanced across at her questioning.

"Catch," she said, "you make them sound like fish." Luca smiled and started to laugh. "Maybe my translation is not good."

"No, it's perfect for a place where seafood is served."

"*Assolutamente*."

Leaving the town behind, the car skirted around another handful of bends before they saw a sign for Sant'Andrea. They turned into a narrow lane that ran parallel to the coastline until it came to an end where a small white house stood, its exterior bleached bone-white after years in the Italian sun. Luca stopped and looked up the narrow track that seemed to lead somewhere, and putting the car in gear he drove past the white house and stopped beside two large stone pillars on which hung wrought iron gates, that seemed to be hanging there by more by luck than their hinges.

"Look," Rachel said. "You can just make out the word, hotel carved into the pillar."

"Then this must be what we are looking for." Luca killed the engine and getting out of the car Rachel followed him as he walked through the gateway into the hotel grounds. The garden was a snarl of unchecked shrubs and waist-high grasses. A large tree loomed up in front of them, its branches dangerously heavy with a climbing rose that scrambled up it. They pushed through the undergrowth startling a cat, which protested with a hiss before seeking refuge in a mass of contorted brambles. Adjacent to a colonnade of cypress, they could make out an arc of gravel, littered with years of dead leaves as it swept upwards, away from them before disappearing beneath unchecked undergrowth.

Stepping around overgrown shrubbery they were able to take in the whole of the property for the first time and Rachel's emotions suddenly went into free-fall. She didn't know how she felt, was it awe and wonder, or was it fear and uncertainty? She was in awe of the three-storey building that was larger than she had anticipated but also uncertain of her ability to do anything with it. She removed her sunglasses to get a better look, mentally noting that it certainly looked very different to the modern hotel she'd left earlier that morning. The walls were rendered in a pink wash that decades ago must have looked regal. Over the years the colour had diminished and in parts, the surface was stippled with moss and lichens.

The front of the property was dominated by an impressive arched entrance where carved into the Maiella stone was, L*e Stelle* – The Stars. Its once magnificent wooden doors were now faded and sundried and fastened together by a thick chain. All the ground floor windows were boarded over, but the windows on the upper levels, each complete with a small, rusting balcony were just empty holes; blind eyes staring forward. "Looks like no one has been here for years," Luca said.

"I wonder what state the inside is in."

The doors had two crescent-shaped handles with the padlocked chain entwined around them. Rachel opened her handbag and removed the ring of keys that Dario had given her. There was an assortment of regular sized keys and one very large old one, she handed Luca the ring and he unlocked the padlock before removing the rusty chain, the redness staining his hands. He let it fall to the ground, snaking noisily against the stone steps. The large old key fitted the lock and with some force it turned, and he pushed the door. The wood fought against him, refusing to open. "It must be bolted from the inside. Wait here, I'll see if there's another way in."

As she stood alone at the entrance Rachel turned to survey the garden, she liked the line of cypress trees and imagined it was once very welcoming. The front of the hotel was facing the coast and as she looked through the old gateway, she could see the sky and the sea framed between the stone pillars. She had a sudden thought. *Had Marco visited the hotel?* or had he died never seeing it, *had he enjoyed this view?* Before her thoughts could take her to a place she didn't want to go to, the sound of a bolt being drawn back pushed them aside.

The double doors opened inwards, and she walked into the lobby, her footsteps sounding dull on the tiled floor. In the corner was a dark wooden structure with faded marquetry panels and pigeonholes behind it with hooks for keys. "This must have been the reception desk," she said. An old chair was the room's only other piece of furniture and she brushed away the dust from the back of the chair to reveal creased leather "This chair is fabulous; it just needs some love and attention to breathe life back into it."

Four tall, slim windows took up most of the wall beside the main entrance and behind the wooden boards, Rachel assumed they looked out over the front garden and down towards the little white house. Another, smaller arched doorway led through into what had been the dining room and like the lobby it had a high ceiling with ornate plaster cornices, their gilt long since diminished.

Rachel suddenly shrieked and Luca turned to see her pointing at a rat skeleton, "I think we'll see more of those before we have finished looking around.

He opened a door and peered inside. A narrow corridor lined with cupboards led down to a door with a sign barely clinging to the wood that read, '*privato*'. The door opened into a suite of rooms and pointing out the small kitchen Luca said, "This must have been the owner's accommodation."

Rachel's ringtone disturbed their exploration and looking at the screen she turned to Luca, "It's Dario."

Luca walked into the kitchen leaving her to take the call in private, when she entered the room he asked, "Good news?"

"Dario says he has spoken with the estate lawyers and they have confirmed the legality of Marco's will so ownership should pass to me in the next few weeks. He also said he has a meeting with the bank later to determine when Marco's money will be released."

"So, it looks like you'll be flying back and returning at a later date."

"I'm not sure. Dario thinks it will all take around three to four weeks, but I can't afford to stay at the hotel in Lanciano for that long.

"I imagine it's quite expensive to stay there."

"It is rather. Looks like I have no choice but to find a cheaper hotel."

Why not let me help you?"

"How?"

"I have a friend with a small apartment in town. Not glamorous, he could let you rent it short term."

"I'm not sure," she said removing her sunglasses and looking across at him. "As I said, I don't know how long I'll be staying, and I wouldn't want to be any bother."

"Bother?" he asked, his brow furrowing.

"Trouble. I don't want to be any trouble."

"It is no trouble. It's only four rooms, not expensive. I will today ask him." Rachel smiled but was evasive when it came to a reply.

Returning to the lobby Rachel looked at the sweeping staircase and imagined it must have looked grand with men in smart suits and ladies in gowns descending on their way to dinner. She suddenly felt overwhelmed and steadied herself on the banister. As her hand met the ball of wood on the top of the newel post she realised it wasn't smooth, its surface had been carved craters, giving it a moon-like appearance. Running her fingers over its surface, tracing the dips and hollows, impressed with the attention to detail she took control of her breathing.

Before they could move up the stairs a cough sounded and turning, they saw two Carabinieri officers standing in the doorway. "*Salve*," the taller one said removing his cap, followed by the customary, "*Documenti*." Luca removed his identity card from his back pocket and handed it over as Rachel looked inside her handbag for her passport and the letter that Dario had given her.

Satisfied, the officers handed back the paperwork and the shorter of the two asked Rachel her intention. "I'm not sure yet," she said folding Dario's letter and slipping it back inside its envelope.

"Well, whatever you decide signora," said the taller officer putting his cap back on. "*Buona fortuna*, and…" smirking he added, "Good luck with Rosa too."

"Rosa?" Rachel asked following the officers outside and the shorter nodded down the lane towards the little white house, where an old woman stood with her arms folded looking up at the hotel.

Aldo III

Aldo carried the bowl holding the remains of Giacomo's dinner into the kitchen and poured the old man a glass of Amaro. His shrunken stomach may not be able to hold a full bowl of *pastina*, but there is always room for the customary shot of bitter digestivo.

Giacomo's hand shook as he tipped the herb spirit over his tongue and a small amount spilled out from the side of his mouth. Aldo leaned forward with a tissue, but his hand was gently pushed away by his uncle.

"I need to talk to you," Giacomo said, "come close, my voice is weak."

Because the old man had been lucid all morning Aldo moved his chair closer and listened.

"You must have heard the story about the Medici diamond?" Aldo nodded his head. "It's now known as the Florentine diamond and used to belong to the Grand Duke of Tuscany. It passed into many hands but after The Great War ended in 1918 it went missing." Giacomo saw the puzzled look on his nephew's face and continued. "Don't ask why I remember these details, just accept what I'm telling you before it is lost inside my head again." Aldo pulled his chair closer. "At first, I thought I was dreaming, but each night the dream has resurfaced and I've come to see it not as fancy but as fact." He paused to cough and spit a gob of green phlegm into a handkerchief.

"Uncle?" Aldo said, the worry evident in his voice. Giacomo took his nephew's hand in his and leaned in closer, the earthy smell of Amaro was still on his breath as he whispered, "The diamond came back to Italy where it belongs, and I am the last person to know of its whereabouts. I cannot die without telling you, otherwise it will be lost to the world forever."

"Where is it?" Aldo asked humouring the old man.

"The images in my head are grainy, but I'm certain a large building with an arched doorway is the stone's hiding place." Another bout of coughing followed, and Aldo assisted him with a sip of water before making him comfortable. Giacomo tried to speak again, but he was too weak to form the words and with his eyes sliding shut Aldo shook his head and dismissed the story as dementia-driven ramblings.

As Giacomo slept Aldo took out his phone and typed, 'Florentine Diamond' into the search bar. He scrolled through the many results, all of which told him that the lost gemstone was yellow and of Indian origin. The stone was sizeable at over 137 carats and there were various theories regarding its disappearance and alleged recutting. The most common myth is that the diamond was stolen from Switzerland and taken to South Africa.

Aldo cleared the screen and shook his head, Giacomo's story must be fantastical, especially as the legend of the diamond appears to be well-documented.

Chapter Five

Rachel woke to birdsong drifting in from the open balcony doors, she stretched and yawned noisily before pulling back the sheet, lying uncovered. She listened to the sounds of the morning as the piazza below awoke. The shutters of the pasticceria clattered as they rolled upwards. The hiss of the coffee machine in the espresso bar was followed by the uplifting aroma of fresh coffee, while the conversations of old men looking forward to a morning *caffè corretto* collided with each other before ricocheting off the walls of the buildings surrounding the square.

A week had passed since Luca had taken her to see the hotel and she was still undecided what to do. Her thoughts now tossed between restoration and making a new life for herself in Italy, or the option of selling it and going back to England. One thing she was certain of, was she couldn't make such a momentous decision without advice.

So much had happened recently, she had moved out of the hotel and into the apartment owned by Luca's friend. It was a charming place on the middle floor of a three-storey palazzo, it had a small open-plan living room with a balcony overlooking the piazza, a kitchen/diner that was tiny but serviceable – as was the bathroom. The spare bedroom was also small with another balcony, but the main bedroom was vast, a large airy space with a high ceiling painted with flowers and cherubs. As she lay on the metal-framed bed, she traced the gold-coloured cornice from one corner of the room to the other counting the plaster roses that blossomed from it.

After pulling on her bathrobe, she padded into the kitchen and made herself a pot of tea. She took a tray from the shelf above the cooker and placed alongside her tea things, a box dressed in a red ribbon. Taking the tray out to the balcony she placed it on the small table, opened the box of pastries she'd purchased the day before and enjoyed her breakfast in the sunshine. Bees in their striped vests buzzed above a flower filled window box. Butterflies danced in the motionless air, and she watched as a small green lizard with the poise of a prima ballerina walked across the narrow balcony rail. "I need to make a decision Mr Lizard," she said.

The green reptile stopped moving and its eyes connected with hers. "I think I need to do some research." She leant forward to select another pastry and the lizard darted into the window box and hid among the geraniums.

She savoured the last of her English breakfast tea before entering the bedroom. She looked across at the cardboard tube on the antique sideboard, "Morning Marco, I have some work to do, then it'll be decision time."

Showered and dressed in a thin cotton dress she came back into the sitting room, opened her bag and removed her laptop. After attaching it to a travel plug, she switched it on and waited for the pre-paid internet drive to kick in. Opening a web browser she typed into the search bar, 'running a hotel in Italy.' As Google searched for relevant links, she opened her email account and clicked through the waiting messages, just a couple of newsletters and a best wishes email from Oli that also asked her what day the wheelie bins were emptied. She left a message from Louise until last, she scanned through the questions asking what the weather was like. What did she think of the hotel and are the men as fit as they are on the television? Rachel smiled and flagged the email as important, intending to reply later that morning before returning to the searches Google had brought up.

She had become engrossed in the overabundance of websites advising anyone wanting to set up a business in Italy and was startled when a knock sounded on the apartment door. She glanced at the clock in the corner of the screen and realised a couple of hours had passed since she'd sat down.

Opening the door, she smiled to see Luca standing in the hallway. "I hope you haven't forgotten our meeting with Carlino," he said.

"No," Rachel said, "I got a bit side-tracked doing some internet research."

She grabbed her summer hat and bag and joined him inside the palazzo hallway where the air was several degrees cooler than inside the apartment.

***

"I'm not sure what I would do if I decided to restore the building," Rachel said as Luca drove along the SS16. "To be honest I don't know if I'd be good at running a hotel."

"Let's hear what Carlino says before you make any decisions. He might tell us it will be too expensive to repair."

As the car rounded a bend Luca said, "This is a good place to come for the beach." He pointed to his right. "No tourists come here, only local families." Rachel caught glimpses of rocky coves and tracks down to small intimate beaches between the clumps of bamboo fringing the road. Luca navigated a sharp bend and a *trabocco* came into view, he slowed to let Rachel get a better view of the wooden structure, which looked like a dragon jutting out into the sea.

"A lady in town told me some of them are used as restaurants," she said.

"This is true, but the fish they serve isn't always caught here. But it makes a nice romantic meal."

"I think I'm a long way away from romantic meals," Rachel said.

As Luca's car turned off the road and into the lane leading up to the hotel both he and Rachel spotted Rosa outside her house. "Slow down," Rachel asked winding down her window and calling to her neighbour to be. "Morning Rosa, are you well?"

"I guess so. I'm still alive," Rosa chuckled before adding, "There's a man with a briefcase up at the hotel."

"That'll be the geometra," Luca said leaning over so he could be seen.

"So, you're going ahead with plans to restore the place?"

"We'll see what he has to say first," Rachel said and waved as Luca drove up to the gates and parked his car.

"When did you and Rosa become friends?" Luca asked.

"I drove here a couple of days ago and introduced myself. She's a real character, but very welcoming."

"Hopefully that's a good omen," Luca said holding the car door open for Rachel before escorting her up to the hotel's entrance.

Inside the foyer, Rachel was introduced to Carlino, the builder that Luca had found to look at the property.

"*Piacere*," he said shaking Rachel's hand. "My assistant, Massimo, is upstairs with the geometra."

Luca excused himself and the two men set off upstairs leaving Rachel sitting in the old leather chair. As she listened to their footsteps on the floor above, she looked around the room as if taking it in for the first time. She glanced up at the ceiling and followed the cornice around the room. Something didn't look quite right; almost as if there had been a false ceiling added to it. She made a mental note to ask Carlino about it when he returned with Luca.

She walked across the reception area, running her hands across the plastered walls wondering what the building had seen over the years. There was something about the hotel that comforted her and she had a good feeling about it. She felt relaxed within its walls. Was she warming to the idea of staying she wondered?

The men returned from upstairs and the geometra continued taking measurements with a laser device as Luca and Carlino leaned on the reception desk studying some architectural drawings. They were deep in conversation and Rachel wanted to know what they were talking about but didn't want to interrupt. Just then in the entrance Rosa appeared. She called out a raspy "*Buongiorno*," then entered the foyer waving aloft a jug "*Caffè*," she said and from the pocket in her apron she retrieved a handful of thimble-sized paper cups which she lined up on the reception desk.

"Thank you, Rosa. This is very kind of you." Rachel said, grateful for someone to talk to. Luca introduced her to Carlino, and the old woman stabbed herself in the chest with an ancient thumb and said, "Rosa."

The geometra packed away his laser and notebook, telling them he had all the information he needed. He drank the coffee Rosa had poured for him and then had a hushed conversation with Carlino in the corner before saying goodbye and leaving.

Rosa took Rachel by the elbow and directed her through to the garden saying she wanted to show her the pool. "The pool?" Rachel replied, "I wasn't aware there was one."

Leaving Luca and Carlino to their drawings, the two women walked through the overgrown grass that looked like a fringe that had grown too long and touched the eyelashes. The air was filled with a sweet perfume, an intense almost sickly smell and Rosa pointed out the hedge covered with tiny white flowers.

"The jasmine hedges surround the pool area," said Rosa as she navigated her way between an overgrown gap in the green border. Stepping through Rachel saw a hole in the ground that was green and filled with what looked like years of decaying leaves. Between streamers of dried green algae, the pale blue tiles of the swimming pool could be seen. The pool was surrounded by wooden decking, most of it too rotten to walk on. Several discarded sun-loungers lay rusting and forgotten, their canvas covers dried out and shredded by the wind, making them look like strange skeletal creatures hiding in the tall grass.

A twig breaking underfoot caused them to turn around and they saw Luca approaching, "Look," Rachel called, "there's a pool."

"I think it will need a deep clean before it's ready for guests."

"Years ago, the pool was very popular," Rosa said.

"Do you think the hotel could attract many guests?" Rachel said turning to Rosa. The old lady shrugged her shoulders, her lips straightening out as she evaded the question.

Rachel turned and looked back towards the hotel's rear façade and a feeling of contentment swept over her. "I'm really quite taken with this place."

"It needs a lot of work," Luca said interrupting her reverie.

"It needs a lot of love," added Rosa who gave Luca a sidelong glance and then winked at Rachel before making her way back to her little white house.

"What did the builder say?" Rachel said as they made their way back inside.

As they walked Luca explained that Carlino had told him that the bones of the property were in good order and being close to the coast it was in a low-risk area regarding land movement. He explained that apart from a small area in one of the bedrooms, the roof was sound and that there were enough old tiles on-site to recycle. The plumbing and heating system would need to be replaced and most of the wiring would need to be updated. "Every bedroom window needs to be replaced and after that, there will be much plastering and painting required."

"It sounds expensive," Rachel said, her look of contentment fading slightly.

"Let's wait for Carlino to give us his estimate. I'll call on the geometra later to ask him about his thoughts."

"Thank you, but you've done enough for me already. I feel like I'm taking up too much of your time."

"I have all the time in the world."

"But what about your job?"

"I don't have one."

"Oh, when I saw you in town, I thought, maybe you worked in an office."

He let out a small laugh, "Me in a suit all day. No. I'm a gardener."

"A gardener, I'd have never guessed that."

"Yes. I was working for the council, but they say they can no longer afford to pay me, so now I have no job."

"But you don't have –" she stopped speaking, embarrassment creeping up her neck.

"I don't have, what?" Luca asked her, his forehead wrinkling with curiosity.

"I meant to say. You don't have what I'd think of as gardener's hands."

"No?" he looked down at his hands and then said, "I always wear gloves." He held his hands out for her to see and she began to blush as she looked at Luca's hands with their smooth palms and slender fingers.

With a crack in her voice, she said, "What time is it? I have an appointment with the bank at five o'clock."

***

Sitting in the bank manager's office, Rachel watched as he tapped away at his computer, "Signora Balducci, I have good news for you," he said looking up. "I have the authorisation to transfer the funds from your husband's account into a new one for yourself. But first." He pushed a pile of forms across the desk towards her and smiled.

Rachel filled out the forms and signed endless sheets of paper before he gave her a plastic bank card and the account details. "Here," he said, pointing to a slip of paper in front of her, "this is the balance on the account."

Rachel looked at the number printed on the paper and then back at the manager, "Are you sure this is correct?"

"Yes signora, it is correct."

"But how –" she started the question but as she was handed another a buff-coloured envelope, she stopped speaking.

"This is all the paperwork for your husband's account. You'll find the answers you seek here."

After leaving the bank and walking back to the apartment, she called into a traditional *salumeria* where she purchased two bottles of prosecco, four slices of San Daniele ham, a wedge of pecorino cheese and a crusty *pane casereccio*.

Back in the apartment she poured herself a glass of prosecco and began slicing the crusty bread and adding the ham and cheese to a plate. Using her fingers, she scooped out some antipasti from jars before dropping a slice of griddled artichoke into her mouth.

Carrying her dinner over to the sofa she picked up her phone and dialled Louise's number, as she waited for the call to connect, she wrapped a slice of sun-dried tomato inside a slither of ham and popped it into her mouth.

The call connected and Rachel heard Louise give a small scream before saying, "Rachel, it's so good to hear your voice. How are you?"

"I'm great. Eating expensive ham and quaffing prosecco."

"What's it like out there?"

Rachel looked around the small apartment, listened to the sound of people below in the piazza and smiled. "It's better than I expected, living here is so different to being on holiday."

"But you're not living there, it's just an extended stay."

"I know." Rachel thought it best to keep any talk of restoring the hotel to herself for now. "I have so much to tell you."

"I was going to email you again later. I've booked some holiday dates from work and wondered if I could come over and spend some time with you."

"Perfect," Rachel said. "When did you have in mind?"

"There's a cheap flight to Pescara on Friday. Is that too soon?"

"No, but what about Ben?"

"He's fine with it. It'll give him free rein to drink beer and eat takeaways in his underpants while playing *Call of Duty*."

Aldo IV

Aldo was beyond tired, and it showed on his face. Dealing with the undertaker in the dead of night following Giacomo's death had taken its toll, and as the dawn broke, he felt he needed the large glass of grappa that he had just poured himself.

With the alcohol warming his insides, he walked over to his late uncle's nightstand and opened the slim drawer. Inside was the usual assortment of odds and ends that end up rattling around inside bedside drawers. A needle threaded with a length of cotton pierced a business card. Several old buttons and a comb shared the space with a lottery ticket, a half-used blister pack of aspirin and a small envelope. Aldo removed the envelope and turned it over in his hand, on the reverse in faded ink was written, *le stelle*. He slid his finger beneath the flap and removed a small silver key. Turning it over in his hand he wondered what lock it could fit and unconsciously, without thinking it may be important he slipped it back inside the envelope and put them both inside his pocket.

He poured himself another grappa and stood on the balcony looking out over the rooftops of Naples. The sun was just beginning to colour the sky but even at this early hour, the city was alive. The scent of diesel rose with the fog that was waiting to be burnt off by the sun. The dull roar of the early morning trains was like waking giants. Street vendors were setting up their stalls in the piazza below and as they worked, they called out to each other, their shouts travelling down the narrow streets to merge with the waspish sounds of early morning scooters.

Closing the balcony doors Aldo went into the bedroom that had been his as he'd cared for his uncle and dropped onto the bed. He forgot how many nights he'd complained about the thin mattress and lack of air-conditioning, and as his eyes closed, sleep took over.

***

Aldo had felt his shoulders relax as drove up the road he'd grown up on and surrounded by fields and lemon groves his family home came into view. He'd

He'd been born in the shadow of the mighty Vesuvius and as a child, it had always been visible from his bedroom window. The volcano had blessed his family with rich, fertile soil which had helped to provide well for their table over the years. As he came close, he saw the rows of tomato plants growing beside the road and he drove into the courtyard, chickens scattered noisily, and a sleeping cat opened one eye to observe him. He parked his beaten Fiat and looked at his watch before he pushed open the kitchen door.

He was late and apologised while hugging his mother who was standing at the stove stirring a pot of bubbling sauce. "Don't blame me if lunch is spoiled," she said, grinning widely.

"It smells good."

"*Pasta Fagioli.*"

"Simple food made magical by Mama."

She playfully whipped his legs with a tea towel before telling him to wash his hands before opening the wine.

At the table in the centre of the kitchen, Aldo sat with a bowl of pasta and beans in front of him while his mother talked about her brother. "As you know Aldo, your uncle Giacomo had a great talent. People often said he was as talented as the famous Renaissance artists. Before the accident, his work had been in great demand. Renowned hotels and grand houses would commission him to paint their murals and frescos. I remember my mother saying he could paint the souls of cherubs and his flowers looked as fragrant as the real thing."

"Tell me again about his accident." Aldo poured himself a glass of wine and listened as his mother explained that Giacomo had been working away from home "Where was this?"

"A hotel on the Adriatic coast."

"Do you remember where?"

Shaking her head, she removed the empty pasta bowl and replaced it with a plate of grilled chicken. Aldo cut a wedge of lemon from the fruit on the table and squeezed the juice over his second course, followed by a drizzle of olive oil as green in colour as the leaves of the lemon tree.

"I can't remember," his mother said, "After he returned home from the hospital, Giacomo had no memory of the job he had been doing and the family thought it best not to pry. His recovery was slow and questions he couldn't answer infuriated him." She walked over to the dresser picked up a small wooden box and brought it to the table. Sitting opposite her son as he ate, she opened the box and removed from it several pieces of jewellery. "The undertaker brought these over this morning and dipping into the box she removed a gold chain on which hung an ornate gold crucifix and a ring set with a large green gemstone. "I think Giacomo would be happy if you took this." She pushed the ring towards Aldo, who stopped eating and picked it up. "Giacomo's emerald."

"He'd spent his first painting fee on it many years ago… Do you mind if I keep this?" she said, sliding the crucifix from the chain. Aldo shook his head and his mother handed him the gold chain. "You take this too. I'm truly grateful for the care you gave your uncle and that you stayed with him until the end."

"No doubt the landlord will want the apartment ready to rent out again soon. You know how difficult it is to find inexpensive property in Ponticelli." His mother nodded, poured a glass of amaro and set it down in front of him. "I shall return to the apartment later and start to pack up Giacomo's things. But first I am going to sit under the lemon trees and sleep off my lunch.

Settling into an old wicker chair he'd slept in many times before, Aldo thought about his forthcoming drive back into Naples. Ponticelli may attract tourists keen to visit the 13th-century *Basilica of Santa Maria della Neve* and to gaze upon the street art in *Murales Pudicizia*, but to Aldo, it was a depressing area with crumbling buildings sandwiched between modern concrete apartments. The congested roads with cars that looked abandoned rather than parked were a nightmare to navigate and the narrow alleyways where old men driving three-wheeled *Piaggio*'s darted out without checking for oncoming vehicles – no wonder the sound of Naples is the car horn.

Arriving back in the city with its oppressive heat and litter-strewn pavements Aldo shuffled along the narrow vico where no light ever seemed to reach the pavement, he pushed open the main door and climbed the stairs up to Giacomo's apartment. Despite having had a sleep in the lemon grove he was still tired, but he knew he must make a start on packing up his uncle's possessions.

He entered the apartment and made his way over to the kitchen table where the bottle of grappa beckoned him. He poured himself a generous measure and sipping at the liquor he took the ring he'd inherited out of his pocket and slid it onto a finger. He looked at it for several minutes before returning it to his pocket, then taking the silver key he threaded it onto the chain his mother had given him and fixed it around his neck.

He swallowed another mouthful of grappa, stood up and began removing Giacomo's books from their shelves and stacking them on a sideboard.

Chapter Six

Louise walked through passport control and saw Rachel already waiting for her. The two friends hugged each other before Louise spoke. "I'm so glad to see you."

"It's a forty-minute drive to my apartment so let's get that out of the way and then we can relax with a glass of prosecco."

"I'm so excited, I could pee myself."

"Best not in public," laughed Rachel, "it's frowned upon in Italian society."

Back at the apartment Louise was arranging her toiletries on the dresser in the spare bedroom when a cork popped in the kitchen. "This place is lovely; how much are you paying for it?" she called.

"It's dirt cheap only two hundred euro a month," Rachel said entering the room carrying two glasses of prosecco.

"Wow, that's a good deal,"

"It belongs to a friend of Luca."

"Tell me is this Luca a looker?" Louise snorted as she laughed. "Is Luca a looker, did you see what I did there?"

"Yes. And yes, he's a bit of a dish."

"So, tell me everything, I need to be up to speed." Louise listened as Rachel explained that she had seen a geometra to ask about restoring the property. "I've also spoken with a builder to get an idea of timescale and money."

"It's a big commitment to take on. You'll need to be certain it's what you want, you could be risking everything if it doesn't work out."

"That's why I need to be sure I make the right choices."

"When will you need to make a decision?"

"When everything is sorted out and the building and the money are transferred into my name."

"Money?"

"Yes, over four hundred and eighty thousand, euro."

"No! Well done Marco," said Louise then instantly she regretted it. She watched as a single tear slowly rolled down Rachel's face and gave her friend time to acknowledge it before she reached over and put her hand on top of hers.

"I have a meeting tomorrow with the builder Carlino, will you come along to help keep my feet on the ground?"

Rachel walked over to the oven, opened the door and removed a baking tray, filling the kitchen with the aroma of rosemary and garlic.

"Of course, I'll come. But before that, what is that? It smells heavenly."

"I picked up some porchetta from a street vendor and popped it into the oven to warm up." Rachel began to divide the slices of fragrant pork onto warmed plates. "Can you lay the table while I finish serving?"

Louise laid the placemats and cutlery and then waved the empty prosecco bottle in the air.

"Sorry I've no more fizz, but if you can open that bottle of red on the table, that'll be a great help."

Louise picked up the bottle and read the label, "*Montepulciano d'Abruzzo*. Don't they do screw tops over here?"

"Not often." The cork was released with a pop and Louise poured the red liquid into their glasses.

"Is this local?" she said putting down the bottle lifting a glass to her lips and taking a large gulp. "Oh my, that is so good. Is it expensive?"

"Less than two euros a bottle."

"At that price, you could bathe in it." Louise then chugged another mouthful.

"It'd be a bugger to clean the bath afterwards."

Rachel picked up her phone and pressed the side button to switch it on; Marco's smiling face beamed from the screen as she opened the camera and took a photograph of Louise sitting at her Italian table. "Send me a copy, I'll forward it on to Ben, show him what he's missing."

"I bet he's missing you," Rachel said.

"He'll be missing someone to pick up his dirty socks and clear away the curry trays from the coffee table." Louise laughed, "And I can tell you, I'll enjoy a break from his early morning bum trumpets in the bed."

"I've still got Marco's last answerphone message saved on here," she held up her phone. "I can't bring myself to erase it yet."

"Tiny steps," Louise said, "tiny steps," and picking up the empty wine bottle she said, "Where does it go? It must evaporate."

Rachel put down her phone and laughing she removed another bottle from the wine rack.

***

Louise stumbled out of her bedroom with a noisy yawn. Her blonde blunt cut was sticking up and she was rubbing the sleep from her eyes.

"Do you have –"

"Paracetamol," Rachel replied pointing to the packet on the worktop before going back to pouring coffee into mugs. "Go and sit on the balcony and I'll bring this through to you."

They sat in silence watching as the shops in the piazza below opened, shutters rolled up noisily and a delivery van pulled up, its engine running as the driver dropped some cardboard boxes onto the pavement.

"What time are we going out?" Louise asked running her fingers through her hair.

"Luca's coming over before lunch."

"I'd better make myself presentable then," Louise rose from her seat and then groaned. "I need to shift this headache first."

"A shower will do you good."

"Or a hair of the dog."

"You'll be lucky, we drank all the wine I had last night."

"Bugger."

***

Dressed in a floaty summer dress, her hair tamed and a hint of coral colour on her lips Louise entered the sitting room.

Luca stood up and held out his hand towards her introducing himself. "*Piacere*," he said and Louise dipped her eyes shyly. "I was just saying to Rachel, I'd like to take you both to lunch at a beachside trattoria."

"Sounds perfect," Louise said huskily and Rachel did her best to stifle a giggle.

Luca pulled into a parking space on *Via Lungomare* at Fossacessia Marina. The pebble beach a few steps away was behind a low wall and on either side of the pavement stood palm trees. The opposite side of the road was lined with holiday apartments, most with cards reading no vacancies. "The restaurant is this way," Luca said indicating up the road. "It's very basic, plastic chairs and paper plates, but the fish is very good."

The restaurant was a square building with a takeaway counter on the roadside and a patio at the rear with tables beneath umbrellas. It was still early in the season and the beach was mostly deserted apart from a couple of people enjoying the early June sunshine. "I thought the beach would be busier," Louise said as she placed her bag on the ground beside her chair.

"It's still early for Italians, the people that come to the beach before the start of the season are the Brits who live here and tourists," Luca said handing out laminated menus.

The owner came to their table bringing three plastic cups and a bottle of sparkling water and after taking their order he delivered a wicker basket of bread and a small dish of olives.

Rachel was captivated by her huge bowl of mussels when it arrived and was eagerly dipping hunks of bread into the tomato sauce. Louise was doing her best to wind her clam pasta around her fork and Luca using his fingers peeled the flesh away from the plate of tiny fried fish he'd ordered. "Here try," he said holding out what looked like a small crown to Louise. Taking it, she dropped it into her mouth and her eyes widened as she marvelled at what she'd been given.

"That's wonderful, what is it?"

"Squid tentacles," Luca said.

"If you'd told me that before I don't think I'd have tried it."

"You must put aside the fear of the unknown when eating," he said.

"Unless it's snails," Rachel said with a shudder and Louise agreed with her.

Pushing her empty pasta bowl forward Louise said, "That was quite simply the best *spaghetti alle vongole* I've ever eaten,"

"*Chitarra*," said Luca, "here in Abruzzo we serve clams with *chitarra*. Did you not notice the straight edges of the pasta?"

"I wondered why it was square shaped."

"It's special to Abruzzo." Luca picked up his car keys and added, looking at Rachel, "I shall pay the bill and then we shall show Louise our fabulous line of coast." Rachel's mouth widened into a toothy smile at his fractured English and she spotted Louise's eyebrows rise.

Luca was a very attentive driver, occasionally slowing to point out places of interest. Rachel told Louise about the *trabocchi* and said that they must spend an afternoon at the beach. Luca took the road that led up the hotel and Rachel held her breath, wondering what her best friend would make of the hotel. As Luca's car drove up the lane, he noticed that Rosa was sweeping up outside the gateposts. "*Buona sera*," he called to her and she stopped what she was doing and shook her head.

"Your men have gone to lunch and look at the mess they leave behind."

"Well, this is now a building site."

"That's as it is, but they should be tidy. Shame to drive a nice car only for the tyres to be punctured by this," Rosa held out her dustpan to show them the pieces of jagged metal left behind from where the gates had been cut from the posts.

"Thank you, Rosa. I shall speak with them when they return."

Rachel grabbed hold of Louise's hand and pulled her through the gates and up the path towards the hotel entrance. Stopping at the three stone steps and arched doorway with the name carved into the Maiella stone, Rachel said, "Welcome to *Albergo Le Stelle*, or roughly translated, The Stars Hotel."

"Wow! This must have been impressive back in the day," Louise said letting a slow whistle escape her lips as Rachel stepped aside to let her friend walk into the foyer for the first time. Walking slowly across the room, her heels clicking on the stone floor and echoing around the vast space Louise took in the enormity of the room.

Louise slid her arm inside Rachel's and said, "Come on, show me around." Inside the lobby, Louise nodded through the open doorway in Luca's direction. "He's gorgeous."

"He's just a friend."

"Just a friend with a great ass," Louise said, "I wish my Ben had hips like that." With a determined stare, Rachel shushed her friend and pushed her forward and up the staircase to the second floor.

After a tour of the upstairs rooms, they returned to the reception area where Luca was now talking with Carlino. Two men in overalls slouched in the corner "Signora Balducci," Carlino said, "my workers, Massimo and his brother Cosmo." On hearing their names, the two men immediately stood up straight and nodded their hello in Rachel's direction. "Here are my drawings and if everything is acceptable, I'll be putting up the work's notice later."

"So soon?"

"Carlino has been very busy on your behalf." Luca said as the builder moved forward towards Louise and held out a hand "*Piacere*," he said offering his hand.

Taking it Louise asked him what a work's notice was and Luca translated. "To tell people that this is a building site, it's for safety. Carlino says it stops idiots walking into death." Carlino chuckled and gave Louise a cheeky wink of his eye.

"I suggest we let these guys get on with their work," Luca said and he shook Carlino's hand as the two men in the corner returned to their earlier slouching.

Outside the hotel, Luca said, "I have one more surprise for you." Louise and Rachel looked at each other and with girlish excitement they allowed Luca to hold the car doors open for them.

The drive back was deliberate, and Luca took a diversion through the countryside. Louise pointed up to a ridge where houses clung to the rock like limpets and Rachel pointed out the ruins of stone buildings peeking out from olive groves. The road took them up high and the valley was laid out below them, a collage of yellows and greens. "Oh my!" Louise exclaimed as the car came over the brow of the hill and a mountain came into view.

"The Maiella mountains," Luca said as he turned off the road and into a gravelled area outside a bar, that if you didn't know was there, you'd miss. "I think it's time for gelato he said as the engine cooled and he opened his car door. He pointed to a table under a striped awning and they understood his instruction as he went inside.

Moments later, Luca returned with a bottle of wine and three tubs of ice cream. "There's chocolate, strawberry and pistachio."

Louise smiled, loving his pronunciation of the 'ch' as a 'k' in his native language, and replied, "I'll have the pistak-yo please," mocking him gently.

Luca handed out the ice creams and then began to open the wine "This is a local frizzante that goes well with gelato." He filled their glasses declining any himself, "I am as you English say, driver *designato*."

"This is the life," Louise said, "Seafood lunch followed by wine and ice cream, what's not to like?"

"If you liked the vongole," Luca said, "Then you must let me cook for you both tomorrow evening."

Rachel was about to decline the offer wanting more time alone with her friend when Louise jumped in with an enthusiastic, "Yes."

"Great. *Ora mangiamo i nostri gelati.*"

Louise may not have understood Luca's Italian language, but she correctly guessed he was telling them to eat their ice creams.

Chapter Seven

Luca's apartment was on the ground floor with a private rather than communal entrance. The décor was simple, greys and creams adorned the walls, and the living room fixtures were brushed steel and glass. Luca busied himself in the open-plan kitchen as Louise and Rachel looked around.

"Very masculine," whispered Louise.

"Nice though," Rachel replied as Luca returned from the kitchen area carrying glasses of orange-coloured liquid. He looked at the women in his living room and thought they couldn't have been so different from each other. Rachel's long red hair fell over her shoulders and her pale skin was accentuated by red lipstick. She wore a white blouse teamed with an aquamarine cardigan over slate grey culottes, whereas Louise with her short blond hair and pale lipstick was less formal in a floral summer dress.

"You'll like this," Rachel said to Louise taking her drink. "Luca introduced me to it when we had drinks in town."

"Aperol spritz," he said, "the best aperitivo in Italy." Louise took a sip of the slightly bitter drink and vocally gave it the thumbs up. "Aperol, prosecco and tonic water," he continued, "not forgetting the slice of orange and the ice." He indicated that they should sit down and quickly the conversation turned towards him.

"Do you live here alone?" Louise asked. "And where is your family from?" Luca told her that, yes, he lived alone, and that his family was from a small village on the outskirts of Lanciano. "Rachel tells me you're a gardener."

"That's right, would you like to see my garden?"

"Yes please," Rachel said, and he stood up and flicked a switch and the blinds on the far wall slid across to reveal an illuminated oasis.

"I thought we could eat outside, it's a lovely night." The women walked towards the window and looked out over the manicured lawn with its raised beds of geraniums and zinnias. Oleanders formed a floral hedge and a purple-flowering bougainvillea clambered up a trellis behind a water feature that trickled lazily. The patio was made from slate-coloured bricks and the table standing on it was dressed for dinner with plates of antipasti covered with netting cloches and several jugs containing wines of different colours. "Shall we?" he said and without a word, the three of them stepped outside. As they took their seats Louise noticed that under the table was an electric fan and Luca told them it was there to keep the mosquitos at bay. "They cannot fly in the wind and so cannot bite your ankles."

"You've thought of everything," Rachel said.

"No, I'm just being a typical Italian." Luca smiled with no hint of an apology. "For dinner, I have white wine or rosé. Red would be too robust for the..." pausing, he tried to find the correct English translation and then just said, "*Scampo*."

He'd just lifted the cloches from their plates of sliced meats and cheeses when a young girl appeared on the balcony next door, "*Ciao* Luca," she called, "*Come va?*"

"*Ciao* Nicoletta," He called back and answered her question telling her he was well, he asked how she was and if her mother was feeling better.

"Mama is feeling better."

"How's school?"

"The usual. Boring mostly." Luca laughed as Nicoletta feigned a yawn before she wished him a good evening and slipped back into her apartment.

"Doesn't it bother you being overlooked?" Louise asked.

"No, why should it?"

"In England, people are very protective of their privacy."

"But this isn't England," he said with a smile, "this is Italy, here we all rub along together – as I think the English expression is said. – Now let us eat."

After the starter had been cleared and wine poured, the primo was a langoustine risotto, the plates were decorated by a head and pair of claws but to save his guests the indignity of shelling the seafood Luca had removed the flesh and added it to the rice. "This is divine," Rachel said as she tasted the dish, "It's got a hint of the sea."

"That'll be the Adriatic," Luca said, "I add a little sea water to the rice."

The second course was a creamy lemon chicken piccata; tender strips of breast served in a lemon and caper sauce with whole roasted baby potatoes with fennel. During the *secondo,* both of his guests complimented Luca on his cooking and the conversation poured from them as did the wine from its jugs.

Louise told Luca how she and Rachel had been friends since college and Rachel told him how Louise could at times be a bad influence. "One day I'll tell you about the time we got arrested."

"What did you do?" Luca asked.

"We stole a car, but that's a story for another time."

"We didn't steal it, we just borrowed it," Louise said.

Luca listened as they told him the story, his gaze shifting from one to the other as they finished each other's sentences and giggled like children.

Once the dishes had been cleared, they retired back inside and bottles of *digestivi* were placed on the table.

"Business is always best discussed in private." Luca laid out the drawings that Carlino had given him that day.

Rachel traced a finger from the hotel's entrance through to the dining room and stopped at the kitchen door. The three of them discussed the hotel layout, but no firm decisions were made, it was more of an exercise in seeing what might work for the property. Luca said he thought it would be a good idea to build a poolside bar and covered seating area at the rear with access to the kitchen adjacent to the jasmine hedges. As they pored over the drawings it became obvious that Luca knew what he was talking about.

"You're quite knowledgeable about construction," Rachel said.

"I used to help my father. He was a builder, as is my brother."

"You have a brother," Louise said then adding with humour, "Is he married?"

"Yes. His wife is fierce, almost as fiery as this grappa." He poured three small tumblers of the spirit and with gusto, they all drank it down and noisily slammed the glasses down on the table.

Chapter Eight

The aroma of fresh coffee and the bubbling of the stovetop percolator in the kitchen greeted Rachel as she opened her eyes. She yawned loudly before climbing out of bed and pulling on her robe.

"Morning," Louise said as Rachel entered the room, "I've made coffee and I'm just about to make us both scrambled eggs."

"What time is it?"

"Half past nine."

"Bloody hell, I didn't mean to sleep so long."

"You must have needed it."

"To be honest it was one of the best night's sleep I've had since losing Marco."

Rachel surprised herself, for the first time she was able to mention his name without feeling as if she had been jabbed in the chest. She sauntered out onto the balcony and took a seat at the small bistro table while her friend prepared their breakfast.

At the open double doors to a balcony opposite stood a smartly dressed man in a linen suit, he was holding what she presumed to be, by its size a cup of coffee. He looked like he was dressed for work and as he glanced in her direction she waved and wished him a good morning, smiling he waved back and repeated the salutation, and with this simple interaction, she felt like she belonged.

"I love the view from here," Rachel said to herself as she sat watching the day unfold below them.

"Yes, it's very... Italian. I think I could live here," said Louise appearing over her shoulder with a plate of fluffy eggs on a slice of toast.

"It's nice now, but I imagine during a festa, it'd be hard work trying to sleep with all the noise."

"Who'd want to sleep," Louise said, "I'd be down there joining in with the festivities." Rachel let out a small laugh and Louise looked at her friend closely. "I hope you don't mind me saying, the dark circles under your eyes have faded... that could just be the sun because your skin is positively glowing, but babe, you need your roots done."

"I have hair colour in the bathroom, will you sort them out for me?"

"Sure," Louise said as a smell of burning drifted out onto the balcony. "Shit, I forgot about my toast," and she darted back inside the apartment.

After wafting a tea towel to disperse the acrid smoke Louise joined Rachel on the balcony and together they enjoyed a leisurely breakfast along with several cups of English tea.

"I enjoyed it last night," Louise said.

"Me too. Who'd have thought Luca could cook so well? He's definitely a man with hidden talents."

"And easy on the eye too. I've seen how you look at him."

"I don't look at him – well not in the way you're implying I do." Rachel blushed – her protestation unconvincing.

As Louise showered complaining about the burned toast smell in her hair, Rachel took Marco out onto the balcony and told him about dinner the evening before at Luca's. "I wish you were here," she said, "I could do with some sound advice."

"Sound advice?" Louise said standing in the doorway swathed in a bathrobe and with a towel wrapped around her head.

"About the hotel. Should I just put the building up for sale, or do it up and sell it?"

"What do you think Marco would do?"

Louise began towel drying her hair as Rachel carried the ashes back inside. She stood looking at the cardboard tube for a while collecting her thoughts and then turned to Louise and said, "Oh, you know Marco. He'd be excited about it and talking about restoring and opening the hotel."

"Is that such a bad idea?" Rachel turned to look at Louise who just shrugged.

"Are you serious?"

"Think about it. Maybe this is an opportunity to change things. Write a new chapter in the life of Rachel Balducci."

"But what is it they say – don't make any important decisions until at least twelve months after a bereavement."

"That's all good and well if you're deciding on whether to buy a puppy. The hotel is a conundrum that needs thinking about now."

"It's not as if the money is an issue, there's enough in the pot for the work and I still have Marco's life insurance and pension. But it feels like a massive risk, what if it doesn't work?"

"There's only you who can make that decision. Why don't we sit down and talk it through properly?" Louise refilled the coffee maker before taking a notebook from her bag and sitting at the kitchen table.

The two women sat drinking coffee weighing up the pros and cons of first restoring the building, deciding it would probably sell better if restored rather than as the shell it was presently.

"If you did decide to change direction, I'm sure with your experience in marketing and management you could run a hotel."

"But I know nothing about hospitality."

"And I can help with I.T." Louise said avoiding the question, "Help with a website etc."

They batted ideas back and forth across the table, moving between positive and negative until Rachel said. "But what about us?" Louise stopped scribbling on the pad and looked at her friend. "We've been friends since forever and I've already lost Marco, I couldn't bear to lose you too."

Louise stood up and moved towards Rachel and placed her hands on her shoulders, massaging them. "You won't lose me; I'll be with you every step of the way whatever you decide to do. And it's only Italy, not New Zealand or some other far-flung destination. I can be here in a few hours. Why don't we forget about it for now and do something else? Maybe a break will help to settle your thoughts."

"Why don't we drive over to Sant'Andrea and walk around? Maybe being around the hotel will help me to make up my mind?"

Rachel drove along the coast road with the air-conditioning on and her iPod plugged in, belting out 90's songs.

"Tune!" Louise shouted as the track changed and the spoken intro to All Saints, *Never Ever* began to play. Turning into the lane Rachel felt a ball of nervous energy knit itself into a blanket around her stomach. She'd been here many times before but today it seemed different, as if the finality of a decision weighed on her shoulders.

Opening the huge doors Rachel and Louise felt a rush of cool air escape from the foyer, illustrating the difference between the temperature inside and out. Heels on stone echoed around the room and they both walked around in silence. Rachel moved into the dining room while Louise said she was going outside to look around.

Running her hand across the stone walls Rachel knew that whoever had made the choice not to plaster them had got it right. The warm colours of the stone worked so well with the creamy floor tiles. She thought about the type of curtains she'd like to hang at the four tall windows; a cobalt blue with small tables and tub chairs for guests to sit in and look out over the front garden.

Upstairs she wandered slowly from room to room, ignoring the cobwebs and dusty old wooden crates, imagining bedroom furniture and colour schemes. People always talk about finding the perfect house – you'll just know, they say – and Rachel had a sensation that the building she was walking through was welcoming her. *That's a bonkers idea*, she thought, *it's just stone and cement*.

Louise joined her in one of the bedrooms and they both screamed as a startled pigeon took flight and escaped out of where the window should have been. "Not nice," Louise said pointing to the huge pile of pigeon poo on the floor, "best get this window boarded up."

They pushed open the door at the end of the corridor and began to walk up the narrow stairs to a third floor. "I haven't been up here yet," Rachel said. Louise pushed open the door at the top and an old newspaper and dried leaves shushed across the floor, pushed into the room.

"Wow!" Rachel said stepping inside, "Look at the size of this space."

The ceiling was high with olive-coloured walls and fitted wall lights, their glass shades dusty and unclean, giving the illusion of frosting. Rachel walked across and ran her finger over one of the glass shades; this was a room she knew she could fall in love with.

A door opened into another large room overlooking the front with a view of the sea from the window. Along the top of the walls were the faded remains of what must have long ago been a painted mural. Cream-coloured cornices shaped to look like swags of fabric butted up against the ceiling with plaster drapes in the corners. "This would make a perfect bedroom."

Another two doors led off the main room where inappropriately a 1970's kitchen was tacked onto the far wall. Formica and floral tiles. One led into a rear room with an equally high ceiling but minus the cornice and swags. "Look at that view," Louise said standing at the open space that had originally been a pair of doors onto the balcony over the rear garden. "You can see all of the villages in the distance, imagine it at night, all the houses lit up."

Rachel was imagining it, and if she needed something to help her make up her mind, it was this upper floor and its potential to be her forever home.

Aldo V

Aldo yawned, rolled over and rubbed his eyes open. His head felt heavy. He'd overdone the grappa the night before and his mouth tasted sour. Groaning, he pulled himself up into a sitting position and stretched his arms above his head. After a few minutes of waiting for sleep to fully retreat, he rose from the bed and pulled yesterday's shirt over the vest he'd been wearing for the past week. He plodded into the kitchen where his trousers were draped over a chair and filled the base of the coffee maker with water – he didn't bother to replace the already used coffee, he just added another spoonful – and after screwing the percolator together and lighting the gas he reached up and took a cup down from the shelf.

After pulling on his trousers, he poured himself a double measure of the dark brown liquid and stood looking at his reflection in a mirror. He had what his mother called, 'a friendly face', round and topped off with an unruly mop of black hair that never lay flat. His large brown eyes were warm and welcoming; doe-like, giving him a simple look. Sadly, Aldo had a face that the opposite sex had thus far overlooked.

He'd spent the previous evening packing up Giacomo's clothes, they'd been sorted into two piles. One for the charity bins outside the church and the other – the good suits were going to go to a cousin who'd just been offered an office job.

Splashing a measure of grappa into his coffee he looked at the box of oddments that he'd gathered and left beside the sink. Kitchen utensils were crammed into a box with well-thumbed magazines and paintbrushes. There was still more packing to do but it could wait until after breakfast.

Naples was now awake and at full volume, he rose from the table and closed the doors that led onto the balcony. The single-glazed doors did little to keep the noise out but did muffle it. How he wished he was at home on the outskirts of the city. Back with his mother, where the air was cleaner and the environment less obtrusive.

Sitting back at the kitchen table he tore apart a crema-filled cornetto and dipped the end into his coffee, the sweet pastry was devoured in just two bites. He was tearing the cellophane wrapper off another when there was a knock at the apartment door. He rose from his seat and the banging on the door became more insistent. A voice in the hallway outside shouted, "I have keys." Realising it was the landlord Aldo opened the door and the aptly named Signor Gallo elbowed his way inside.

He was a tall man who like the rooster he took his surname from preened and strutted like a cockerel. On his head was a thatch of hair, his artificial cockscomb – people knew he wore a hairpiece, but no one dared to mention it. He was slender and wore expensively tailored suits and, on every finger, he wore a gold ring and around his neck hung more precious metal.

Gallo owned many properties in the area and although his rents were considered cheaper than most landlords the quality of the accommodation often reflected this. He flaunted his wealth in much the same way a bird displays its plumage and the endless speculation about his involvement with some of Napoli's less savoury individuals was enough to keep him in his position of power.

"I need the apartment cleared. I have new tenants moving in tomorrow." Gallo barked as he walked around opening cupboards and looking inside. He threw a sheet of paper onto the sideboard, "These are the fixtures belonging to me, you cannot take these."

"I need more time," Aldo said.

"No more time, what you leave will be thrown out onto the street."

Gallo wandered over to Giacomo's bedroom and pushed open the door. Aldo watched as he walked over to the bed opened the bedside drawer and looked inside. He took the photograph from the wall and looked at the faded image of the woman behind the glass. Grabbing at his crotch he licked his lips and Aldo's nostrils flared. His eyes closed in anger and he turned away before he said something he knew he'd end up regretting.

Gallo threw the frame onto the bed and pushed his way into the living room again and after reminding Aldo he had just one more day he left the apartment, his oppressive aftershave retreating much later.

Aldo finished his coffee before opening a glazed wall unit and began packing up the years of accumulated knick-knacks and religious icons that along with the boxes of half-used tubes of oil paints had sat upon the dusty shelves untouched for years. The simple task of removing items and wrapping them in a newspaper was made more tiring by the heat. The start of June had brought with it temperatures bordering on thirty degrees and with no air-conditioning the apartment became oppressive. Needing some relief Aldo went back into Giacomo's bedroom and turned on the portable fan beside the bed. The air around him shifted, barely cooled but bringing some relief. He picked up the photograph of the unknown woman that had hung on his uncle's bedroom wall and noticed that when Gallo had thrown it onto the bed the image had moved behind the glass revealing another picture behind the photograph. Curious, Aldo removed the pins holding the frame together and from behind the photograph slipped several sheets of old, yellowed paper.

The hidden papers were sketches, more likely drawn by Giacomo and slipped into the frame to keep them safe. Aldo looked at the drawings in turn, one was a clock, another an eagle and there were several sheets of floral studies. Aldo remembered as a child seeing his uncle work on similar designs for his customers. "Why had Uncle Giacomo kept these," he asked himself as he looked at a rough sketch featuring a building with an impressive arched entrance. Turning it over, written in pencil in his uncle's hand was, '*Sant'Andrea. CH*'.

Going back to the task of packing his mind kept returning to the sketches. "Why were they hidden?" he said aloud, pausing to think.

"What if?" he walked over to the kitchen sink and chose a book from the box there. He opened the atlas and ran his finger down the index stopping when he found the name he was looking for. He flicked through, counting the numbers until he reached the page he sought and looking at the map he saw what he was searching for, a village on the Adriatic Coast. "What if?" he said again and his heart fluttered in his chest. "What if?"

With Giacomo's clothes and the few possessions he had owned packed into his car, Aldo drove out of the city. On the passenger seat was an old, battered suitcase, brown, scuffed and containing his clothes. He drove to a house on the outskirts of the city and there he left Giacomo's things with the cousin who was expecting the good-suits and after filling his Fiat with petrol he took the A1/E45 signposted Pescara.

Less than an hour later, he pulled off the motorway into a service area, walked into the Autogrill ordered a coffee and a panino and took his mobile phone from his pocket. He scrolled through his contacts and punched at a button waiting for the call to connect.

"*Dimi*," his mother said as the call connected. The line wasn't clear, the signal at the family home was patchy and the conversation stuttered. Aldo explained that he was tired after looking after Giacomo and needed some time away. "But what about work?" his mother asked between clicks and pauses.

"Don't worry, I'll sort something out."

"I don't understand why you need a break, it's not yet Ferragosto." Her voice disappeared as the connection died completely.

Aldo put his phone away, ate his sandwich and then continued his journey across the middle of Italy towards the east coast.

***

After spending an uncomfortable night sleeping in his cramped Fiat, Aldo drove along the coast road towards Sant'Andrea, the area was studded with villas set back from the main road and further along there were smaller stone-built houses. Unable to find anything that suggested the name his uncle had written down. Thirsty, he spotted a small bar beside the road, pulled up outside and walked inside.

Aldo couldn't risk anyone else knowing anything about Giacomo's diamond story and knew he had to be discreet. He ordered a beer and selected a table in the middle of the room to allow him the opportunity to eavesdrop on the conversations of the men wearing overalls and taking a break from their work.

He'd barely touched his beer when he heard the name, *Le Stelle* from the table beside his. He glanced across at the tall moustachioed man who was sitting opposite a smaller, chunky man and listened into their conversation.

"Carlino is hoping the English lady decides to restore the hotel."

Hotel, thought Aldo, turning slightly in his seat to hear more.

"I could do with the work," the little round man said. "This could be a good job for us."

Aldo decided to take a chance and speak to the men, leaning over he asked them if they knew of any labouring work available. "Just basic lifting and carrying," he said.

"There may be some in *Sant'Andrea*," the taller man said brushing the beer froth from his moustache. "But it'll be down to the boss to decide."

"The smaller man emptied his glass and said, "Off the main road," he pointed in the direction he was talking about and continued, "There's a lane that leads to the sea and an old hotel. There's a chance a restoration will start in a few weeks."

A few weeks. That would give him time to get inside and look around before builders were on site, thought Aldo, how fortunate he was to have chosen to visit this bar today.

Thanking the men for their conversation, he downed his beer, rose from his seat and walked out of the bar.

Chapter Nine

Rosa was deadheading roses when she became distracted by the sound of clattering metal. She looked up from her gardening and watched a flatbed truck make its way up the lane and drive past her house. It parked up outside the gates to the hotel and two men got out, they puffed at the cigarettes hanging out of their mouths and leaned against the truck. Checking the knot under her chin, Rosa straightened her headscarf and marched over towards the smoking men.

"*Buongiorno signora*," a short man with a face the colour of hazelnuts said as she approached him.

"What's happening here?" she asked.

"Scaffolding," said a taller man sporting a moustache so thick you could hide a kitten inside it.

"The English lady is repairing the building," the short man said as he ground his cigarette butt into the ground. "We need to get this lot unloaded before the other builders arrive."

"More people, more vehicles," she moaned, with a wry smile. "My life is ruined."

The men forced the rusted gates open before getting back into the truck. "Just one moment," Rosa said, and bending down she picked up the extinguished cigarette butt and handed it to the short man. "Now you can continue," and with a smirk, she watched as the truck drove up the path beside the trees and up to the hotel.

The clang of metal on metal rang out all morning, scaffolding poles collided with each other as they were unloaded and erected. A radio began blaring, the music inaudible, just noise and Rosa decided it would be best to retreat inside.

The kettle on the stove whistled as a knock sounded on her front door. Rosa stopped what she was doing to open it.

"*Buongiorno*," Rachel said from behind a potted geranium. "I've come to apologise for the noise."

"What noise?" shrugged Rosa.

"The noise from the hotel. I have decided to restore it." Rosa felt a pinprick of warmth begin to swell in her breast at this news. Rachel handed her the plant, "I got this for you."

"Compensation?" Rosa asked, causing Rachel to stammer.

Rosa seemed to enjoy the awkwardness her question had raised and then taking the geranium she beckoned Rachel inside where the kettle was wailing.

"The kettle," Rachel said.

"What?" Rosa said ignoring the whistling and busing herself with the potted plant.

Rachel moved across to the stove and removed the howling kettle and Rosa started laughing. "Now it is I who must apologise for the noise."

Sitting at Rosa's table with their drinks Rachel began to tell Rosa how after their day at the hotel she'd talked it over with Louise again.

"Where is your friend today?"

"We were up into the early hours and drank too much wine," she said. "I'm letting her sleep off the Montepulciano. This afternoon, I thought we could spend an afternoon on the beach at Le Morge."

"The weather is good for a beach. You will miss Louise when she leaves?"

"Yes. But I'll hopefully be busy here."

"And you can always come to talk with old Rosa. She leant over and placed her hand on top of Rachel's. "I am happy the hotel has found a new owner."

"It may be a reckless decision, but I think this could be a new beginning for me, and I want to see where it takes me."

Minutes after waving Rachel off, Rosa watched as a mud-coloured Fiat with Naples numberplates coughed its way up the lane and came to a stop outside the hotel. She watched as the car door opened, and a short man with wild hair climbed out and walked through the gate and up the drive. Going outside she walked a few paces up the lane to get a better look and through a gap in the trees, she saw him stop in front of the main entrance where he removed his phone from his pocket and took a photograph of the arched doorway. Just then Carlino's white truck appeared in the lane and stepping aside Rosa let it pass and it parked up beside the Fiat.

"The English woman. Rachel told me she's decided to renovate," she called out to Carlino.

"Yes. We are starting straight away." Carlino waved, picked up a battered briefcase and made his way up the drive to the hotel, stopping briefly to speak with the man who'd arrived in the Fiat.

Rosa watched as they shook hands and as the man walked back to his battered old car she turned and headed home.

Chapter Ten

When Rachel and Louise arrived at the hotel the next day, Carlino's men were already busy at work. Entering the foyer, they saw that the joiner had started work on the new window frames and a new man, Aldo was busy sweeping up wood shavings. The women were greeted by a chorus of "*Buongiorno signore*," from the workmen and Aldo touched the brim of his cap while keeping his eyes lowered. Peering through his eyelashes he watched as Rachel walked over to Carlino, said a few words then placed a gold-coloured tray of cakes and pastries down upon a trestle table. Carlino called to his workers and pointing to the pastries told them to help themselves.

Work stopped briefly and Aldo asked, "Who are the ladies?"

"The lady with the red hair is the hotel's new owner," Carlino said biting into flaky pastry, releasing a bright orange blob of apricot jam that ran down his wrist. He licked up the jam before it fell to the floor and said, "I have a new job for you. I'd like you to demolish the fireplace in the dining room." Then wiping his chin with a paper napkin, he swallowed the last of the pastry.

"I'll start immediately," Aldo said.

"*Piano, piano*," Carlino said emphasising the phrase, "Take your coffee first."

The men had returned to work when Luca arrived. Rachel was showing Louise the pool when he called, "Thinking of going for a swim?"

"Maybe when it's been cleaned up," Rachel said.

The sunlight caught her hair and Luca said, "You've coloured your hair. It looks very nice."

"What a catch," Louise whispered, "a man that notices when you've had your hair done." Rachel gave her the side eye.

"I've been thinking about your offer," Luca said.

"Yes. And?"

"I'll take on the job with one condition." He looked serious.

"What's that?"

"That you allow me to build an orto."

"Orto?" Louise asked.

"Vegetable garden," Rachel said. "Very well, where do you plan to put it?"

"Over behind those trees, away from the guests, but not too far from the kitchen."

The arrangement was agreed upon and as Rachel shook Luca's hand, his skin felt good on hers and she felt a strange surge of electricity run up her arm. The moment was interrupted by the sound of raised voices coming from inside the hotel. Carlino appeared at the kitchen door and shouted, "Come see," before he disappeared back inside.

Entering the dining room, they joined the other workers who were standing looking at an ornate wrought iron fireplace that had previously been covered by a hideous plaster hearth and mantlepiece. "Looks like the previous owner had the original fireplace covered over," the moustachioed builder said.

"This was hidden inside," Aldo held up a wooden box.

"Looks like it needs a key to open it," the shorter, portly builder added.

"Let me see," Rachel said and taking the box she ran her fingers over the surface and traced the faded pattern that decorated the lid. "Was there a key with it?"

Aldo shook his head saying he had looked through the plaster but couldn't find one.

"I'll open it," the smaller man said holding aloft a screwdriver.

"No," said Rachel, "it could be valuable." Rachel carried the box through to reception and set it down on the desk.

"A mystery on day one of the build, whatever next." Louise joked. "You don't think… looking at the size… it could be like Marco's box."

"Someone's ashes?" Rachel said appreciating her friend's candour. "Now that would be weird. It's a similar weight, but we'll have to wait until we find the key.

Carlino clapped his hands and ordered his men back to work. Aldo began sweeping up the broken plaster as Rachel walked back into the dining room to speak with Luca. "Do you mind if we leave?"

"Not at all."

"Louise flies back to England later, so, I'd like us both to have another day looking around like tourists."

"Good idea," Luca said, "Is she booked on to the evening flight from Pescara?"

"Yes, 21:45. I thought we could take the coast road and take a look at Lido Riccio."

"Why don't you join us?" Louise said.

"I cannot. Now I am a manager, I have too much work here," Luca winked at Rachel and she felt the blush begin to rise on her neck. "And I need to plan the orto."

Rachel turned to Louise and quickly said, "Well that's sorted, we need to go back to the apartment and collect your suitcase."

Louise said goodbye to the workmen, and hugged Luca, whispering into his ear that she hoped he would look after Rachel, and with a practised "*Ci vediamo presto*," she picked up the box from the reception desk and Rachel followed her outside to the car.

"*Scusi, capo*?" Luca turned to see Aldo standing beside him.

"Just call me Luca," he said before Aldo told him he was feeling unwell and asked for permission to leave early.

***

After collecting Louise's suitcase, Rachel drove them along the coast road. As usual, they sang along to the songs that shuffled on Rachel's iPod and before they knew it, they were parking in a small beachside car park at Lido Riccio. Putting on their sunhats and sunglasses they strolled along the sandy beach, looking at the yellow beach huts and regimented umbrellas lined in perfect rows. Louise took her camera out to take some photos, saying they'd be ideal for the hotel's website.

The hotel's website thought Rachel, how definite that sounded and she realised she was now at the point of no return. She hugged Louise who complained she'd spoiled a shot of sunbeds she'd lined up. "Let's go and check out the nearby hotels and see what the competition is like."

Louise grinned and took several shots of Rachel as she posed for her, pouting on the beach like an Instagram influencer.

They collected brochures from hotels on the beach, chatted to staff about their guests and discovered that they mostly catered for Italian guests, with much of it being repeat business. "The same families come each year."

"You'd think they'd want a change," Louise said as they walked over to a small bar to buy some lunch.

"Italians seem to like what they know," Rachel said before ordering two *panini*.

"That's good," Louise said, "If they like your place then they'll keep coming back."

"I dare not think that far ahead yet. Come on let's get going to the airport."

"One quick question," Louise said as Rachel pulled into the airport car park. "When did you ask Luca to be the project manager?"

"Yesterday, and he said he'd think about it."

"Good choice. I think he'll be a good fit for you."

"For me?" Rachel said.

"For your project." Louise opened the car door and went around to the boot to retrieve her suitcase before she said anything else that could be misinterpreted.

"I hope you don't mind my leaving you a little early," Rachel said, "I've not done the drive at night, and I'd like to get through those hairpin bends before it gets dark."

"I'll be fine, you get off and drive carefully. Text me when you get back to let me know you've arrived safely. Ben's already left for Stansted, so he'll be there when I land."

Away from the electric lights around the airport, the afternoon light was softer, the bright sunshine replaced with a hazy hue that seemed to cling to the surface of the road. The SS16 was now filled with vehicles as people began to return to work. Buzzing scooters with university students wearing backpacks weaved in and out of the lines of cars heading into town. Thankfully as the road moved out of the populated areas the flow of traffic became less frantic and Rachel began to enjoy seeing the sea in a new light. As she passed through Marina di San Vito the seafood restaurants were already starting to fill with tourists eager for their dinner. Knowing that these were the people who would be her target guests, she slowed down and pulled over to watch people sitting at kerbside tables drinking beers and eating fried calamari and prawns. The Ice cream parlours already had queues forming outside and the warm air was filled with a mix of conversation and laughter.

"I hope this works," she said to herself as she indicated and drove towards Lanciano.

***

Aldo had been sitting across the piazza looking up at the apartment ever since he'd followed Rachel's car there earlier. His cap was pulled down over his eyebrows to hide his face, and even when he'd been addressed earlier by an elderly gentleman, he kept his head bowed. About to leave he sighed with relief when opposite the main door to the palazzo opened and a woman with a pushchair and a toddler struggled out onto the street. "*Signora*," he called rising to his feet and crossing the square to hold the door open for her. Placing his foot in the space between the door and its frame he grinned as she exited the building.

"*Grazie*," she said and took hold of the toddler's hand and as they walked away, Aldo slid around the door into the palazzo's *cortile*.

Exhaling silently, he opened an exterior door and climbed the stairs. Reaching the second floor he stopped for a moment to gauge his position. Deciding that the green door on his left must be the one to the apartment overlooking the piazza he knocked gently, just loud enough for anyone inside to hear, but not enough to bring the occupants from the apartment opposite out to see who was on the landing. Getting no response, he inserted a lock pick into the keyhole, nothing happened and shaking his head he selected another and inserted it and after turning it several times he heard the lock click open. Wasting no time, he entered the apartment and closed the door behind himself.

The room was tidy, a jacket was draped over a chair in the kitchen and a pair of shoes were placed neatly side by side underneath. He wandered around the perimeter of the room, opening drawers to the sideboard on one wall – they were empty – as was the drawer in a table beside the sofa where a novel written in English lay.

He skirted around the bathroom quickly, briefly picking up the electric toothbrush before moving into the bedrooms. The smaller room was empty; the bed had been stripped but the larger looked like it was slept in nightly. A suitcase beneath the bed was empty and the wardrobe and chest of drawers all contained ladies' garments. His attention was caught by the dressing table where a bracelet containing coloured gemstones was lying, he picked it up and turned it over in his hand just as a breeze from an open window shifted the curtain and the tall box hidden behind the voile was exposed. Aldo dropped the bracelet back onto the dressing table and picked up the tall box. He weighed it in his hands and shook his head seeing that it was cardboard and not wooden – and not the box he'd discovered hidden behind the fireplace.

Aldo replaced the box and after a few more minutes of fruitless searching he let himself out of the apartment pulling the door silently closed behind him.

***

Rachel drove into the side road where the parking zone for the piazza was situated. She parked and walked to the rear of the car where she collected her bags from inside the boot. She looked at the wooden box found earlier that day and ignoring it, she picked up the tube containing Carlino's drawings and then closed the boot and pressed the key fob to lock the car. With the cardboard tube under one arm, she hitched up her shoulder bag and walked around the corner as at the same time, in the opposite direction drove a battered old Fiat.

Inside the apartment, she dropped her bags onto the sofa took out her phone and quickly fired off a text to Louise as promised. In the kitchen, she took a bottle of wine from the rack and poured herself a generous glass of red before moving to the balcony to watch as the last of the piazza's human traffic began to slow down. Sitting in the warm evening air she watched as the doors to the *farmacia* and the *tabacchi* closed for the evening leaving only the boutiques and bars open.

Across the square, a shuttered door opposite opened, bleeding light onto its balcony and the man stood there. Dressed in jeans and an open-necked shirt; his suit put away for the day, he lifted a hand and gave her a friendly wave.

Her eyes began to feel heavy and stifling a yawn Rachel couldn't decide if her tiredness came from the wine or the sea air and decided she ought to go to bed. Walking into the bathroom to brush her teeth she stopped and stood looking at her electric toothbrush for a few seconds something about its position wasn't quite right. She shook her head and picked it up.

She dropped her clothes onto the chair by the dressing table and pulled the window shut, adjusting the curtain so that it was behind Marco's box. Naked she looked at herself as she brushed her hair and talked to Marco, she told him about the large rooms at the top of the hotel, the views from the windows and how the property seemed to feel right. She placed her brush down and her eyes glanced down at the bracelet. "That's odd," she said, "I'm sure that was lying straight, not pooled into a circle." A shiver brushed across her shoulders before she decided that maybe Louise had picked it up earlier and stretching, she rose from the dressing table and pulled back the cool cotton sheets and slid between them. Within minutes she was sleeping soundly.

Chapter Eleven

Rachel stepped out of the shower and was dripping onto the mat when there was a knock at her apartment door. She grabbed her robe and wrapped a towel around her hair and leaving wet footprints on the tiled floor she walked to the door. "Oh, hi," she said shocked to see Luca standing there. Flustered for a moment she hesitated before inviting him inside.

"I bring breakfast," he said, and Rachel's heart sank, she didn't think she could spend another morning eating Italian pastries. Luca placed a carrier bag on the kitchen table and continued, "I found this in the supermarket and I thought you being British would like it."

Intrigued Rachel opened the bag and removed a box of Weetabix. The yellow packaging gave her a sudden rush of homesickness before she took down two bowls and fetched the milk from the fridge. "Give me a couple of minutes to get dressed and we can both have a bowl." The look of fear on Luca's face registered with her and she laughed as she walked into her bedroom.

Returning a few minutes later wearing shorts and a floral blouse, she chuckled as she watched Luca trying his best to enjoy the breakfast cereal, "You Italians really are the least adventurous people when it comes to new food."

"We have enough good food of our own."

"I remember Marco's parents were the same. They'd never try a curry or even Chinese food."

"We have Chinese food here in Lanciano," Luca said, "I can take you one day."

"I'll keep you to that."

"Did you look at Carlino's drawings?"

Rachel shook her head as she filled the coffee maker, "I was too tired last night."

"Never mind, we can go over them later as he's invited us out to lunch. But before that, I'd like to take you to see the town my family is from. If you are going to become a hotelier, you must know the area."

As Luca drove them out of the town centre the roads became less congested and he overtook the occasional tractor pootling along the pot-holed road. After another frightening hairpin bend obscured by tall bamboo, they came to the crossroads at Guarenna. The village was little more than a handful of houses, a couple of bars and restaurants and a small church. "How can such a small village support two restaurants?" Rachel said.

"People will travel for good food," Luca said pointing ahead to another restaurant a short distance down the road, "See all the cars in the car park already. A very good place to eat, expensive but worth it." Rachel made a mental note to try to remember the names of all the places he was pointing out to her but guessed she'd be relying on Google later.

"Perhaps I should put a book of recommendations on the reception desk."

"That would be a good idea, but you need to start now because you will not the time have when you are full of guests."

The two of them spent the morning in the medieval town of Casoli. Rachel had held her breath as his car tackled the steep, almost vertical road up the hill and seeing the T junction at the top she hoped his brakes and clutch were in good working order.

After parking they sauntered through the streets that twisted ever upwards towards the castle perched at the top of the town. People going about their day stopped to say good morning as they walked past and a man tending to his window boxes picked a flower and handed it to Rachel.

Luca pointed out things like market days, pizzeria opening times and the names of the shops and as the sun became oppressive, he took her to a bar where they sat in the shade watching the people who were gathered outside the post office, each person knowing where in the jumble of bodies their place in the queue was. "It's like organised chaos," Rachel said smiling.

"It's Italy," Luca replied with a smile.

They took a different road out of the town; this one was less steep and at the foot of the hill Luca pulled over to allow Rachel to take some photographs of the sun looking like a sunflower behind the castle's tower.

"This place is good for lunch," Luca said as he parked the car. Rows of workers' vans and cars lined the road and he pointed out what looked like an unassuming bar. "*Il Bucaniere, menu fisso*. Set price, two courses and wine and water."

As they stepped inside it was clear to see that the place was popular, every table was occupied and although basic, the setting had a convivial charm. They spotted Carlino sitting in a corner and made their way over and after much handshaking and air-kisses they were approached by the waitress who gave them the choice of three *primi* and two second courses.

Rachel ordered a *pappardelle ai funghi* first course followed by *a parmigiana di melanzane secondo* then turned to Carlino to ask him when the main work would start.

"Please, we speak *Inglese*. Carlino needs practice. We eat, then go see the hotel." Carlino said at the same time as he took a mouthful of pasta, his words becoming muted.

The meal was eaten slowly. The Italian relaxed style of dining suited Rachel; she liked their attitude towards food, and the respect shown to the cook, by taking time to enjoy the eating. She much preferred this to the haste in which she had often eaten lunch in England, the rushed business lunches that would often result in indigestion. This, she thought is a more civilised way of doing business.

That afternoon, back at the hotel, as they walked from room to room Carlino discussed the drawings that he held in his hand. "I agree with Luca that we should build a bar area at the back of the kitchen meaning it can serve the pool without bar staff walking through into the dining room. I have also had a thought about the previous owner's accommodation, I think it should become the pantry and stores.

They followed him out into the reception and looking up he pointed out the cornices that had looked strange to Rachel. "Here, is a false ceiling. Not good, needs to come down."

"Will the plaster underneath be all right?" Luca asked.

"Who knows," Carlino said, his nose and cheeks glowing from the wine with lunch. He smoothed his long grey hair into a ponytail and tied it up with a piece of electrical wire as he walked past the reception desk. "This steps. *Come si dici in inglese?*"

"Staircase," Rachel said.

"Yes. Staircase. Very good, sturdy. Last forever." Carlino slapped the wooden banister to validate what he had said. "On the second floor, there are twelve rooms and on the third, I think six should be for guests."

"What about the remaining rooms?" asked Luca.

"Plumbing to these is not good, so I think Rachel's idea of these becoming her apartment is the best solution. Two or three bedrooms, bathroom and living room."

"Sounds good to me," Rachel said, secretly pleased that her suggestion had been agreed upon. she wanted the apartment upstairs more than anything.

Back in the foyer gathered around the reception desk Carlino asked, "When do you want to open?"

"As soon as I can. Hopefully December."

Carlino sucked his teeth and shook his head. "Six months, not possible to open all the hotel." His eyes closed and moved up and down as if he was counting; he seemed to be doing mental arithmetic, behind his eyelids.

"For all the job, I think twelve maybe thirteen. Remember we have the August holiday next month. I think in six months, if we work every day, we can restore downstairs, second floor and Rachel's apartment."

"Really?" Luca said, "That much?".

"*Certamente*. Then we finish the last rooms at the end of tourist season."

Rachel liked Carlino's suggestion, thinking, *maybe it would make perfect sense to refurbish half the hotel and see how the business develops.*

"Also, don't forget," Carlino said pointing out of the window towards the dishevelled garden.

"Leave that to me," Luca said.

***

"Over here," Luca shouted to the man delivering skips to the hotel, "One by the entrance and another around the side." The driver nodded and did as he was instructed while several men; a collection of Luca's friends and previous co-workers clambered from a minibus. They looked around and some whistled while others shook their heads. "*Pazzo,*" one exclaimed telling Luca he was crazy, while another asked him if the English woman was beautiful enough for all this effort.

Each man was given his instructions and without argument, a whirlwind of activity began. The waist-high grass was scythed and then cut shorter, revealing a scrappy lawn that looked beyond saving. Men using giant vacuums sucked up leaves from the gravel while others tamed the overgrown cypress trees. Brambles were cut back sending snakes into the open to search for new safe havens.

Within a few hours, the skips were full of green waste and the driver was returning to collect them.

"The lawn is disappointing," Rachel said after parking her car outside the gates.

"It is difficult to keep a green lawn in an Italian summer," Luca told her. "Many litres of water will be needed, it's not economical."

"But I'd like a large green space here," she said, "but not one of those fake lawns."

"We could plant it with a creeping thyme, it's tolerant of hot summers and grows low to not need cutting. It also has purple flowers in summer. It will look very pretty."

The pruned cypress trees stood in a straight line, slender sentinels leading the eye up the garden towards the arched entrance. The gravel path beside them had been given a power wash and as the moisture evaporated in the midday sun, the Maiella stones shone like autumn-coloured gemstones.

Following Luca around to the rear she saw that two of the workers had cleared the pool of its coating of decaying leaves, the smell was still unsavoury but as the sides had been hosed down, she could see that the tiles were still intact.

"I can't believe so much has been achieved in just one day," Rachel said after everyone had packed away their tools and climbed back into the minibus.

"Now I just have to pay them and buy many bottles of Peroni to say thank you."

"Do you need me to pay you now?"

"It can wait until next week. This will be black money, no need to pay taxes." Luca gave her a wink and then taking the driver's seat of the minibus he beeped the horn and drove away.

After everyone had left Rachel walked around the garden. Now it was tamed it looked so much bigger, with ample room for her guests to enjoy it. Standing at the hotel entrance she stared at the cleared driveway, it looked welcoming, as it meandered up from the gate posts. She took out her phone and fired off a few photographs.

Feeling a sense of achievement, she hugged herself before driving back to Lanciano.

Chapter Twelve

The day before, while standing at the supermarket checkout, Rachel had been approached by an English woman. "Sorry to bother you," she'd said, and Rachel turned to see a pale-skinned lady with oversized sunglasses and a huge floppy hat. "Are you the English lady with the hotel just passed San Vito?"

"Yes, that's me," Rachel replied, "in Sant'Andrea, why?"

"There's no secrets between the ex-pats," the woman said hitching her bag's strap back onto her skinny shoulder. "Word gets around here quicker than a virus in a care home. I'm Penny by the way."

"Pleased to meet you, Penny, by the way," Rachel replied.

"No, I'm not named, by the way, I'm –"

"I know," interrupted Rachel, "I'm just being silly. Pleased to meet you, I'm Rachel." She smiled and after paying the cashier she left the store.

Rachel had just placed her shopping in the boot of her car when Penny walked over and apologised for approaching her. "I'm sorry I barged into your day earlier. I don't normally accost strange people in supermarkets."

"I wasn't aware I was strange."

"No … Sorry … I –" Penny stopped abruptly, frowned, and said, "You're joking, right?" Rachel nodded before asking if Penny wanted to join her for a drink. She pointed past the fountain in the supermarket car park towards a small bar with umbrellas shading the tables.

Waiting for their lunchtime spritzers to arrive Penny asked Rachel about the hotel and seemed pleased when Rachel told her that the work was motoring along faster than she anticipated. "Carlino has been a godsend."

"That's great. Things usually move so slowly here in Italy." The waiter delivered their drinks and they sipped at the cool mix of white wine and lemonade Penny told Rachel that she lived outside the hilltop town of Atessa and by the end of their drink-date Rachel had been invited to lunch the next day.

***

Despite having a thermal cover over the windscreen, the car was blisteringly hot inside and as Rachel opened the door it was like heat escaping from an oven. Thankful for the air conditioning she drove towards the town of Atessa.

Rachel pulled up outside a cream-coloured villa set behind a pair of impressive iron gates. She introduced herself to the intercom and the gates slid open without any sound. Driving through she parked on the short, paved driveway and opening the car door was bathed in the floral fragrance coming from a pink rosebush that was surrounded by crimson cosmos. The front door opened, and a wiry hound bolted from between Penny's knees. Rachel froze as the dog reached her its tail oscillating like a fan and its tongue lolling out of its mouth. "She's very friendly," Penny shouted, adding, "Come here *Sale*."

At the door the women air-kissed and Rachel commented on the perfume from the rose. "It's an old one called, Apothecary, I brought over from England, it seems to like it here."

With her ankles being whacked by the dog's wagging tail she said, *Sale* is an unusual name for a dog."

"I had two, *Sale e Pepe* – salt and pepper – but *Pepe* passed away last spring. Now, come inside, out of this infernal heat."

Penny led Rachel through into a spacious open-plan room with two large white sofas and a tatty red chair. Penny offered her a seat, and she chose the sofa nearest the window and the dog jumped up on the red chair, its long legs hanging over. "Tea. English breakfast?" Penny asked before moving into the kitchen area. "I'm a fan of good Italian coffee but just can't shake the need for a good old British cuppa."

As the tea brewed in its pot, Penny sat and listened as Rachel told her about Marco and the discovery of his inheritance – she chose to leave out the financial details – and she talked about how she had come to the decision of restoring and maybe opening the hotel up to paying guests. "But it's pretty much early days yet."

"You will have a lot of work ahead of you?"

"I know and I haven't started to think about decorating the rooms yet, and the thought of looking for laundry supplies and staff fills me with dread."

"You need to get on top of things. Time will start to run away with you and you don't want to be advertising rooms without the bedding already on the beds." Penny stirred the tea in the pot and poured it out into the two china cups on the tray.

"I don't know where to start, I was going to do a few Google searches this weekend."

"You don't need Google, what you need is local knowledge." Penny handed Rachel the tea and nodded her head towards the biscuits arranged on a plate.

"I suppose I could ask Luca… he's my project manager."

"Or I could help you."

"You?"

"Yes. I have to be honest I didn't run into you yesterday purely by accident. I've been hoping to meet you for a while now." Penny placed her hand on her throat and then said, "Oh my, that makes me sound like a stalker."

"A stalker who serves tea," Rachel chuckled.

"You see. I run a holiday business from my office just through there," Penny indicated towards a door across the room." I'll show you after we've had our tea." Rachel wondered where the conversation was leading and was worried she'd given Penny too much information about her plans.

"Don't worry I'm not in direct competition with your hotel if anything we could hopefully help each other out. But we'll get the that later."

Penny topped up Rachel's teacup. "Thanks. So, Penny, how long have you lived here?"

"How long have you got?" Penny laughed, put her tea down and after wiping her mouth on a napkin she said, "I moved here with my husband twelve years ago. No need to tell you his name as he fucked off with a fishmonger after eighteen months – well I say fishmonger, the truth is she worked behind the counter of her father's fish shop in Whitby. I used to run a consultancy business back home in Preston and one night after a chance conversation with a lady who lives locally, I set up my company, and if I say so myself, it's doing very nicely. If you've finished with your tea, I'll show you my office."

Rachel followed Penny into a large room dominated by a huge desk on which was sitting two large computer screens. Posters from the Abruzzo region were framed and hung on the walls and on the top of a filing cabinet in the corner were what looked like looked awards.

"Welcome to, 'Aspire Abruzzo'. My little corner of the international holiday business."

"It all looks very impressive."

"It's a lot of hard work and hair-pulling at times but it's kept me sane. Why don't I fix us lunch and I'll tell you all about it?"

Back in the kitchen, Penny opened a packet of *chicche di patate* and dropped it into a pan of boiling water, "I do prefer this smaller gnocchi to the normal size," she said reaching for and opening a jar of sauce. Rachel helped by slicing a warmed focaccia and within minutes the two women were sitting together at the table.

Rachel listened as Penny explained that her business booked holidaymakers into local hotels and self-catering rentals, "I started off advertising a handful of holiday lets for Brits looking to make an extra bit of cash while their holiday homes are empty and now, I have a portfolio of over forty self-catering properties and five Italian owned hotels."

"I'm impressed," Rachel said as she stabbed at the gnocchi in her bowl, and you do this all by yourself?"

"Not now. I handle the bookings and fees, but I have several people who do change-overs, airport runs and hospitality. People often don't realise what a huge area Abruzzo covers."

"So do you cover the whole region?"

"I concentrate on Chieti and over into Pescara and a few properties over the border into Molise. I leave L'Aquila alone and Teramo is just too far away for me to look after."

Penny rose from her seat and opening the fridge removed a lemon meringue pie and placed it down on the table. "I made this yesterday," she smiled, obviously pleased with the results. "I'd love to tell you it's made with the best lemons from a Neapolitan lemon grove but it's a packet mix from an online shopping company in Leeds." She laughed and Rachel joined her not out of politeness, but because she genuinely liked Penny's sense of humour. "Seriously though," Penny said cutting a slice. "Let me give you some addresses for local businesses that will be able to help you, and once you're up and running maybe we can both discuss a partnership to benefit us both?"

"How would that work?" Rachel said, keeping her voice even so she didn't sound suspicious.

"I think it would be good to have a hotel managed by an English-speaking owner to promote. We can discuss finer details later if you want to consider it once you're up and running. Until then, I think you should consider starting up a blog where you can post updates and photos and people can use it as a link to your website."

"I don't have a website yet."

"But you will." Penny popped a cork from a bottle of frizzante and poured the foaming fizz into a glass and continued, "Enough of business let me tell you about that husband-stealing bitch of a fishmonger from Whitby."

***

Fired up after her lunch with Penny, Rachel decided to drive over to the hotel and see how work was progressing. She was amazed by the amount of work that Carlino and his men had managed to get done since the start of the restoration. With the gardens at the front now looking presentable, the overgrown mess at the side of the property had been dug over and levelled, in readiness for a vegetable garden. The upper floors were cleaned up, and roof tiles replaced where needed, and then the stairs were closed off to the third level. The rewiring was completed quickly following the existing channels and the plumbing was less of a problem than first thought, this meant that work had progressed quickly.

Rachel had discovered the names of Carlino's main builders; two brothers so dissimilar that you'd never guess they were related. Massimo was the tall gangly man with the giant moustache that looked at odds with his narrow face and small mouth. A mouth that was permanently pursed, as if it had stuck one day as he was whistling. Carlino had joked with Luca on Massimo's first day on the job, saying he had a mouth that looked like a cat's arse.

Cosmo was the opposite of his brother. He was a robust man with a thick head of curly hair that sat upon an equally robust neck. His podgy hands with their short sausage-shaped fingers looked like balloon hands on the ends of his hairy thick arms. Cosmo did all the labouring, being responsible for lifting the sacks of plaster and mixing it, whereas Massimo did all the plastering, taking great care to leave as smooth a surface as he could. The two men had been working daily at the hotel and had already replastered ten of the twelve bedrooms on the second floor leaving the joiners to fit the new windows as they finished off the final rooms.

Downstairs the noise of saws, drills and hammering filled the dining room. Luca helped a miserable-looking man put up a scaffolding tower in the reception area, while Carlino explained to Rachel that they were going to remove the false ceiling in the foyer. "Can you see where the cornice has been damaged to fit what looks like boarding?"

"I hope it's nothing that can't be repaired."

"Now we discover," Carlino said as Massimo began to climb up the scaffolding tower. At the top, bent double because of his height he started to remove nails that fixed the hardboard to the ceiling. Flakes of painted plaster began to rain down and it was only as the ceiling cover was finally removed that they could that a portion of the cornice was missing.

"It's a shame that it's damaged," Luca said.

"Maybe that's why it was covered up," added Carlino, "Looks like water damage."

The ceiling appeared intact but in need of some work to bring it back to its former glory. Rachel looked up at the pale magenta paintwork with what looked like constellations painted in gold.

"*Sangue di Pecora*," a voice behind them said and they all turned to see Cosmo standing looking up at the ceiling in awe. "The colour," he said, "It's mixed with a little sheep's blood to get that shade of…" his voice trailed off as he tried to describe the colour, then he pointed through the window at the oleander flowers, "*Come questo*."

"I'm guessing we won't be able to restore it," Rachel said.

Carlino was shaking his head when Cosmo said, "I can." Everyone looked at the stout man with a nose the same colour as the ceiling as he folded his arms in a defiant gesture and grinned.

"Are you sure?" Rachel asked him, hope evident in her voice.

"*Rachele*," he said, his pronunciation of her name in Italian melting the air around her, "I promise, it will be perfect when I have finished."

"But what about our work on the building?" Massimo said from the tower.

"I shall do the work in my own time," he turned to Rachel. "It will be my pleasure."

"Very well," she said shaking his outstretched hand, "If you let me know the cost, I'll let you have the money for materials… and you will be paid a little over the hourly rate for your extra hours too."

"Not essential, normal rate is good with me," said Cosmo beaming like a teenager.

The moment was put aside by Carlino clapping his hands and ordering everyone back to work, adding, "Massimo, get down from that tower and get upstairs to your plastering."

Rachel hugged Cosmo – he blushed – before she rushed outside to fetch her camera from the car to take some pictures of the ceiling to email to Louise later that day.

Chapter Thirteen

Rachel was determined to achieve as much as possible in the short space of time before the August holidays began. There were just five working days before the men downed tools. Grabbing her sunglasses and hat, she closed the balcony doors as the piazza began to move from restful to restless and set off for the day.

She opened the car door, threw her briefcase onto the passenger seat and set off for the hotel, she was beginning to enjoy the drive to the hotel, and although the coast road was scenic it added time to her journey, so today she opted for the more direct route. It had taken her a few days to get used to the baffling one-way system that took her through the historic centre of Lanciano with its grand palazzos and streets so narrow she'd sometimes have to stop to pull in the wing mirrors.

The streets on the edge of the old town were soulless; modern apartments and geometric family homes were squeezed into narrow spaces, almost hiding the sky from view. Once out of town, the world looked enormous, the road widened, and the sky took over. Villas built over the past fifty years rubbed shoulders with ancient crumbling farmhouses. Some of the newer properties looked as if they'd just been plonked down beside the neighbouring vegetable plots and olives. Houses built by Mussolini's government for impoverished farmers remained – most abandoned – their owners untraceable after so many years and next to them were shiny new builds with rendered walls and electric gates. Rachel liked this juxtaposition of dwellings; it was almost as if time had been captured and locked into a clockface that developed into the modern while still retaining the obsolete. She sometimes thought it strange how time moved on here. Modern trends were apparent, yet there was still a measure of the traditional in the daily Abruzzese life.

The hotel reception was filled with workers getting ready for their day. Some were putting on their overalls, others talked about football: as is the usual topic of conversation between Italian men. Rachel looked across at Cosmo who was painting a pinkish stripe on a piece of hardboard. Looking up he called out, *"Niente Sangue,"* telling her there was no blood, in the paint he'd colour-matched. Rachel waved to him and wished him a good morning then made her way over to the chair beside the windows. After removing her notebook and phone, she sat looking out at the front of the hotel.

The hedges had been trimmed and standing beside them, like watchmen were two large yellow skips filled with rubble. Rachel looked at them her desire to see the garden open and welcoming was a strong emotion she'd not experienced before. The morning soon became filled with the sound of hammering and drilling and the chatter of the men working and as she imagined rose bushes and cosmos in the garden a feeling of achievement washed over her.

Working through her 'to-do' list lunchtime soon crept up and the workers began to filter off for their midday meals. Opening a paper bag to reveal a cheese panino Rachel was disturbed by Luca who beckoned her over. "Come to see what I have done outside," he said, she put down her lunch and walked towards him. "I want you to see this." Luca led her between a gap in the trimmed jasmine hedge into a wide-open space.

The scrub had been removed revealing a small stone building and bare earth. "This will be the orto." Rachel listened as he pointed out the places where different vegetables would be grown, he showed her a spot for a poly-tunnel and then opening the sun-dried wooden door to the discovered outbuilding, he said, "This will be perfect for storage." His smile disappeared behind his ears, "You like?"

"Yes, I like it," Rachel said, "I like it very much. But how you can grow anything in this stony soil is beyond belief."

"Good for drainage, bad for fennel. Look here." He pointed to a long row already sieved and stoneless in readiness for his aniseed-flavoured bulbs.

As they walked around the garden he told her of his other plans to improve it. Rachel told Luca about her meeting with Penny and the contacts she had given him. "I've booked an appointment with two local laundries and I'm meeting a representative from a catering supply company in Ancona.

Luca shook his head and said, "So you want to spend more money than you should?"

"I don't understand."

"Laundry, yes, you need. But buying pots and pans from big suppliers is not needed. Wait."

Rachel watched as Luca took out his phone and dialled a number, "*Ciao, Edoardo…*" Rachel left him to his call and wandered away looking down at the end of the garden. A fence separated the hotel grounds from the olive groves beyond; between the trees the grass was clipped to within an inch of its life to prevent it from taking the nutrients needed for the olives and red painted stones denoted each owner's boundary.

"This is like being in another world," she said as Luca joined her.

"For you, yes. For me, it's already my world." He looked out over the countryside as Rachel looked closely at him. The work at the hotel was showing on his face. His nose and forehead were more bronzed, and the whites of his eyes seemed to be clearer and there were a couple of new lines at the edges. Her eyes dropped to his lips for a second and she feared he'd notice if they lingered there. She broke the silence by asking him who Edoardo was. "He comes here tomorrow to talk about kitchen supplies. Local and best prices."

"You seem to know everybody," she said.

"No," he shook his head. "Here we do community business, we all look after each other and keep our money in Abruzzo."

"Puts another perspective on the phrase 'shop local'," Rachel said. Luca looked confused and she brushed it away as they turned and walked back towards the hotel.

Returning to the hotel they were taken by the silence and murmuring of voices from the reception area. Massimo held up something small and silver, "Look Rachel, one of the men has found this." He dropped a small silver key into the palm of her hand.

"Do you think this could be the key to the box that Aldo found?" Luca said.

"Where was it?"

Massimo pointed, "Over by that pile of rubbish waiting to be cleared away."

"Perhaps it was in the plaster from the fireplace after all."

Rosa handed out cups of coffee and as Rachel left to go to her car, Luca turned the key over in his hand and Aldo reached up to his throat to discover that his necklace had come undone; no one heard the curse that escaped his lips. Coming back into the lobby Rachel carried the wooden box that had been in the boot of her car. The chatter in the room halted as everyone watched as Rachel inserted the key inside the tiny lock. "It fits but feels stiff," she said.

"Here," one of the men handed her a small can of oil and after a few drops the lock relented and the box was open. Reaching inside Rachel removed an ornate pewter coloured clock and placed it down on the desk. No one spoke as they all looked at the timepiece and Rachel pointed out that fastened to one of the feet was another small key.

The silence was broken by Rosa: "Many years have passed since that has been seen."

"What do you know about this clock?" Carlino asked her.

"The old woman shook her hand with a 'so, so' expression before she began to collect up the cardboard coffee cups. Shuffling over towards the open spaces waiting for the window frames Rosa poured the remnants of her coffee flask out onto the grass as Carlino ordered everyone back to work.

Rosa sat at the table where Rachel had been working earlier and beckoned her over. "I was a young girl, barely at my mother's knee in height when we came here to live with *Nonno*. He was old and needed to be cared for and mother being the eldest daughter the task fell upon her shoulders. One evening after too many glasses of wine *Nonno* told me tales about the house that this once was. During the Great War, the house was for a short period a hospital for soldiers and much of its artefacts had to be locked away. When the war ended it became a convalescence home for soldiers from the Alpini Regiments. The house was repaired and re-opened everything was laid out once again and paintings were re-hung, and the clock was placed back where it belonged on the dining room mantlepiece, with its blue face with mother-of-pearl stars and second hand shaped into a crescent moon moving across it."

Rachel was becoming impatient and Carlino was looking at his watch. "The clock?" Luca said, attempting to move the old lady's story along.

Rosa held up a hand and said, "*Va bene,*" she smoothed the front of her apron before continuing, "One day it went missing, assumed stolen and now here it is once again, ready to chime once more."

Heads turned to look at the clock on the reception desk, and eyes fixed upon the tiny crescent moon hovering above the cobalt face. Rachel untied the key attached to the foot slid it into the winding arbour and turned it. The crescent moon remained static and no sound came from the inner workings.

"Looks like it's so old it's seized up," Luca said. "It needs oil maybe." Rachel handed him the clock and as he took it a rattle was heard. He shook it and the rattle became louder.

"Sounds like there's something broken inside," Rachel said taking it back and returning it to the wooden box. "Maybe when the hotel is completed, I'll have it repaired."

Aldo VI

That evening Aldo watched Rachel remove the wooden box from her car and walk around the corner to her apartment. He kept himself hidden, tucked into an unlit vico so even the whites of his eyes were unseen. He watched her open the entrance to the palazzo and as the large doors closed behind her, Aldo stepped out into the green light from the *farmacia*.

The windows of Rachel's apartment lit up indicating she was now inside. How funny that the foreigners never close their shutters when they go away, Aldo thought as he slunk back into the vico as she opened the bedroom window. He remained motionless, watching, expecting her to open the balcony doors but they remained closed. He could see her moving around from room to room, her silhouette illuminated from inside against the sheer voile drapes.

Leaning against the damp and mossy wall, that was denied sunlight he took a bottle from his pocket and took a swig of grappa and settled down to wait. What he was waiting for he did not know; he just knew that he needed to get his hands on the box.

Time passes slowly when your eyes are fixed on one point, and because of a mix of boredom and grappa, Aldo felt his eyelids start to droop. The light in Rachel's apartment was extinguished and he looked at his watch, poking his arm out into the green glow from the chemist's sign to read the dial. *Nineteen-fifty, too early to retire for the evening,* he thought as he watched a slim woman enter the piazza, she took out her mobile and he heard her make a brief call before minutes later the palazzo doors opened and Rachel stepped outside.

Aldo watched as the two women embraced and walked away together. He waited until he was sure they'd be far enough away and then stepped out of the gloom.

Rachel's apartment looked as if he remembered it from his first clandestine visit. There was an unwashed coffee cup on the drainer and a pair of discarded trainers beside the sofa. He pushed open the door to the bedroom and there on the dressing table stood the wooden box and beside it was Giacomo's key.

Aldo picked up the box, felt the weight and pocketed the key. He looked down at the gemstone bracelet and for a second considered stealing it. He shook his head and told himself, "I'm not a common thief." He swallowed hard, the experience made him feel uncomfortable, "I'm a *contadino*, not a burglar." Aldo wasn't comfortable breaking the law, he was just a peasant farmer who grew up on the outskirts of Naples, and now because of Giacomo's legacy he was a jewel thief and it didn't sit well with him.

The boot of the old car squeaked as it opened, and Aldo held his breath fearing alerting any passer-by. He placed the wooden box inside and covered it with an old blanket before climbing onto the driver's seat and starting the engine. Pulling away from the kerb and with the headlights unlit the rusting Fiat Panda made its way out of the town centre.

As he left Lanciano, Aldo realised he hadn't given much thought to where he'd go. Could he risk going back to Naples? He dismissed that idea quickly, returning there with the diamond would be foolish. Besides trying to sell it in Naples could bring serious trouble to his door. I could lose myself in Rome, he thought but again dismissed the idea as he knew no one there. As he approached the retail park at the autostrada entrance, he saw a sign for L'Aquila and his mind was made up.

He parked outside the shopping centre and was contemplating buying something to eat when his eagerness got the better of him. He looked around before moving his car to the far side of the car park and away from the evening shoppers and bright lights. Checking he was not drawing attention to himself, he got out of the car and walked around to the boot. He could feel the sweat beading on his forehead, not because of the evening warmth, but the anticipation of finally seeing the Medici diamond. He knew it would be foolish to remove it here in public, but just to look inside the box would be enough. He grinned, how clever of Giacomo to have hidden it inside the clock, he thought as he opened the box. His grin faded faster than an ink bloom on a blotter. There was no clock inside just a cardboard tube, he took the tube out and realised he'd seen it before on the dressing table back at Rachel's apartment. He read the name printed on the sticker, Marco Balducci, the rest of the words were useless to him, he understood no English, but the word 'crematorium' stood out. A word similar to the same in his language, "*Crematorio*," he said under his breath, and the realisation of what he was holding struck him.

He fumbled the ashes back inside the box and locked it. He was sweating, panting like a dog as he sat in the driver's seat again trying to figure out what to do next. Anyone else would probably just ditch the ashes, but Aldo couldn't do that. He'd just nursed his uncle through his final days, and his death was still a shadow clinging to him. "I must return them."

Arriving back at the piazza Aldo looked up at the lights shining inside Rachel's apartment and realised he'd lost the opportunity to return the box. He was considering creeping up the stairs and leaving it outside her door when a scream pierced the evening stillness.

Chapter Fourteen

When Rachel opened the door and saw Luca standing in the hallway, her anxiety began to fade; if anyone could help her in this dilemma, she felt it would be him. He placed the black rucksack he was carrying on the table and took both of her hands in his. His dark brown eyes looked into hers; red and puffy, searching for the story behind her urgent phone call. She was sniffling, the gulping sobs having subsided and after taking a deep breath the words plummeted from her lips. "It was on the dressing table... I was with Penny... Someone has stolen Marco... We only –" Her words ended as a fresh batch of crying started, and she allowed Luca to pull her close and hold her until the shaking of her shoulders lessened.

Pushing him away she was about to start speaking again when he put his finger to her lips, and she stopped and listened.

"Take a deep breath and slowly tell me everything," he took a pristine linen handkerchief from his jeans pocket and handed it to her. Rachel blew her nose on the handkerchief as Luca reached inside the rucksack and removed a bottle of something amber-coloured. "Sit," he said as he poured two glasses. He turned to face her. Rachel's shoulders were once again rising and falling with rapid breathing. "Here. This will calm the nerves."

Rachel took the offered glass and nervously sipped at the brandy before telling him about leaving the apartment for dinner with Penny and returning to find Marco's ashes had been taken.

"Are you sure they have been taken?"

"Yes," she said her voice cracking. "Do you think I'd call you if they hadn't gone missing?"

"Of course not," Luca said, reaching to top up her glass.

"I don't want any more fucking brandy. I want my husband."

"Tell me again what has happened," Luca said, hoping Rachel would calm down and not disturb the other people living in the palazzo.

"I've already told you. I came home from the hotel, and I took out the clock and put it beside the bed in that room," she pointed to the smaller bedroom and Luca walked over and opened the door to look inside. "Then just before I went out for dinner with Penny, I placed Marco's ashes inside the box. I just thought it would be better protection for them, the tube is only made of cardboard you see, and it's travelled so far and…"

Luca placed his hand over hers and she stopped rambling. "I returned from dinner and went to change my clothes and saw that the box had gone." She stood up and taking the hand that was on hers she led Luca into the bedroom and pointed to where the box had been.

Rachel sat down on the bed as Luca checked the locks at the window before saying I think we need to call the carabinieri. Do you have your documents at hand?"

"They're in my laptop case." Rachel pointed out into the sitting room. Luca left the bedroom and looked around before calling to tell her he couldn't find it. "Maybe it has been stolen?"

Rachel appeared in the doorway, "It might still be in my car, I don't remember bringing it inside." She took her keys from the countertop and handed them to Luca. She had a huge knot in her chest as she heard Luca's footsteps on the marble steps outside. She sipped at her brandy and grimaced as the heat bathed her throat.

Within minutes Luca returned and standing in the doorway he was holding the wooden box, with her laptop bag hanging from his shoulder.

Rachel's eyes were wide and questioning as she placed her glass down. "How... Where... No, it... She grabbed at the box and putting it on the counter she scrabbled at the lid trying to open it. "Key," she yelled at Luca, he shook his head. Grabbing a knife from the drainer Rachel inserted it between the lid and box frame and the sound of splintering wood was followed by the retrieval of Marco's ashes from inside.

Luca was now beside the sofa and as Rachel turned to face him, he shrugged and said, "They were in the boot of your rental car."

It was Rachel's turn to shake her head. "I don't know how." Much calmer now. "I did bring the box inside; I did put the clock in the other bedroom and I did put the box on my dressing table."

"But –"

"I don't know."

"If someone did take the box then I'm sure they weren't after Marco's ashes."

"What do you mean *if*. Of course, someone took the box. I'm not making this up." Rachel stopped speaking placed Marco down and walked towards the spare bedroom. Before entering she turned to Luca and said, "The clock."

Sitting side by side on the sofa Luca and Rachel examined the clock closely. They wound it up again, but it failed to start, the crescent moon remaining where it had stopped years before. Turning it over Luca looked for a maker's mark but found nothing he recognised. As they turned it over, it rattled again; something inside had broken off. "What if it was the clock that they wanted," Luca said. "Not the box, but what was inside it."

Rachel felt the colour drain from her face before saying, "I don't want that clock in this apartment a minute longer than necessary. Can you look after it?"

Luca nodded and after offering Rachel another brandy he placed the clock inside his rucksack. "You look tired," he said.

"I am."

"It's getting late, and the night has been eventful. Maybe you should rest."

"Yes," Rachel whispered.

As she got ready for bed, Rachel looked at her face in the bathroom mirror. Her eyes were sore, red-ringed and swollen. Mascara trails ran down her cheeks and what was remaining of her lipstick had bled into the creases at the corners of her mouth. Her hair was wild where she'd raked her fingers through it and down the front of her blouse, an amber stain from the brandy had dried.

She slipped between the sheets and lay looking up at the ceiling, occasionally tossing a glance over to check on Marco's ashes when she suddenly became anxious again as she realised, she was in another country and apart from Luca she had no friends and family for support.

Suddenly Rachel felt lonely.

Chapter Fifteen

The following morning arrived with a breeze that was a welcome change from the hot stillness of the previous days. Rachel had showered, dressed and eaten breakfast and after putting Marco in the car drove over to the hotel early.

Sitting on one of the balconies and watching the day wake up, she listened to the sound of lazy waves in the distance. The garden was filled with natural sounds, clicks of insects, the song of a thrush and the clack-clack of a nearby woodpecker. In the distance, two figures moved through an olive grove inspecting the trees as a dog bounded ahead of them, stopping now and again to sniff at something that had caught its attention.

Luca's Alfa Romeo pulled up, the wheels scattering gravel and Rachel watched as he lifted the boot and removed a pair of boots and several gardening tools. He walked around the side and past the kitchens, through the jasmine hedge and she heard the clatter of tools being dropped onto the ground.

Rachel leant over the balcony to shout her hello to Luca as his phone rang and she listened to his one-sided conversation held in dialect, a muddle of very fast staccato phrases. As the call ended Luca reappeared below and from her vantage point Rachel could see that his black hair shone in the sunlight, she took in the full width of his shoulders and the sleekness of his form. "*Ciao,*" she shouted, amused when he was startled.

He looked up, using one hand to shield his eyes before he called back, "*Ciao, Rachel, aspetta li.*"

Within minutes Luca was joining her on the balcony and together they stood watching as the figures in the olive grove below were joined by someone on a tractor, the driver navigating the steep incline as the dog rushed up to play chase.

"I want to apologise for last night," Rachel said breaking the silence.

Luca's raised hand stopped her, "No need. Yesterday is gone, today is a new day. Have you put Marco's ashes somewhere safe?"

"They're on the reception desk, I'll move them when Carlino's men arrive," Rachel said as the builder's pick-up pulled up in the driveway.

Carlino dropped down from the driver's cab and walked up to the hotel entrance and as he entered the reception area he was greeted by Luca and Rachel coming down the stairs. "You're early too," Luca said.

"I've asked everyone to put in a few extra hours," he turned to Rachel, "No overtime, just normal rate," turning back to Luca, "I want the last of the window frames fitted before the holiday. When we return, we shall start work on Rachel's apartment."

A shuffling sound came from above their heads, "That's upstairs," Luca said turning and walking back to the second floor. He looked along the corridor and seeing nothing began to climb to the third floor. Carlino followed with Rachel behind.

The third floor was dark, hardly any light got through the boards up at the empty windows. Their footsteps echoed along the corridor. The only door was to the space designated to become Rachel's apartment, and as Luca pushed it open light spilt into the corridor.

"Someone has been living here," Carlino said as they stepped inside the room. On the floor was an old mattress and sleeping bag. A camping stove with a coffee maker stood on the floor and beside the makeshift bed lay cornetti and pre-packed sandwich wrappers.

"*Vagabondi*," Carlino said, moving the food wrappers with the toe of his boot. "I'll speak with the men today and ask if it is one of them. Maybe Cosmo has slept here after working on the ceiling." Rachel and Luca nodded in agreement; his assumption was plausible.

Carlino and Luca went downstairs to greet the arriving workforce as Rachel stayed behind and picked up the food wrappers, she was stuffing them inside a supermarket carrier bag when she became aware of someone on the second floor, she opened the door to the room where she had stood on the balcony earlier and there at the window was Aldo. "*Buongiorno Signora,*" he said holding up a paintbrush to justify his being there. Rachel wished him a good morning and carried the rubbish she'd collected downstairs.

"*Va tutto bene*?" asked Luca as Rachel appeared in the reception area. She looked towards Rosa who had arrived with breakfast and coffee for the men; this was becoming a daily ritual and Rachel feared it was becoming expensive for the old woman. "Yes, all is okay," she said as she reached Luca's side, "I'll move Marco's box to somewhere safer."

As she placed the box inside one of the laundry cupboards in the kitchen corridor Rachel was joined by Rosa. The old woman was cradling one of her small cardboard cups of coffee and she held it out to Rachel. The coffee was as strong as tungsten but as sweet as honey and as Rachel drank the tar-coloured liquid Rosa observed her closely. "You have seen much sadness," the old woman said placing her hand on Rachel's arm, "but I see happiness behind your eyes. Maybe it is the hotel, maybe something else?"

"Thank you for the coffee," Rachel said avoiding the question.

"You looked confused earlier as you came down the stairs like something was on your mind. I heard Luca ask if you were all right."

"I was just wondering what my apartment would look like when finished."

"I'm sure it will look grand."

"I'd like it to look like it would have done years ago, oh, I wish I knew more about the history of the hotel." Rachel released the cup Rosa took it crushed it placed it inside the pocket of her apron. If these walls could talk, I wonder what they'd say,"

The old woman turned to walk away then looking back said, "Old buildings are like vaults, they hold memories securely. The stones that make up, *Le Stelle* hold its secrets inside them." The door swished as it closed behind Rosa leaving Rachel standing alone in the corridor.

Chapter Sixteen

August arrived, and as if it knew the date the weather ramped up and the temperature rose by a further few degrees. The mountains had been cloaked with summer fog earlier and now at seven-thirty the morning air was steaming, the mist had started to burn off and the air was becoming humid. Olives dotted with small green fruits soaked up the warmth, knowing the searing heat of August would ripen the fruit – Luca had already promised to take Rachel to an olive harvest in November, but for now, she was content to wait in anticipation of the peppery oil that would be produced.

The day before Rachel had enjoyed being at the hotel in the early morning and so had chosen to do the same today. She used the time alone to compare wallpaper samples that Louise had posted over. She was holding the paper squares next to the small blocks of paint in a brochure trying to imagine how the finished walls would look.

Hearing her mobile ring, she crossed to the trestle table where her bag was and picked up her phone. It was Louise's boyfriend, "Hi Ben, everything okay?"

"Hi Rach, yes everything is great. Louise asked me to call, she said – now let me get this right, she's written it down for me – Can you let her know which paint and wallpaper you want before the end of this weekend as there's a sale on."

"Oddly enough I'm at the hotel now choosing them," Rachel said.

"What's it like there at the moment?" Ben asked.

"Hot. There's no breeze to speak of, so I think I'll go to the beach later and take a dip in the sea."

"Lucky you. Listen I'd best go, I'll let Lou know I've told you and take care, see you –"

Before she could respond he had gone.

Rachel spent the remainder of the morning wandering from room to room holding up paint charts against walls and matching them to website images. She'd already decided that all the linen and towels would be white so she could choose to have two different colour schemes for her rooms. She decided that the bedrooms facing the front of the hotel would be duck egg blue, with a pale-yellow bird of paradise patterned paper and those facing the rear garden would be a washed-out sage teamed with a more dramatic floral mulberry paper.

Opening a bottle of sparkling water and taking a sip, Rachel sat down and composed an email to Louise, she double checked the colours and names before pressing send and then packed everything away inside her bag. She looked across at the stairs leading to the upper floor and found herself moving towards them. She made her way up to the third floor opened the door and saw that the mattress had been moved and the sleeping bag was gone. "Looks like our unknown visitor has checked out," she said to herself as she entered the room. Walking around she began to imagine how her apartment would look. Taking out her phone she began to take photos, sure that she'd need them for the future discussions with Carlino.

***

The morning had slipped away peacefully, she'd not seen another soul – it seemed it was true, everything in Italy stopped in August. – Sauntering down towards the beach she wondered if she'd see Rosa, but the lane was deserted and she felt a sense of calm being the only person there.

She noted that the steps down to the small sandy beach were wide and easily accessible for her future guests as she walked down them. The cove was hidden behind swathes of tall bamboo that rattled in the gentle wind coming off the Adriatic. This is better, Rachel thought allowing the cool air to cover her. She'd changed earlier and wore her swimsuit beneath her summer dress and after finding a spot to rest she pulled the dress over her head and waded into the crystal-clear water. As she paddled small silver fish-like coins darted away and then returned the swim around her ankles. At waist height she fell forward and swam in a languid breaststroke, there was no hurry to reach anywhere. She flipped over onto her back and floated there, her body gently bobbing in the water. Allowing a thought about Marco to elbow its way into her head she considered whether this could be a place to release his ashes. It was tranquil enough and close to his hotel, and it was somewhere she could visit regularly.

Shielding her eyes from the sun that was creeping over the frames of her sunglasses she looked up and saw a figure at the top of the steps. Dressed in black and standing as straight as the bamboo canes. She knew it must be Rosa and waved and the figure returned it. "I bet you'll feel lost without all the workers to make coffee for now the holiday season has arrived," she said aloud making a conscious decision to drop in to see the old lady during the holiday.

Later as she lay on a towel with her eyes closed she let the sun bake her skin as she thought how much better being here would have been if Marco hadn't died. She hadn't noticed the lack of sadness in her daily activities lately and how the tears had ceased to arrive at inopportune moments. She thought about how being occupied had staved off the mourning and apart from the night his ashes went missing, she realised that the hotel-shaped surprise from Marco had been the best antidote to the sadness of losing him.

When the afternoon sun became too hot, she dressed and made her way back to the hotel where she found Penny parking her car outside. "I was passing so thought I'd see how you are after the drama."

"I'm fine thanks," Rachel replied, part of her thinking that maybe Penny's remark was edged with a little disbelief about the theft. Just then her mobile rang. Apologising she answered the call, "Hi Louise, did you get my email?"

"Yes, I've ordered everything for you, it's in stock and should be delivered fairly quickly." There was some interference on the line and Rachel asked Louise to repeat what she'd said. "That's good, thanks for doing that for me. Where are you, it sounds noisy there?"

"We're in the car. Ben is taking me shopping." Louise said almost shouting. "He's got his window open."

***

The restaurant Penny chose for dinner was cool, the air conditioning doing its utmost to keep the evening heat at bay. The soft rose-coloured walls were lit by electric wall lights that resembled burning torches and suspended from the ceiling above each table were wrought iron baskets filled with fresh flowers. The waiter, a wasp-waisted man with tight trousers and a tighter white shirt showed the women to their table, with a flick of his glossy black mane he handed them a menu and walked away. "The food here is just as attractive," said Penny with a wink, and Rachel allowed herself a backward glance at the departing waiter's bottom. "How are things coming along at the hotel?"

"I'm more than pleased with how it's progressed, it's just a shame we're so quiet now.

The waiter delivered two glasses of Aperol as Penny said, "In a few years, you'll be used to the inactivity of the locals during August. Besides, if all goes well it'll be one of your busiest periods."

"I hope so."

"Now, I've been thinking," said Penny as she looked at the menu at the same time as speaking. "You need to think about what your season will be and work towards getting interest up."

"Well," Rachel said as the waiter hovered at her side, "I'm guessing Easter through to September. The summer holidays."

Penny didn't look up from her menu, instead, she caught the waiter's attention. "I'll have the ravioli with goat's cheese, followed by the *coniglio alla stimpirata*." Penny's attention moved away from the menu, "I think you should begin by losing the English summer holiday mentality." She nodded to indicate the waiter was waiting for her order and Rachel said she'd have the same as her friend. "Hotel demand is so different from self-catering. As well as being catered for during the summer, people will want to be hosted through Easter and Christmas and New Year." Penny picked up her drink and sucked the orange liquid up the straw before carrying on. "Now if I'm telling you something you already know, then stop me. There's a market for *Pasqua* – Easter, families come together over this period and a hotel is the perfect place for those who live further afield to stay, not to mention the obligatory lamb lunches that you could turn to your advantage." Rachel removed the straws from her drink and sipped at it as Penny continued. "The New Year is great for a younger crowd; it'll be noisy and bloody hard work but can be profitable. All they'll need is accommodation, breakfast, and booze. The Italians are very different to the groups of young Brits you'll be familiar with. And of course, there's Christmas, to make use of, lunches and dinners and a limited capacity. All of these things will extend your season and hopefully bring in a healthier profit."

"I hadn't given it much thought other than summer." Rachel leant back to allow the waiter to deliver their ravioli to the table.

"Far be it for me to tell you how to organise your own business," Penny said cutting into the pasta to let the goat's cheese inside join the almost transparent broth. "But please, do tell me if you think I'm interfering."

"I appreciate all of your advice, as you know this is all new to me and I'm happy to learn from you. I just hope it doesn't seem like you're doing all the work for me."

"I'm happy to help. Think of yourself as a sponge and the experience I have as the water. Now eat up, wait until you taste the rabbit."

Chapter Seventeen

"Bloody hell," Louise said, "I thought Dover was depressing but this place comes in at a close second." She was sat in the passenger seat of Ben's transit van as it chugged along the A25 from Dunkerque to Lille. "I thought France was supposed to have better weather than England. So far, we've had fog and now it's pouring down." Louise hated being in Ben's van, and this led to increased moaning. The interior was typically working male, chocolate and screwed-up burger wrappers littered the floor, and the glove box was filled with everything from used sealant tubes to drill bits. "You should have cleaned this out before we left. We can't rock up at Rachel's in a glorified litter bin on wheels."

"For goodness sake, Lou, give it a rest. You wanted to surprise her."

"I know but you could have made the effort."

"If it bothers you that much at the next service station, I'd be happy to go for something to eat while you give it a clean." Louise folded her arms and sulked as the van skirted around Lille and headed over the border into Belgium heading for Luxembourg and its low-priced fuel.

The drive was tedious, flat carriageways with nothing on either side to stimulate the onlooker. Eventually, as they filled up with petrol, Ben took the van through a carwash and gave the interior a quick once over with a car-vac. With both the van and their stomachs topped up they headed in the direction of Metz and Nancy and the rain gave way to sunshine.

"I hope she doesn't mind us turning up unannounced," Ben said later as the van crossed the border into Switzerland.

"Rachel will love it," Louise said unwrapping a bar of chocolate and handing him several squares. "Besides, she'll be getting free painting and decorating."

After thirteen hours of driving, they were almost at the Italian border when Ben said he needed a rest. "I could do with a few hours' sleep," he said rubbing his neck to ease the stiffness.

"Let's get over the border and find somewhere to stay," Louise folded the map in her lap and watched as the uniformed guards stopped some of the cars crossing into Italy. Ben was just about to take the exit when a guard stepped forward and holding up a paddle directed him into a parking bay. Ben killed the engine and as instructed opened the back of the van allowing two guards to look inside "What is this for?" A guard said pointing to the cans of paint with his baton.

Ben looked at Louise and she knew she must take control. "It's paint."

"Do you have importation documents?"

"Oh, "Louise said thinking on her feet. "It's not to sell. We have a small house in Abruzzo and it's to paint our walls."

The guard looked at her, picked up a can and looked at the colour swatch then shrugged and said, "You can go."

Louise was still thanking him as Ben put the van in gear, and they pulled away from the checkpoint.

Just outside Como, they found a small family-run bed and breakfast and as Louise lay splayed out on the bed, Ben eased his bones beneath the hot water in the shower. "How long will it take to get to Lanciano tomorrow?" Louise called.

"About seven hours, but I think we should stop off for a rest halfway," Ben said, coming into the room towel-drying his hair. He lay down on the bed beside Louise and within minutes they were both asleep.

Breakfast the next morning was a simple affair, slices of cold meats and cheese and a bread roll. Both of them had woken hungry after falling asleep without any dinner and within minutes of leaving the bed and breakfast, they were pulling into a service station for something more substantial.

The second part of their journey had begun badly with Ben getting lost on the orbital around Milan and taking the wrong exit. This led to another argument with Louise; "This wouldn't have happened if you'd let me use the Satnav,"

"It's pretty straightforward," Louise had said holding up her map, "It's virtually one straight line down the country."

Ben managed to find the toll booth directing him towards the A41 and escaping from the urban sprawl they joined the mind-numbing autostrada.

As the van continued south Louise sat looking out of the window and saying very little. She was thinking about the journey and how it had not lived up to the road trip notion she had had, now she wanted nothing more than for it to be over. Three hours later, as if sensing Louise's boredom, Ben took the exit for Bologna and following the signs for tourist parking drove into the city. "Come on," he said, "let's go for a walk and find somewhere for lunch." Louise shrugged her shoulders and dropped down out of the van and just minutes later as Ben led her by the hand through the narrow streets lined with shops her mood lifted.

They found a simple trattoria and decided that being in Bologna the home of Bolognese, it would be rude not to sample some. Ben commented on the lack of tomatoes in the sauce and Louise said, "You have to savour the richness that only slow-cooking can impart into a dish."

"Get you," Ben said, "The travelling gourmet."

After lunch, before resuming their journey they walked to Piazza Maggiore and ate ice creams, they marvelled at the openness of the space in comparison to the previous slender streets. "We must come here for a weekend one day," said Ben.

Back on the road, Louise's mood was more positive and as the van slipped into Le Marche, she was telling Ben about the places she'd visited during her stay with Rachel, the restaurants, the town centre and the rugged coastline. "We'll have to spend at least two days on the beach," she said, "and eat seafood and gelato until we're fed up with it."

"I'm looking forward to just taking some time out with a beer and pizza."

"Philistine," Louise laughed.

They arrived at the outskirts of Lanciano early evening and after finding the rail station to get her bearings, Louise took over the navigation, sending Ben towards the historic centre.

Finding a parking space big enough to accommodate the van was a problem as the *comune* spaces were designed for the small compact cars that were parked inside them. Ben was about to give up when a pick-up reversed out of a space and drove away. Climbing out of the cab Ben stretched and groaned then looked around at the old buildings with modern shop fronts and the brightly lit bars where people were gathering for aperitivi. "Shall I bring the suitcases?" he asked as Louise slipped her arm through his and began to lead him away.

"No let's surprise her first," she said as they turned the corner into the piazza. Louise pointed to the large palazzo doors and was about to ring the bell for Rachel's apartment when a shriek rang out across the cobblestones and her name was yelled. Turning around Ben and Louise saw Rachel across the square standing outside a bar.

The two women ran toward each other and embraced in the middle of the piazza, words tumbling from both of their mouths as they tried to talk. Someone clapped and a voice beside Rachel said, "*Una sorpresa per te*?" Louise looked up from her hug to see Luca standing beside them, she broke away and hugged him too as if he were an old friend. Ben stepped forward and Rachel introduced him and the two men politely shook hands. "I think we need more drinks," Luca said, and everyone followed as he indicated towards the table on the pavement outside the bar.

"You should have told me you were coming," Rachel said.

"And spoil the surprise."

"How long are you staying for?"

"Two weeks if you'll have us. We have your paint and wallpaper in the van so we thought we could help decorate the rooms at the hotel while the builders are on holiday." Rachel hugged Louise again before she continued, "I've been working on some website ideas for you, so you can take a look at that too."

"Have you eaten?" Luca said.

"Nothing since Bologna," Ben said as he took a long slug of his Peroni.

"Leave it to me," Luca rose from his seat and walked a few steps away to make a phone call before returning. "All sorted, there's a table for us at Osteria 101."

Luca paid for the drinks, and they all took a slow walk to Via Roma, Luca pointed out places of interest to Ben as the girls lagged behind catching up on the latest office gossip. The restaurant wasn't large, its tables were close together with each one dressed in an immaculate starched tablecloth. The menu was just one sheet of printed paper and Luca explained that they served fresh homemade cuisine that was seasonal. "It's a case of whatever they've cooked, they serve. It's traditional Italian home cooking."

Ben struggled with his bucatini; the pasta seemed to have a life of its own. He glanced across as Rachel delved into her mushroom pappardelle, rolling the pasta ribbons around her fork like an expert. The secondo was a slice of rolled meat slow-roasted and served with bitter greens which Ben finished well before anyone else at the table and then sat looking at Louise expectantly. She passed him the remains of her dish and afterwards, sitting back and rubbing his belly Ben marvelled at how simple the food had been, yet so delicious.

Luca ordered digestivi. "I'd be happy just doing this every day," Ben said sipping his limoncello.

"We're going to help Rachel decorate the bedrooms at the hotel," Louise told Luca.

"In August," Luca asked. "It will be hot."

"I don't mind a bit of hot weather," Louise said, and Luca's eyebrows raised knowingly.

"What about Ferragosto?"

"Ferra - what?" Ben asked beckoning the waiter over for a refill of limoncello.

"Penny's invited me to a party for ex-pats on the fifteenth." Rachel said, "I'm sure she won't mind if you come along. What about you Luca?"

"Sorry, but I have family dinner that day, but I'm sure you all will have a great time."

"I'll call Penny first thing tomorrow," Rachel said and clinked her glass of limoncello against Louise's, leaving them both grinning like schoolgirls.

Later that night as Ben snored in the spare room Rachel poured two glasses of plum-coloured Montepulciano and the two friends caught up on gossip from back home until the empty wine bottle indicated they should turn in for the night.

Chapter Eighteen

August 15. Ferragosto

Standing at the fence, Ben sighed as his eyes travelled over the valley below. The land was divided up into odd-shaped parcels of ownership; some square, others triangular and one in the centre of the valley was heptagon shaped. The fields were now burned yellow by the sun with the only greens coming from the trees. A thin lane wound its way down one side of the valley and back up the other like a line of white cotton threaded through the earth. "That's the sea in the distance," Rachel said joining him at the fence and handing him a bottled beer. "Can you see how the edge of the sky looks like it's been smudged?"

"This is one hell of a view," he said, "I don't think I'd ever get fed up with this."

"Penny told me it's lovely in spring and autumn when the grass is green."

In the distance, several black shapes were running across the golden fields and Rachel pointed them out to Ben. "Look," she said. "Wild boar. Something must have spooked them as it's rare they're out in the open by day." Suddenly the reason for the running boar appeared over the brow of the hill, a burgundy-coloured campervan.

A woman with pink and blue hair leaned out of the passenger side window and called out, "Have you seen Penny? Is it okay to park here?"

Rachel and Ben both shrugged their shoulders as Penny arrived and shouted back "Yes, it's okay there," then turning to Rachel said, "I'd better make sure they've secured the handbrake, last time they were here their van started to roll down the hill." Penny set off across the grass towards the newcomers then turned and called back to Ben, "Did Rachel tell you to bring swimming togs if you fancy a dip in the pool?" Ben nodded as two children launched themselves into the blue water with a splash.

Rachel thought about how much her life had changed over the past weeks, she watched Ben saunter over towards the bar constructed from old fence panels with a straw roof giving a Caribbean look and for the first time since her arrival in Abruzzo, she felt as if she was on holiday. *I've certainly got a lot to be thankful for* she thought. She looked around at the other guests and even in their summer fashions and sunglasses they still looked quintessentially British.

The guests were mostly ex-pats ranging from owners of holiday homes to permanent residents and she smiled as she remembered Penny had once with a grin disparagingly called them ex-perts, saying, "Say hello to a Brit over here and they'll instantly tell you where you're going wrong."

Joining Ben at an old farmhouse table stacked with various bottles of spirits and bag-in-a-box wines from the local cantina she opened a cool box filled with ice removed a bottle of Prosecco and poured herself a drink when an elderly man with a red face and a much redder nose approached them. "You looking to buy out here?" he said offering a podgy hand to Ben.

"No," Ben said, "I'm on holiday. Staying with Rachel."

She introduced herself.

"Really, where?"

"In Lanciano, but Rachel has a place along the coast," Ben said, being prudent as he was unsure how much information Rachel was sharing with the guests.

"Nice area," the red-faced man said and after downing the drink he was holding, he poured himself another and sauntered off to join some people standing beneath a fabric-covered gazebo.

A laugh rose above a group standing beside the kitchen door and Rachel recognised it. She looked over and saw Louise standing on the smaller of two patios with four men gathered around her as she chatted animatedly. "She's always been a social butterfly," Rachel said. "She'll soon have them running backwards and forwards to the bar for her."

"It's a good job I'm not a jealous boyfriend."

Rachel slipped her arm through Ben's and the two of them wandered over to join a group of people sitting in a shaded area surrounded by white oleander. After introducing herself to two women, both wearing floppy sunhats she sat down. "Kenneth tells us you have a place on the coast," The younger-looking of the two women said.

"Kenneth?"

"Yes," said the other woman pointing towards the red-faced man standing at the bar once again.

"Is this your husband?" The first woman said holding her hand out to Ben who looked confused not knowing whether to shake it or kiss it.

"No," Rachel said, "He's a friend. He's here with Louise." Rachel indicated towards the patio where her friend was holding court. The two women looked across the garden and swiftly back, their faces, blank but very telling.

"She's a terrible flirt," Ben said.

"She's certainly keeping our husbands entertained. If you'll excuse us." The two women rose and walked across to the patio and after a brief conversation, they led their husbands away.

"I see you've met Helen and Rita," a man in a loud floral shirt said as he dropped into one of the vacated seats. "Todd," he held out his hand and Ben shook it. "I have a place over in Paglieta."

"Beer?"

"Sure, Peroni please." Ben walked over to fetch two more beers as Rachel introduced herself to Todd. "I'm restoring a hotel in Sant'Andrea," she said.

"So, you're the enigmatic English woman who's restoring The Stars. Nice to finally make your acquaintance." Todd's grin widened and Rachel noticed the white ring of skin on his finger where his wedding ring usually sat.

"I'd hardly call myself, enigmatic," Rachel said. "But I'm intrigued to know how people know about me."

"Small community, big gossip," he said. "Who is doing your restoration?"

"A builder named Carlino."

"Ahh," Todd opened his legs and pushed his hips forward filling the fabric in the crotch of his linen trousers. Rachel tried not to snigger at his posturing as he told her he knew Carlino. "a fine tradesman, a bit pricey compared to many of the locals who'll work cash in hand, but a decent sort." Ben returned with the beers and after handing a bottle to Todd he left and walked over to Louise. "You're husband?" Todd said.

"No, he's a friend."

"Oh… I see…" Todd smiled, his lips parting to reveal snow-blindingly white teeth. Rachel could imagine the cogs turning in his head, his ego fuelling his desire.

Before Rachel could respond she was interrupted by Louise who slipped her arm across her shoulders letting her hand dangle tantalisingly above Rachel's breast. "Who is this darling, I don't think we've been introduced?" Louise said.

"This is Todd," Rachel said looking across at Ben who was giving her the thumbs up. "He was telling me he has a place near Paglieta. Have we been there yet sweetheart?"

"Not yet. Maybe Todd would be free to show us around. Do you have a number we could call you on to make arrangements?"

"I… err," Todd was flustered, his face flushed, making his cosmetic dental work look even brighter. "Do excuse me, ladies," he said rising from his seat. "This Italian beer goes right through me." They both laughed at his obvious squirming as he walked away.

"Ben said he looked like a letch, so I thought I'd come over and rescue you."

"When was the last time we pretended to be lovers to get rid of a man?" Rachel said.

"When Ben asked me out," Louise said.

"And look how well that subterfuge turned out."

"What have I missed?" Ben said joining them as they hugged each other and laughed.

The August sunshine was blistering, and Rachel and Louise were glad to have claimed a chair each in the shaded area of Penny's garden. People walking past to go to the bar or pool stopped to say hello and introduce themselves and Rachel was surprised by the age differences within the guests.

"I expected the party to be full of pensioners who'd retired but there's so many young people here. When I say young, I mean around my age," laughed Rachel. "I was talking to a couple in their early thirties who've moved here to live on the side of a hill with just a mountain view for company. I thought most of the people would be holiday homeowners, but they're mostly people who've moved here full-time."

"Well, that goes to show that if they can all make a go of it then there's hope for you too," Ben said, his comment earning him a look from Louise who'd still not come to terms with losing her best friend to Italy.

A woman with a toddler perched on her hip said hello; the child dripping after playing in the pool. "Penny said to tell everyone the food will be served in five minutes."

"That's good, I need something to soak up all the prosecco I've had," Rachel said introducing herself.

"I'm Mole. Originally Sally, but I hate my given name. It was great when I was ten but now… well, you know what I mean."

"Mole?"

"It's a nickname I earned ever since a primary school production of *The Wind in the Willows.*"

"What brought you here to Abruzzo?"

"We've been here seven years now," Mole indicated to a man who Rachel noticed was older than the woman with the wet child. "My husband was suffering with stress – work related – we came here for a holiday, and he was so relaxed that we decided to sell everything and come here initially for a year's respite, that said, we've no plans to return yet." A man with impressive tresses of blond hair joined them and as Mole handed him the child she introduced him. "Everyone, this is my husband, Ivan. The women and Ivan air-kissed, and Ben shook his hand.

"Has Mole been boring you all with tales of our self-sufficient lifestyle?"

"I'll have you know that boring is not a word anyone has ever used when describing me," Mole said as she gave her husband a playful punch on the arm.

"You're self-sufficient," Ben said, "how does that work?"

"Mole has lots of ideas and I do the work," Ivan said moving out of range of his wife's fist. "Mostly we manage to grow all the fruit and veg we need, and Mole has adopted the Italian practice of preserving what's left over. If you need any passata we have enough bottles left over from last year to float a cruise ship."

"And drinking all the beer to collect the bottles was such a hardship, eh?" smiled Mole.

"Seriously," Ivan said. "We get by with my doing airport transfers for the ex-pats and tourists, and I do some garden maintenance for Penny's clients. We're not wealthy compared to our life before but we're richer now than we ever were when I was working myself into an early grave." Rachel felt the realisation move across her face as she remembered Marco, but the moment was erased as Penny shouted that it was time for the food and the assembled guests began to file inside the villa.

Back in their seats with plates balanced on their knees, Rachel listened to Ivan telling Ben about the local football team and their lack of achievements. "My husband, Marco told me that football is taken very seriously in Italy?" she said, instantly hoping no one asked her to point him out.

"He's right," Ivan said out of the side of his mouth as he tore meat from a chicken drumstick. He swallowed and then continued, "It's like another form of religion, every boy has his loyalty to the local team and then there's the additional allegiance to one of the big five. My neighbour is a huge fan of Juve yet he's never been to Turin to see them play he's never left Abruzzo."

"How come he's never left the region?" Louise asked.

"Many of the people here never have, for centuries the Abruzzese have been hemmed in by the Apennine mountains, they've kept them protected. When the locals say, 'Why would you leave somewhere so beautiful', one look around proves that they're right to think that way."

Kenneth appeared at the edge of the seated area and asked if everyone was having a lovely time, he held a bottle of limoncello aloft and handed it to Ben. "Make sure you all have your digestivo," he said before staggering off to talk to another group of people.

"Kenneth is a darling," said Mole.

"He looks like he enjoys a drink," Rachel said.

"He does bless him. He's been here longer than anyone else and what he doesn't know isn't worth knowing."

"He'll help anyone out." Ivan added, "When we first arrived, we had problems with the utilities, our lawyer was worse than useless, Kenneth took control and within a week we were connected."

"What about those two ladies," Rachel said nodding in the direction of Helen and Rita.

"Oh, those two. I'm not normally the kind of person who speaks ill of others, but that pair have more faces than Ali Baba had thieves, and to be honest, after Ivan's illness we try to steer clear of negativity."

"That was very diplomatic of you," Ivan said, and Mole gave him a tiny little bow from the waist triggering a bout of laughter within the group.

"So, what is Ferragosto all about?" Ben asked as he levered lids off bottles of beer and handed them around.

"Traditionally it's the celebration of the end of the harvest dating back to Emperor Augustus. Mussolini was a big fan and he used to lay on trains to take the poor out of the cities and into the mountains or to the coast to celebrate. Most families now drag it out over a few days to make the most of the party atmosphere."

"Well, any excuse to get together with friends old and new can't be a bad idea," Rachel said.

Ben picked up the limoncello Kenneth had left and cracked open the seal, everyone held out their glasses chanting, "To Ferragosto."

Chapter Nineteen

"Well, that's all the sage-coloured bedrooms painted," Ben said dropping his paintbrush into the empty paint tray. "It's a good job we bought extra paint; this Italian plaster soaks it up like a sponge."

"Thanks for the help, I appreciate it," Rachel said.

"In the words of Dionne Warwick, that's what friends are for."

Louise entered the room carrying a tray of fruit juice and panini. Ben reached for a ham and cheese panino and despite the bread becoming smudged with green paint, he began to ram it into his mouth hungrily. "Slow down," Louise said, "You'll give yourself indigestion."

A shout from downstairs announced Luca's arrival and Rachel called to him saying they were upstairs.

"*Bravi tutti,*" he said entering the room, telling them they'd done a good job. "The colour is very nice."

"Just wait until the paper is on the walls," Rachel said, "it'll look great."

"I am free all the day," Luca said rolling up his sleeves, "What you want me to do?" Rachel handed him a paintbrush indicated towards the bedrooms across the landing and said, "Duck egg blue next." Luca made to move but she placed her hand on his arm to prevent him. He looked down at it and then up. Their eyes met before she let go and told him to help himself to some lunch.

During the coming week with the decorating taking shape, Rachel felt that the end was finally in sight.

They had a minor setback when Ben had papered two of the bedrooms, they arrived the following morning and the paper had peeled away from the walls. "Must be the heat," Louise said.

"More likely this bloody white Italian plaster. I bet it's sucked the moisture out of the paste."

"I'll call Luca," Rachel said, and he arrived an hour later with several cans of sealant.

"We Italians are new to wallpaper," he said, as they all began to give the plaster a coat of what looked like PVA glue.

One of the advantages of Italy in August was that paint and sealant dried quickly, one of the disadvantages was the amount of sweat produced while applying it to walls. "I swear I'll be a stone lighter after this," Ben said.

"You'll end up putting it back on later in the bar," Louise said before grabbing at his midriff and giving it a jiggle making him laugh and drop the corner of the paper.

"Now look what you've made me do," he joked, "I'll need more paste now."

"Are you two looking forward to the drive home?" Rachel asked as she held a roll of paper open for Luca to cut.

"Not really." Louise stirred the paste and handed her husband the brush. "Ben did say I could fly back, and he'd drive, but I can't let him do the journey on his own."

"And I'll have to put up with her constant moaning." He almost fell off the ladder as his girlfriend pinched his bottom in retaliation.

"We shall be finished here today," Luca said. "Why don't I cook for you all tonight?"

"We can't let you do that," Rachel said.

"Nonsense, it'll be my pleasure."

"Okay, but we'll bring the wine." Rachel watched as his brow furrowed. "What?"

"Not sounding… *come si dice… arrogante*?"

"Arrogant," both Rachel and Louise said at the same time.

"Not sounding arrogant, how can you buy the correct wines when you don't know the menu?"

"So, what do you suggest," Ben said, "Peroni or Moretti?"

Luca laughed, "You bring the beer I'll get the wine. Now come along there's more strips of paper to hang first."

***

Rachel was dressed in a floaty floral dress, her legs bare and her feet, complete with nails painted the colour of poppies slipped into sandals. Louise had opted for baggy linen trousers, cinched in at the waist and teamed with a sheer blouse while Ben had gone for the shorts and T-shirt combo he favoured. "You could have made an effort," Louise said as he entered from the bedroom.

"Why? I don't think Luca will be interested in what I'm wearing, you two however…" he let out a whistle as the two women posed and pouted for him.

"No doubt Luca will have made an effort," Louise said.

"Of course, he will, he's Italian and –"

"And what?" interrupted Rachel only for Louise to shut down any response from Ben with a raised eyebrow.

They decided to walk to Luca's apartment, the evening air was hot and seemed to catch in their throats, so for much of the way they walked in silence. To stay cool, they chose to take a more meandering route through the shady *viale* and *vias* of the historic part of town. All around them, the sound of families on balconies and behind open windows trickled out, and the musical-sounding Italian language became the soundtrack to their walking. Conversations snaked through the narrow streets, clinging to the town's old walls like lint to velvet; occasionally a heated debate met with children's laughter and the rattle of cutlery and cooking pots becoming the percussion section.

They were ready for a drink as Luca opened the door to his apartment and beckoned them inside. Ben handed him two packs of Italian beer and as Luca placed them inside his fridge, he removed a jug of *Cerasuolo* and began pouring four glasses of the chilled rose-coloured wine.

"As it's so hot tonight I thought you'd all prefer to stay inside with the air-conditioning." Everyone nodded their agreement as they each took a drink from him. "The first course will be ready in a few minutes, so why not take a seat and I'll be right back." Louise and Ben moved into the sitting area as Rachel hung around the kitchen to ask what they'd be having. "Lobster raviolo," Luca said dropping two of the large round pasta parcels into boiling water.

"Lobster, how nice."

"I did not make them," Luca said adding two more to the water, "Nicoletta upstairs - you remember?" Rachel nodded. "Her mother made them for us, she has the patience to roll the pasta until it is, how you say, *trasparente*."

"What are you two talking about?" Louise said entering the kitchen area.

"Lobster ravioli," said Rachel.

"Not ravioli but raviolo," Luca corrected, "Ravioli are small square-filled pasta but a raviolo is a larger, filled parcel."

"Well," said Louise, "every day's a school day."

"School day?" questioned Luca his brow furrowing.

"Ignore her," Rachel said as she leant over a small pan of sauce on the hob and breathed in. "It's an English phrase."

The raviolo was a success, served in white china bowls with a lobster-flavoured sauce and a handful of mantis shrimps for good measure. Ben had managed to dribble some down his T-shirt and Louise in mother-hen mode wiped it away with a napkin. Rachel poured more wine for everyone as Luca cleared the table before returning with another jug of wine.

"This is a local wine," Luca said placing it on the table. "It's from the cantina at Santa Maria Imbaro. It will go well with our dinner."

"What are we having," Louise asked.

"Miale alla romana"," said Luca, "Pork fillet with sage wrapped in *prosciutto*."

The three guests watched as a bowl of roasted potatoes with garlic and another filled with green beans and cherry tomatoes were placed on the table. Ben exhaled loudly as a large platter with a thin, amber-coloured butter sauce surrounding the pork arrived at the table. "I don't know how you're single," Ben said. "If I was on the lookout for a husband who could cook like this, I'd have snapped you up years ago." The table fell into comfortable laughter with Louise asking Ben if he had a secret he'd like to share.

After dinner Louise helped to clear the dishes and Luca reached up into a cupboard to remove several bottles containing digestivi. "So," Louise said, "how come if you can cook so well there's no Mrs Travaglini?"

"There is," Luca replied collecting thimble-sized glasses from another cupboard.

"Oh, really!"

"Yes, my aunt."

"Now you're just being evasive," Louise laughed as Luca lifted an eyebrow to show her he knew what she was implying. "You're a handsome man in good physical condition yet still single. How come?"

"I'm only thirty and I'm still too young by Italian standards."

"Okay, putting marriage aside, how come you're single?" Luca shrugged his shoulders, but Louise wasn't going to let the question go. "Okay, just answer one question and then I'll let you serve the grappa. Has there ever been a special lady in your life?" she paused before adding, "apart from your mother."

Luca smiled and with a tilt of his head said, "Yes. *Nonna*." Louise folded her arms in mock annoyance.

"Very well," Luca relented. "It was a long time ago. It just didn't work out, and since then, I've stayed single. But don't get me wrong, I've not been living like a priest. Before Louise could ask another question, Rachel appeared and asked what was keeping them.

"We're coming, I couldn't find the glasses," Luca said with a wink in Louise's direction.

Dropping onto the sofa beside Ben, Louise snuggled up to her boyfriend and watched as Luca poured four glasses of clear liquid. "What's this?" Ben asked taking a glass.

"Grappa. A popular digestivo after dinner." Rachel said.

"Not for the faint-hearted," added Louise before she could stop Ben from tipping the contents of the glass into his mouth. Three pairs of eyes watched him as he swallowed, screwed his eyes together, coughed, and then coughed some more.

"That's fierce," he said, his voice almost a whisper.

"Wuss," Louise said as she swallowed her measure, and everyone laughed."

Chapter Twenty

Things began to get back to normal after the August holiday. Rachel busied herself checking out the competition in the area, spending hours scrolling through websites and booking platforms while Carlino and his men carried on working at the hotel. Cosmo and his brother Massimo had stayed over each evening, Cosmo to continue working on the reception ceiling and Massimo to strip out the old kitchen. As usual, Rosa had appeared as if by magic to deliver coffee and cornetti to the men each day. "You will soon be ready to open?" questioned Rosa, screwing the top onto the coffee flask. "Have you thought about hiring the staff you will need?"

"I'm going to sit down and discuss it with Luca at a later stage."

"No need to do that." Rosa took a modern smartphone out of her apron pocket; it looked out of place in her wrinkled hand. She dialled a number. The call was as brief as the rapid exchange of dialect it contained and after she'd disconnected the phone Rosa looked up and said "All done. Silvana will arrive on Friday."

"Who is Silvana?"

"The answer to your prayers," Rosa said, and she collected the disposable cups and shuffled away leaving Rachel puzzled.

The bedrooms were completed and now just needed the furnishings. The beds were on order and Rachel was torn between buying new or looking for antique pieces for the remaining furniture. Italians are not keen on second-hand and apart from a store in Pescara, there were very few antique sellers in the area. Rachel was happy with the bedroom colour scheme; the green rooms echoed the colours of the valley at the rear, while the blue of the others echoed the light from the sea and the lavender hedges that Luca had planted at the front of the hotel. At the far end of the corridor, Carlino had had a secure door installed to prevent anyone going up to the third floor and during the day his men were starting work on Rachel's private accommodation. Rachel strolled back into the reception area and stood looking up at the ceiling. Cosmo had painted the smooth half of the ceiling with the sheep's blood paint and was starting to tackle some water damage over by the windows. She could make out a series of faint gold-painted lines and was wondering what they were when Rosa sidled over and said, "Aquila." The old woman put her hand on Rachel's shoulder and moving her position slightly she pointed upwards. "The capital of Abruzzo is *L'Aquila*, meaning the eagle and decades ago the original hotel owner had the Aquila constellation painted onto the ceiling there."

"What a good idea," Rachel said. "It ties in with the region and the hotel name. I must ask Cosmo to repaint it."

"Come. It's lunchtime." Rosa directed Rachel over to the rear patio where on a small table was set a jug of wine and two covered bowls. Rachel thanked Rosa and watched as she removed the napkins from the bowls. "*Pallote cace e ove*," Rosa said revealing golden-coloured balls in a tomato sauce. "*Fatti a mano da me.*"

"Hand made by you?" said Rachel as Rosa poured two glasses of wine and nodded her head. "I've heard about these and have wanted to try them for so long," Rosa told her that the cheese balls were a traditional Abruzzese recipe. Cutting into one with her spoon Rachel saw the inside was fluffy, an indication of the delicate cheesy flavour that was promised by the dish. As the two women ate together Rosa began to tell Rachel about the hotel's history.

"The hotel was originally a family home," she said putting her spoon down. "But they lost it to great debts and gambling. The government took possession of the property and land and as I've already said, during the First World War it was used as a military hospital."

Rosa rummaged inside her apron pocket and removed a small bottle of straw-coloured liquid. "*Genziana*," she said then adding in a whisper, "*Non legale.*" She poured a measure of the illegally made spirit into two of her ever-present paper cups and handed one to Rachel, observing her reaction as she sipped at the liqueur, her half-closed eyes unable to hide her reaction to the bitter earthiness spreading over her tongue.

"That's... unusual," Rachel said with a shudder.

Rosa smiled and drank her measure then continued with her story. "My grandfather told me that, shortly after the war it became a convalescence home for wounded Alpine soldiers and in 1920 one of the doctors, an Italian speaker from Switzerland bought the building and a year later the soldiers all left."

"When did your family work here?"

"My grandfather became the gardener in 1923 and my grandmother the housekeeper. The owner lived alone, with no wife or children. I remember my grandmother telling me he was a quiet man who loved to sit in the garden and listen to music, he didn't seek out the company of others."

"What happened to him?" Rachel shook her head as Rosa held up the bottle of Genziana before pouring herself another drink.

"What happens to us all? He died leaving my grandparents in service for several more years, looking after the house until their wages stopped being paid and the house was boarded up. One day a relative of the doctor arrived and opened it up again, this time giving it a new name and turning it into a hotel."

"Maybe I should investigate Marco's family history. Perhaps he's related to the doctor."

"The house has had many owners since then, some staying less than a year." Rosa removed a white handkerchief from beneath the cuff of her dress and wiped her mouth. "Over the years the hotel has been sold and resold many times. Men came with ideas of making a fortune, but the work needed to build up the business lessened their enthusiasm, and it was eventually locked up and abandoned."

"And when did you work here?"

"I was fifteen years old when I started as a chambermaid and remained here until it finally closed in 1971."

"So, it's been closed for over fifty years?"

Rosa nodded and collected the bowls and paper cups, looking up from the table, she said, "I am hopeful that you will breathe life back into the walls where the ghosts of previous guests are waiting to return."

A car horn sounded, "That must be Penny," Rachel said, "We're having a day out."

Rosa stood up and collected the bowls from the table and after wishing Rachel good afternoon she sauntered away.

***

"Have you got everything I asked you to bring?" Penny said as Rachel slid into the passenger seat beside her.

"Yes," she said holding up her bulging beach bag. "Towel, camera, notebook and I'm wearing my swimsuit underneath my clothes."

"Good. This is going to be a whistle-stop tour."

"Where are we going?"

"You'll see. Today is all about education because when the hotel is up and running, you'll need to be the fount of all knowledge for your guests." Penny gunned the engine and directed her sporty white convertible south.

Once on the coast road, she released the roof and Rachel had to put her hand up to stop her sunhat from blowing away. "First stop, Vasto," Penny called making herself heard over the sound of the air rushing past them.

The drive to Vasto took forty minutes and before they reached the seaside town Penny took a detour to Punta Aderci and parked the car in a spot overlooking a wide stretch of beach hidden behind a row of grass-covered dunes. After parking the car Penny pointed out to the beach and said, "First stop the nature reserve." The roof slid back into place and the two women exited the car and Rachel allowed Penny to lead her down some wooden steps.

"Wow! What a lovely spot," Rachel said looking along the sandy beach. "Are we staying here for a swim?"

"Sadly, no." Penny said, "We've too much to see before we can relax."

Rachel listened and took notes as Penny told her about the nature reserve. "People often come here to snorkel and just down a little further is *spiaggia punta penna,* where most of the tourists gather. Because of the grassed dunes, it's quite sheltered and this makes it popular. It might seem quite a distance from the hotel, but holidaymakers will travel quite a distance each day." Dropping her bag onto the sand Rachel took out her camera and started to take photos of the beach.

"Make sure you get a shot of the wooden steps; it'll prevent people from asking how to get down from the parking area."

Back in the car, they headed to Vasto where after a quick walk around the town and a drive along the coast they began the trip home. Penny pointed out Aqualand, a water park, telling her that she could do a deal with them and her guests could get a discount on day passes to enjoy the shows and slides.

They pootled back northwards, slowing down to take in the views and for a stop off at a cantina, where they tasted some local wines and purchased some homemade salami.

The car left the SS16 and after a few minutes along winding lanes, they drove into the car park at the Sangro River War Cemetery. "This might not seem like an ideal holiday destination," Penny said. "But you'll be surprised how many people who holiday here make a beeline for the place. There are over 2,500 British and Commonwealth soldiers remembered here and on a sunny day the contrast between the green of the grass and the white graves can be breath-taking." The two women took a stroll through the memorial garden with Rachel's camera clicking as she caught images from as many angles as possible.

"I'll have to email the photos over to Louise and she prepare them for the website."

"How's it coming along?" asked Penny.

"It's looking good, much better than I'd be able to achieve."

"Perhaps she'd let me take a look, and give you a few pointers regarding local things?"

"Sure," said Rachel, "I'll ask her to send over the latest update. I'm sure she'll appreciate any input."

"Just as long as she doesn't mind, I'd hate to step on anyone's toes."

"She'll be fine." Rachel turned to take some shots of a sitting area shrouded by white flowered shrubs and Penny declared it was time at last for a swim.

As Penny pulled into a parking space, she remarked to Rachel that although the beach was a pebble one the sea here was deeper and better for swimming. "I'll grab the picnic basket if you carry the umbrella."

Once settled on a spot Penny popped a cork and poured prosecco into plastic tumblers. "I've packed us some nibbles.

The beach was a long strip of smooth pebbles, man-made, but perfect for an afternoon in the sunshine. "I'm glad of a break," Rachel said.

"Me too." Penny said, "I've been so busy since the holidays."

"I'd have thought there'd be a lull after August."

"I wish. It's mostly people wanting to rebook for next year and a few confirmations for Christmas. Mind you it'll be too chilly in December for the people on the nudist beach." She tipped her head to the left.

"Nudist beach?" Rachel said, her eyes wide.

"Yes, just down that way," Penny pointed. "There's another beach and half of it's a nudist area. It's quite popular."

"It's not for me."

"Where's your sense of adventure?" laughed Penny.

"Don't tell me, you…"

"What! At my age. Maybe twenty years ago, but not now, there's more I want to keep hidden than have on show."

The two women spent their afternoon swimming and sunbathing. Rachel listened and took notes as Penny told her about the local points of interest and after packing the boot of the car, they made their way back along the coast to Fossacessia Marina where they walked along the seafront with ice creams.

"I have an idea for the hotel," Penny said, "but let me give it more thought and I'll run it past you in a few days."

Later that evening Rachel called Louise to tell her she'd emailed her the day's photos. "I'm absolutely shattered, "I've taken so many notes that it'll take me another day to organise everything. For now, though, I'm just going to sit on the balcony with a glass of red and watch the world go by."

Rachel poured herself a drink and putting her feet up on the balcony rail, she sat watching the people below as they sauntered up and down. She liked passagiatta, the act of seeing and being seen. Young couples talked in hushed tones, looking into one shop window after another. Husbands held hands with their wives, both dressed smartly for the walk before dinner and the late teens, influenced by music and videos from the US pulled their baseball caps down over their eyes and with their hands thrust down the front of their joggers added their strolling habit into the mix.

Chapter Twenty-One

Rachel felt enthused after her day out with Penny. It was early morning, and she was already copying the notes from her hastily written scribble into a more decipherable format. The kettle on the hob whistled and, she poured the boiling water over instant coffee, *not very Italian*, she thought as she dropped in a sweetener. She placed the mug on the kitchen table where she worked and then stepped outside onto the balcony.

In the piazza, the shops remained shuttered, and only the sweet smell of baking from the pasticceria crossed the cobbled square. The sky was flat and cloudless, like a stretched canvas, just a vast expanse of forget-me-not blue and with the sun behind the palazzo, the piazza reminded her of a stage, illuminated but waiting for the players to arrive. She became distracted by the smell of warm pastries and so decided she would continue working at Sant'Andrea. She closed the balcony doors, drank her coffee set off to buy freshly baked cornetti.

***

Luca stepped from the shower, wrapped the towel around his waist and padded from the bathroom into his kitchen. The coffee pot had finished bubbling and he poured a measure and took it over to the dining table where he'd laid out his drawings. As he sipped at the strong black liquid, he leafed through the pages of drawings he'd made, dividing his orto design into sections.

Droplets of water dripped from his nose onto the page, and he put down his coffee and removing the towel rubbed it over his hair. Standing naked with his black hair sticking up in spikes he looked out at his garden, his reflection in the glass looking back at him. He patted his stomach, noticing that a small bulge had appeared where it normally remained flat. "I need to do some digging," he said aloud as he squeezed at the tiny paunch below his ribcage. The remainder of his body was taut, his chest was covered with just a smattering of hair across his pectorals and with shoulders in a perfect V shape and a pinched in waist, he had a physique that women desired and other men envied. Covering himself up again he moved into the bedroom where he dried off and dressed ready for his day working in the orto.

Luca was already digging when Rachel arrived at the hotel, and he leant on his spade as he watched her walk towards him. She was wearing a floral camisole dress with a scalloped neckline and spaghetti shoulder straps that accentuated her neck. Her hair looked more claret-coloured in the sunlight and Luca wondered what her eyes were doing behind the large sunglasses she was wearing. *Was she looking at his bare chest or his face?* He shook his head to dismiss the thought; he knew that all they were was friends, and neither one was looking for more than that.

"Ciao," Rachel said leaning in with a kiss to his cheek. "What are you up to?"

"Arranging the orto into beds ready for next year's seed sowing." Luca bent down and picked up his drawings and handed them to her.

"This looks impressive, do you think we'll be able to grow a lot of the produce the kitchen will use?"

"I don't see why not. This is, after all, Italy, we can guarantee the sunshine, we just need to keep the plants watered." Luca went back to work, measuring out a new bed in strides across the soil counting aloud as Rachel stood chatting inanely but watching him until Rosa appeared holding out a cup of coffee. Stopping to grab his shirt she told him not to dress on her account as he accepted the paper cup from her.

"You now have the responsibility my grandfather had." Luca looked at her, puzzled. "He was a gardener here and this is exactly where he planted his orto."

"Most logical place," Luca said, "Sheltered from the sea wind by the building and bathed in sunshine most of the day."

"And when you're not working here will you bathe over there?" she gave him a cheeky smile as she nodded towards the empty swimming pool. "I hope so, it will make an old woman very happy to see a handsome young man in his speedos. It will save me a trip down to the beach." Luca blushed like a teenager and with a cackle Rosa turned and left him to his coffee and counting.

***

Rachel opened her notebook but was distracted, watching Luca through the window. Every time his spade pierced the soil she watched as his shoulders flexed and relaxed in the sunshine. He was tanned – not too much – his skin was the colour of honey and with the sweat glistening on it she thought about salted caramel. Her thoughts must have been printed across her face, making her grateful she was alone.

Luca tore the top off a packet of seeds, and with the dexterity of a pianist took a pinch of the small brown orbs and sprinkled them lightly along a depression in the soil. He gave them a light covering of earth before a sprinkling of water darkened the drill. Rachel continued to watch him, the slender frame disguising his strength. A dash of black hair made a trial from his navel down to the waistband of his jeans before disappearing beneath the denim. "A hidden delight," she found herself muttering. Her phone buzzed in her pocket and turning around, she saw Rosa standing in the doorway. The old lady just smiled and tapped the side of her nose before walking away to welcome the small silver Alfa Romeo that had just pulled up at the entrance.

"I was going to call you later to thank you for yesterday, Rachel said and was still talking when Rosa returned followed by a serious-looking woman with grey hair scraped back into a tight bun that shone like the paintwork of a showroom car. "I have to go now. I'll call you later."

Rachel disconnected the call and then as if an explanation was needed, she told Rosa it had been Penny. The old lady nodded with a blank expression and then introduced her companion as Silvana.

"*Piacere*," the newcomer said nodding her head. Rachel returned the greeting and indicated that they should move into the reception area. Silvana sat down in the solitary chair and Rachel listened as Rosa explained that the visitor was a very experienced housekeeper. "Silvana has worked in many hotels, big hotels with many rooms."

"Is she…" Rachel stopped and then directed her question directly, "Are you working in a hotel at the moment?"

"I am," Silvana said. "The hotel and golf club at Miglianico. I live in Tollo. It's not too far to travel each day, but a golf club is different to working in a hotel."

Rosa interrupted. "You will have so much to do Rachel when the hotel opens, you cannot be manager, host and housekeeper. You need someone with both the skill and the knowledge to keep things running like as you English say, a well-oiled machine."

Silvana coughed and took over the conversation, speaking for herself. "Signora. I understand that work is still to be completed before your hotel is ready for guests." Rachel agreed with her, "But there is much that I can help you with. I can organise the laundry, interview chambermaids and complete work rotas for everyone from gardener to kitchen staff." Rachel allowed a small smile to cross her lips wondering how Luca would take to being given his instructions from Silvana.

"I think before we discuss my suitability any further, I should look around." Silvana's request took Rachel aback; it was almost as if being offered a position at *her* hotel was inevitable.

Luca stepped into the reception and seeing Silvana, he wiped his hands on his handkerchief and offered his hand. As they introduced themselves, Rosa said that she was about to show the visitor around. "I think, as Luca is the project manager he should show our guest around," Rachel said.

"Project manager?" Silvana said, "I assumed you were the gardener."

"I am designing the orto," Luca said attempting to assert his authority. "If you'd like to follow me, we'll start with the bedrooms." Luca handed Silvana a yellow hard hat before saying, "Please be aware there are still builders on the site and care must be taken when moving around." Silvana stood up and smoothed down her skirt and with a raised eyebrow she indicated she was ready to follow him upstairs.

"She looks fierce," Rachel said to Rosa after they'd been left alone.

"She's stern but fair."

"Have you known her long?"

"Many years," Rosa said. "In her youth, she'd had many suitors and was said to have been the best catch in the village, however since she reached her fiftieth birthday some of the locals unkindly refer to her as, the old maid of the village – that said," Rosa giggled. "No one would ever have the nerve to say this to her face. What Silvana lacked in romance she made for with spirit."

That evening as they sat enjoying aperitivi in the piazza Rachel asked Luca what he had thought of Silvana.

"I think she's very capable of doing the job of housekeeper, and to be frank, if you want the hotel to succeed you will need someone with experience."

"So do you think I should hire her?"

"I think she thinks she's already been hired." He laughed a little then said, we need to discuss Rosa's frequent visits each day."

"But the men look forward to her bringing them coffee."

"That's okay for the builders, but when the hotel has guests, she needs to know that she can't just turn up and disrupt things."

"I'll speak to her tomorrow," Rachel said to him and as he raised his arm to order another couple of drinks, she began to wonder how long he'd stay at the hotel once it was up and running.

Chapter Twenty-Two

When Rachel arrived at the hotel a few days later the entrance hall was crowded. Luca was talking with Carlino who was barking instructions to his men while Rosa doled out cups of coffee. Silvana was sitting in the leather chair, leafing through a folder oblivious to the commotion around her. As she entered the room, her name was called and looking up she saw Cosmo at the top of the scaffolding tower. "*Signora Rachele*," he called.

"Morning Cosmo," she replied as he began to descend rather ungainly from his sitting position just centimetres away from the ceiling.

"The men will continue working on your apartment today," Luca said joining her as Carlino walked over to speak with Massimo.

"Why is Silvana here?"

"She says she needs to speak with you."

What about?"

"I'm not sure, she wouldn't tell me anything." Rachel sighed and walked over to the woman sitting in the chair and wished her a good morning. Silvana rose from the chair and did not attempt to disguise the look she gave to her wristwatch, making a silent point about how long she'd been waiting.

Cosmo bounded over almost colliding with Rachel in his eagerness to speak with her. "Signora, I have made an unusual discovery."

"Rosa tells me you need advice regarding linen," Silvana said moving in front of Cosmo before ordering him to get back to his duties.

Cosmo's normally cheerful expression faltered and became confused, he was used to the hierarchy on site and now this new woman was giving instructions. Rachel was horrified by Silvana's attitude and quickly took control. "If you'd care to wait until I am free," she said indicating the empty chair then moving to Cosmo, she slid her arm through his and walked him away to speak in private. As they walked away neither one dared to look back, although they both were grinning, they imagined Silvana to be stony-faced.

"What have you discovered?" Rachel asked Cosmo and he opened his podgy fist to reveal a faceted glass orb the size of a cherry. "What is it?"

"*una palla di vetro. Sfere di cristallo.*"

"Yes, I can see it's a crystal ball, where did you find it?"

"In the ceiling." Cosmo pointed upwards as if needing to validate what he was saying. What he then tried to say became confusing and so taking a pencil from behind his ear he took Rachel over to the window and picked up a piece of scrap wood. On it, he drew lines to resemble those in gold on the ceiling. "*Stelle nelle costellazioni.*" Rachel nodded and he then drew circles at the points where the stars would have been to make up the shape. He held out his hand again displaying the glass orb, grinned and shrugged, his head almost disappearing into his shoulders as his eyes asked her if she understood him.

"Are you saying the stars in the ceiling are glass balls?"

"Yes," he nodded. "At first I didn't see them as they are covered in paint, dirt and glue."

Rachel and Cosmo both stood looking up, turning around as they studied the ceiling and she noticed for the first time that the uneven surface of the ceiling was dotted with small bumps. "Oh Cosmo, this is magnificent." She leaned down and kissed his cheek and he blushed.

"I will return to glory the ceiling," he said in English and then dropping the glass ball into his pocket he took his leave and went to join the other men gathered around the reception desk as Rosa handed out warm pastries.

Smoothing down her skirt Rachel walked over to Silvana thinking, that if the two of them were going to work together she should make sure the other woman knew who was in charge. "Now, Silvana. I don't believe we have an appointment, but how can I help you?"

***

At lunchtime, Rachel and Luca left the hotel and walked down to the beach. "How was your meeting with Silvana," Luca said dropping down onto the sand beside her.

"It was okay, I just wish she'd lighten up. She's so serious."

"I think everything is black and white with Silvana, there's no shading."

"But look at all this," Rachel indicated towards the sea and the beach where they had escaped to share lunch. "How could you not be happy."

"Oh, I think she's happy, but what you forget is this is all normal to her. The beach and the sea are all she's ever known." He looked at her as she nodded her head and he noticed that the sun had brought out a smattering of freckles across the bridge of her nose. He took a long shallow breath as he watched her reach into her beach bag and retrieve a bottle of prosecco, *if things could only be different*, he thought.

"Can you do the honour," she said handing him the bottle and looking at his confused face.

"Honour? I don't understand."

"It means can you do this for me - open the bottle."

"Your English phrases can be so confusing." The cork popped and she held out two plastic tumblers. "I hope you have some food inside there."

"I have *panini. Prosciutto* and *provolone.*"

Hidden behind his sunglasses, he watched her as she bit into her panino; a sideways glance he hoped she'd not notice. Her hair shone in the sunlight, as shiny and rich coloured as a freshly picked aubergine. He took in the length of her slender neck, halting his gaze at her collarbone, imagining the depression filled with his prosecco – oh, how he could drink from the dip beside her shoulder.

"This little beach is perfect; it'll be such a shame to share it with the hotel guests," Rachel said, filling the silence. "I like how most days there's no one here, it's almost a secret place."

Luca mentally pulled himself together and agreed that it was nice. "Look at the Adriatic, it's so still. I wish I could swim today."

"What's to stop us?" Rachel said.

"We don't have swimming costumes."

"There's no one to see, we don't need them." Luca removed his sunglasses and his eyes widened. Seeing this Rachel laughed. "I wasn't suggesting we swim naked, there's a beach further away for those shenanigans."

"I see, so you know all about *la nostra spiaggia per nudisti*?"

"Yes, but it's not really my thing. I thought we could maybe just go in for a paddle."

"Paddle?"

"Come on, roll up your trousers and follow me." She got to her feet and raced down to the edge of the water. Lifting the hem of her skirt she stepped into the lethargic foam of lazy waves, she was up to her knees when he joined her, and they splashed in the shallows giggling like youngsters.

Luca was enjoying the break away from the day-to-day managing of the building project. Distracted by his thoughts he failed to dodge the large wave of water that had crept up behind him and he stumbled forward, his arms windmilling as he fell face-first into the surf.

Pulling himself up, his clothes plastered to his body he looked at her and she was laughing. Laughing like he had never seen her laugh before. She bent double and gasped for air. Her mirth was infectious, a viral giggle that enveloped him and sopping wet he began to laugh too. Rachel stumbled backwards and he lunged for her, too late and she fell backwards into the sea, which led to more laughter.

Back on the beach Luca peeled off his shirt and walked over to lay it out on the rocks to dry before joining Rachel where she was topping up his tumbler. "It's flat and warm," she said as the last of the prosecco dribbled from the bottle. "I've not had so much fun in ages."

"It was fun, even if we are soaking wet."

As they continued with their lunch and dried off in the sun Luca asked Rachel again about her meeting with Silvana.

"She's bringing over some samples from local suppliers and says she can get me a good deal on laundry services with a *lavanderia* in Castel Frentano. Apparently, they'll also look after the kitchen and dining room's laundry too."

"Sounds good, one less thing for you to worry about."

"She also wants to be part of the hiring and training process, which to be honest is a good thing as I have no idea how many members of staff I'll need. Silvana insisted that if she sets them up to her high standards, the new staff will have no excuse, not to replicate it."

"I'll help too," Luca said picking up a handful of sand and letting it trickle through his fingers. "If you need me to?"

They both lay back under the sun and chatted as their clothes dried, until with lunch over, Rachel repacked the beach bag as Luca slipped back inside his shirt. Before they climbed the steps Luca took Rachel's hand and lowering his sunglasses; his heavily fringed brown eyes peering over the rim he said, "I'm so glad we met. I'm grateful for the work you have given to me but I'm also grateful for the friendship you have shown to me." Pushing his sunglasses back to hide his eyes he fought the sudden desire to kiss her.

"And I'm grateful to you too, I'd never have got this far without your help." She gave him a friendly punch on the arm and said, "Now get back in the orto and get it ready for next summer's harvest."

Chapter Twenty-Three

Sitting beside the beach, the sound from the waves was calming and the ink-black sky overhead was made more appealing by the candlelight from the table. In the distance a boat could be seen, its lights illuminating the sea around it.

The restaurant was quiet with just a handful of diners mid-week. The waiter delivered their primi to the table and Rachel couldn't resist leaning over the bowl of tomato sauce and breathing in the aroma. "I've eaten so much seafood since coming to live here," Rachel said as she delved into the bowl and spooned a plump orange mussel from its shell.

"That'll be because of that," Penny waved her fork in the direction of the Adriatic and for a few minutes the two women sat looking out at the large expanse of darkness that was the sea.

"I did want to speak with you about organising some promotion for the hotel, give you a leg up in the marketplace so to speak," said Penny.

"What did you have in mind?"

"A weekend break for journalists, travel writers and bloggers and assorted tourism chiefs."

"Sounds scary."

"Not really. As long as their glasses remain topped up and they sleep well most of them will mention you favourably."

"When are you thinking of? The bedroom furniture only arrived yesterday and we've no mattresses yet, not to mention linen, staff and —"

"Whoa! We're a few weeks away yet." Penny smiled and winked at her across the table. Reassurance that she knew what she was talking about. Rachel felt blessed to have had that chance to meet with Penny, she'd turned out not only to have become a valued friend but also her business mentor. Yes, Rachel was aware that Penny would benefit from any bookings that she organised for the hotel, but there was also a good deal of help and advice she'd handed out for free.

The waiter came to clear their bowls – both mopped clean with bread and as she was driving Rachel covered her glass with her hand as he attempted to top it up.

"So, what will this promotion entail?"

"Free food and drinks for a weekend with accommodation thrown in. Leave it with me and I'll draw up a list of people we should consider inviting and we can discuss it another day."

The main courses arrived, and Rachel looked down at her sea bass, remembering the mess she'd made of the first one she'd been served and smiled, as this time she lifted the skin and removed the fillets cleanly.

"I have a good feeling about your venture," Penny said, "and I don't say that lightly. I've seen so many new hotels open and close within a year, but I think you'll do well."

"You do?"

"Yes, you're in a great spot, close to good local amenities but far enough away to deliver the peace and quiet most tourists look for. The private beach is a real gem and the pool will attract families."

"I hope you're right."

"I don't doubt it, and I'll always be on hand to give you any advice."

The following morning, sitting up in bed with her mug of breakfast tea and cornetto crumbs down the front of her nightshirt Rachel decided to call her brother. Breaking a biscuit and dunking it into her mug she dialled his number.

"Hello Sis," Oli said. "How's things?"

"Things are good. I'm calling to… oh shit –"

"Rachel, what's wrong?"

"I've dropped a digestive in the bed and sat on it. Crumbs in the bed are never conducive to relaxation. I need to pick your brains Oli."

"Just get up and vacuum the bottom sheet."

"Not about the crumbs, about something important."

"Sounds interesting, what do you need to know?"

"It's about stars."

"Celestial or celebrity?"

"Those in the sky at night.

"If you say astrology I'll hang up," he laughed.

Rachel told him about the ceiling in reception and the painted constellations, Oli promised to email her links to some websites and a – as he called it – brilliant PDF. "Any problems just send me a photo and I'll do my best for you. So, what you up to later?"

"I'm going up into the mountains to check out some towns."

"Well, have a great day, I'll have to go I'm already late for work." They ended their call and Rachel showered and dressed she picked up a pamphlet from the kitchen table. She decided to leave the Satnav behind and headed out.

***

The journey from Lanciano to Casoli had become familiar to her, yet as she cleared the village of Brecciaio, which was just a straight road with houses on both sides ending with a hairpin bend, she slowed to take in the view. The road was flanked on either side by agricultural land and ahead of her was the Maiella Massif in the distance, its top awaiting its winter dusting of snow. The sky above it was a watery blue and the land at the base of the mountain was a mix of olive greens and silver with lilac pockets of borage where the herb grew wild in great swathes. A horn hooted and looking in her rear-view mirror she saw an aged couple sitting on a tractor behind her. She increased the pressure on the accelerator, there'd be time to dawdle and gaze at the view another time.

As she passed through the hilltop town of Casoli; vowing to spend another day there soon, the roads became steeper and her hire car climbed upwards, passing olive groves and ortos. A man leaning on his spade waved to her as she drove past and she tooted her horn and waved back.

She navigated a scary stretch where the road seemed to disappear into the sky and no barriers had been erected and a tight almost ninety-degree bend later, she saw her destination ahead, the mountain town of Gessopalena.

Italian villages always seemed to have adequate parking provision and Rachel pulled into a small, cobbled car park on the edge of the village – she'd stopped looking for payment machines a long time ago – she locked her car and strolled up the main street in the direction of a bar with seating outside. "*Prego*," the owner said indicating a seat outside under an umbrella. "*Turista?*"

Rachel shook her head, "No, I live on the coast." She ordered a cappuccino and a bottle of sparkling water and as she waited, she watched as women chose fresh fruit and vegetables from the crates stacked outside the supermarket. "The coast is very different to the mountains," the man said bringing her drink to the table. "Are you here to see *il borgo antico*?"

"Yes," Rachel said removing her sunglasses so he could see her eyes, "Where can I find the old village?"

He pointed across the road, "The path to the museum and the ancient village is just behind the church." He then shook his head and muttered, "Terrible thing, the people do not forget." Rachel had read about how the retreating Nazis had thrown grenades into the houses of the villagers, destroying their homes and massacring 42 women and children. "There are many places here that do not forget, many bad things happened. If you have time, visit the town of Torricella Peligna they also suffered from Nazi crimes." He moved away to serve a new customer and Rachel thought she heard him mutter the word '*Tedeschi*' meaning Germans before he spat on the pavement. It was apparent that the ill feeling from the war was still strongly prevalent.

The sun was high in the sky and despite being up high in the mountains the heat stuck to her clothes like a clinging baby. The destroyed houses were a poignant reminder of a time she couldn't comprehend, and those that had been restored and turned into museum buildings looked out of place. She took photographs; stopping to frame the memorial against the backdrop of the mountains in the distance before taking a few minutes to sit and just enjoy the view and the silence.

Just months before she'd never have guessed she'd be sitting here overlooking the Abruzzo countryside; opposite were mountains and below a wild valley of greens and yellows. In the distance she could see the cobalt blue of a lake and perched on the slopes were white houses with red-tiled roofs looking tiny against the whole vista laid out for her to enjoy. She took a few more photographs but she knew even before she'd checked them that no camera could ever do justice to the scene.

How things change, she thought. *Would Marco have brought her here?* How different would things have been if he'd not died and as she thought about him, for the first time in weeks, tears sprung from her eyes and she allowed them to roll down her cheeks. They were silent tears, no shoulder heaving accompanied them, or vocal sobs and she felt bad about this. She'd already started to feel that she was ignoring Marco. She did still notice his ashes on her dresser, but because of the time required to complete the hotel she'd stopped speaking to him every day. Was it grief passing into acceptance or was it just time taking over? She wiped away the tears and took a sip of water before making her way back to her car.

She drove away slowly, allowing herself to take in her surroundings She stopped beside the road to gaze down at Lake Sant'Angelo. She marvelled as she drove downhill how the landscape appeared to surround her like a pair of welcoming arms.

Rachel's was the only car on the road, there were no people to be seen yet all around was evidence of the land having been worked. Regimented olive groves and fields with enormous rolls of hay drying in the sun. Coming around a bend she slowed to look at a square patch of earth that was filled with tomatoes, the red fruits hung from parched vines and she wondered how with so little water they'd become so plump. She was about to pull back into the road when she heard a voice call to her and a woman appeared between the rows of plants and waved to her. "*Buongiorno signora.*"

Rachel called, getting out of her car. "It's a nice day to be outside."

"It's too hot," the woman said reaching her, "but good for the tomatoes."

"They're impressive," Rachel said, and the woman fished a couple of large fat ones from her basket and held them out to her. "Thank you, how much?"

"*Niente*," the woman said with a toothless smile. "They're a gift. We have more than enough for the family. Try please." The woman urged her to take a bite and Rachel bit into the soft-skinned fruit; remembering what had happened to Marco in Mallorca, she leaned forward to prevent the juice from staining her blouse and showed her appreciation with a nodding smile.

"Thank you very much. I'll enjoy the other in my salad tonight."

"Here," the woman reached into her basket removed a supermarket carrier bag and told Rachel to help herself, adding, "These are good for cooking, they make a good sauce." The woman helped her to fill her carrier bag and after seeing she had enough, she wished Rachel a good day and then trudged away up the field, disappearing over the hill.

Back at the apartment, she placed the tomatoes in a bowl on the kitchen table – Italians' know how to protect the taste, tomatoes must not be put inside a fridge. Rachel thought about the kindness she'd been shown. "It's true what they say about the Italian people," she said to Luca who was pouring chilled Pecorino into glasses.

"What's that?"

"That they're very friendly."

"That's a matter of opinion," he smirked, "I know some unsociable ones."

"I know it's a generalisation," Rachel said taking the glass he offered her, "But in my experience so far everyone has been welcoming and generous." She then went on to tell him about the woman who had given her the tomatoes. "Though what I'm going to do with this many I don't know. She said they are good for sauce, but I don't know how to make it."

"You cannot live in Italy and not know how to make passata or a good *salsa di pomodoro.*"

"Back in England, I just buy a jar of ragù from the supermarket."

Luca feigned a heart attack, and after much cod-coughing, he said, "Ragù! You don't even know the difference between tomato sauce and ragù. You will need to learn these things if you are to stay here in my country."

Rachel saluted him and they both laughed before taking a seat on the balcony to enjoy the warmth of the Lancianese evening.

Chapter Twenty-Four

With his hands covering her eyes Luca led Rachel along the corridor. His chest was pressed against her back and she felt his warmth pass through to her skin. His aftershave, woody and spicy invaded her senses, making the experience of being close to him more pleasurable. He stopped and told her to keep her eyes closed and, in her darkness, she heard him open a door. "Step forward two steps," he said and she obeyed. "Open your eyes."

Rachel opened her eyes and saw that her apartment had been completed. Carlino's men must have been putting in extra hours to get it ready for her. The walls had been plastered and given a coat of cream-coloured paint and on the main wall was the same wallpaper that had been used in the green bedrooms. At the windows opening out onto a balcony hung a sheer green voile and as a lazy breeze moved it, its surface looked iridescent. "Wow!" Rachel exclaimed doing a one-hundred-and-eighty turnaround, "This is fabulous."

"The kitchen was fitted against the far wall of the living space, white units with Calacatta marble work surfaces, the dark veins will look good against the chrome of the coffee machine and toaster that she would bring from Lanciano.

"Follow me, I have another surprise for you." He opened a door to show her into a cool bathroom with pewter-coloured wall tiles and a modern set of sanitary wares. "Carlino says he can fit a bathtub later if you want one."

"The shower is just fine," she said running her hand across the glass screen. "This is perfect." She stepped back into the living space and said, "I'll need to start buying furniture."

The bedroom was bigger than she expected, and the view of the sea gave it a calming feel. The walls had been painted in a watered-down version of the sage-green paint and below the plaster cornices a frieze of summer flowers had been painted. "Cosmo?" she asked and Luca nodded. "That man is such a sweetie." Luca's face creased as he questioned her use of the word 'sweetie' but she didn't feel the need to explain it to him. "I just hope I can find a bed as comfortable as the one I'm sleeping in at the moment."

"You like the bed in Lanciano?"

"Oh yes, I love it."

Luca showed Rachel the second and third bedrooms, both of which were bare plastered walls with no decoration leaving his best surprise until the end. He took her hand and showed her a door at the rear of the smaller of the bedrooms, opening it, sunlight barged in revealing stone steps. He took her by the hand and led her up and out onto a roof terrace just big enough for two chairs and a table. "Your own private space in the sky," Luca said, watching as her eyes became teary. "*Cara Mia,* don't cry, this is a time to be happy."

"Oh, Luca. I am happy. After Marco –" she paused knowing she didn't need to explain herself. "I never dreamed I could be this happy again."

***

The following week Rachel had been in a buying blur; she'd originally planned to shop for everything at IKEA but now her apartment was finished she didn't think contemporary, modern furniture would work in the space. She found a second-hand store in Pescara and there she purchased a sofa and bookcase for the living room, a massive ornate mirror for her bathroom and a wardrobe. She was currently occupied in a store that sold rugs and throws when her phone rang. "Hi Rachel, it's Mole. Ivan has said he can collect your furniture from Pescara later today. Will that be okay?"

"Yes, that'll be great. Would you like to join me for dinner later? We could eat in San Vito. It'll be nice to catch up."

"Sure, I'll see if my neighbour can look after Sprog."

"No, please bring your daughter along, it'll be lovely to see her."

"Okay, but don't blame me if all she wants to do is eat ice cream and hide under the tables."

Later laden with bags and parcels Rachel climbed the stairs up to the apartment in Lanciano and as she dropped her purchases onto the sofa, she felt a pang of sadness. She'd be leaving here soon to move into the hotel and this place had been instrumental in her finding happiness again. Luca had assured her that the owner was happy with her moving out and once again she seemed to be living surrounded by black plastic bags. However, these were filled with the promise of a new beginning and new adventures.

She pushed open the door to her bedroom and stopped, her mouth opened in astonishment when she saw that the bed had disappeared. Her first thoughts were that it had been stolen, but who'd steal a big old antique bed? In the living room, her phone began to ring and she rushed to answer it.

"Rachel," Luca said, "are you coming to the hotel today?"

"Yes, I'm meeting Ivan, he's delivering my furniture from Pescara."

"I'll see you later then."

"Luca," Rachel added quickly before he could disconnect the call, "Do you know anything about the bed in my apartment, it appears to have vanished?"

"Maybe the owner has removed it." Luca's lie wasn't very convincing and as Rachel ended the call, she had a sneaking suspicion that the bed had been taken from Lanciano to Sant'Andrea.

When she arrived at the hotel, Ivan and Luca had already carried the furniture up to her apartment and now as she opened the boot of her rental car, they each took out some of the bags jammed inside. "It's all soft furnishings, nothing breakable," Rachel said as Ivan dropped one of the bags he was struggling to carry inside. Mole stood on the steps holding her daughter's hand as the young girl fidgeted trying to break free from her mother's grip. Rachel called to say hello and Sprog said she wanted to help carry in a bag. Mole released her daughter and she flew down the steps and across the gravel to pull a plastic bag from the car boot. "What's in here?" she asked expectantly as she heaved the bag into her arms.

"Probably bedding," Rachel said.

"I've seen your bed and it's supposed to be a surprise. Mummy helped."

"Shh, don't tell anyone but I think I'd already guessed."

"Is it our secret?" Rachel nodded and the girl wriggled with pleasure.

Once everything had been stacked inside and Luca had opened a bottle of pecorino and poured everyone a glass, he told Rachel she had a new surprise in her apartment. "Oh really," she said giving Sprog a wink, thinking, *I must ask what her actual name is. I wonder what it could be.*

"There'll be no awards here for believable acting," laughed Mole as Luca led Rachel up the staircase to her living accommodation. Throwing open the door she saw that the men had positioned her furniture for her. "Over here," beckoned Luca like an excited child. He opened the bedroom door and there was the bed from the apartment in Lanciano. It wasn't the surprise he'd hoped it would be but Rachel didn't give away anything that could spoil the moment. She flung her arms around his neck and kissed him before stepping back quickly and blushing. "I'm sorry… I… got a little carried away."

"I got it for you. It's, as you English say, a house-burning gift."

Rachel erupted into laughter and with tears in her eyes she said, "Thank you, it's the best house-burning gift I've ever had."

Rachel grabbed some towels and they all made their way to the private beach. As they passed Rosa's house, she opened a window and waved to them before calling over Sprog and pressing a *caramello* into her hand.

"*Buona serata,*" Rachel called to her before the three of them vanished down the stone steps to the sand below.

Smoothing her towel on the sand, Rachel watched Olivia run into the surf and jump over the waves thinking the name Sprog suited her better. Mole was stretched out enjoying the residual warmth of the day when the men arrived and began handing out boxes of fried fish. "I think *frittura di paranza* is much nicer from a paper box," Mole said as Olivia ignored her chips and dived into her ice cream first.

"There's something feral, but enjoyable about stripping the flesh from these little fishes," Rachel said as she popped a piece of white meat into her mouth.

"I never ate fish until we moved here," Ivan said lifting a little crown of crispy squid tentacles from his box and devouring them. "Now I can't get enough of the stuff."

"Ivan's a big fan of *vongole*, aren't you babe?"

"I sure am, and the best *spaghetti vongole* I've ever had was from a beach bar in Fossacessia."

"We must go and check it out," Rachel said. "I've got to start compiling a book of local restaurants and bars for my future guests."

"I'll give you a hand if you like?" Mole said.

"Penny said she'd help too."

"Even better, the three of us can drink wine and eat cake as we do it."

"Cake?" Sprog said, her attention caught.

"You concentrate on eating some of your chips," Mole said, "Then we'll both go for a paddle in the sea."

"So, Rachel," Ivan said as he stole one of Sprog's chips. "Now your private accommodation is completed, have you set a date for moving in?"

"I haven't but hopefully within a week."

"If you need a hand moving anything, just give me a shout."

Ivan stood up and stretched out his lean body before picking up Sprog placing her on his shoulders and striding away towards the sea. His daughter laughed as he threatened to throw her into the deep as Mole joined them in the shallows. Rachel sat watching in silence as the young family splashed each other.

Luca collected their empty takeaway boxes and turning to Rachel asked if she was happy. "Yes, more than I thought I could be. Why?"

"You looked like something was troubling you."

"It's nothing. I was just thinking about moving into the hotel and I also need to sort out a car, it's too expensive to keep a hire car."

"Come on, don't just sit there," Mole called up the beach to them and nodding his head Luca stood up and held out his hand to Rachel and together they walked down to join their friends in the sea.

Chapter Twenty-Five

Rachel was confused. She'd sat on the balcony with her morning coffee and wrestled with her emotions. Originally when she'd come to Italy, she'd had no fixed plans so leaving her home – the house she and Marco had shared hadn't been an overly emotional experience. But now as she spent her final morning in the apartment in Lanciano she felt a strange kind of sadness. She looked across at the apartment opposite and thought it was a shame she'd not seen the man in the suit this morning; she had never spoken to him, but she knew she'd miss seeing him. "I've loved being here," she told the green lizard that lived in her window box, "And I'll miss being here every morning to see the piazza wake up, and of course you." The lizard winked and went off in search of its breakfast.

Earlier she'd wandered from room to room, recalling every space she'd occupied, as if she feared the memories would dissolve when she locked the door for the final time. She had made a point, last night, of listening to the sounds of the piazza; the noises that she'd grown accustomed to and had stopped hearing. The whoosh of the coffee machine in the bar below and the tinkling of spoons as patrons stirred coffee in tiny cups. The laughter of children as they walked to school and the calls of the shop owners as they opened up for the day. It will all be very different from today, she thought, new sounds to get used to.

"I think we've been here before," she said picking up Marco's ashes from the table and walking over to the door where her suitcase was waiting. "You, me and a suitcase off on an adventure."

Arriving at the hotel felt strange. "You've been here so many times before," she told herself as she got out of the car, "but now I'm moving in, it feels different." She stood for a few minutes looking up at the building, it seemed to be much bigger now that she was alone. The windows – all polished were blinking in the sunlight and the huge doors at the top of the stone steps looked daunting as she was about to open them and step inside. "Stop it," she told herself, "There's nothing to be frightened of, it's just a big old building."

Walking across the reception area her footsteps sounded hollow on the tiled floor, she placed her suitcase at the bottom of the stairs and leaned over the desk to switch on the computer. As the screen faded up from black to reveal a picture of a trabocco she clicked on Spotify and chose a saved playlist from her account. George Benson began to sing 'Moody's Mood' filling the room with the familiarity of a favourite song. Humming along Rachel stood looking up at the ceiling. The scaffolding tower had been taken down. Cosmo's restoration was completed. The plaster cornices had been painted an aubergine colour making the silver astrological symbols above and the gold lines of the constellations dotted with crystals pop. The crystal stars sparkled as the sunlight filtered through the windows. "I must find out soon what all these star formations are called," she said, knowing that at some point a guest would ask her a question about them and she wanted to be knowledgeable.

George was now singing, 'Give Me the Night' when she picked up her suitcase and headed upstairs. She paused on the landing looking along the corridor where the guest rooms were and she felt a sense of accomplishment, knowing that a few months ago the rooms were empty shells and now they were ready to be dressed for paying guests.

She climbed up to the third floor, opened the door stepped inside her apartment. On the kitchen table stood a bottle of wine and a vase of flowers, a piece of card propped up against the vase simply read, *'Welcome to your new home.'* Certain they must have been left by Luca she plucked one of the lilies from the vase and breathed in its heady aroma. Her head snapped to the side as she heard her name being called from downstairs and stepping out onto the landing, she called to let Rosa know she'd be straight down.

Still holding the lily as she descended the stairs, Rosa smiled at her and said, "I see you found the flowers that Cosmo left for you."

"Cosmo?"

"Yes, he dropped them off yesterday, just before Luca closed up for the day." Rosa then pointed up to the ceiling and said, "It's good to see this back to its original glory."

"Hasn't Cosmo made a good job of it?"

"I feared that the original painter's work wouldn't be matched, but I am happy that Cosmo has managed to make it look like it did when it was newly painted." Rosa was staring at the gold lines but there was something sad about her smile. Rachel was about to ask her if she had known the original artist but looking into the old woman's watery eyes, she decided it was a question for another day.

"I know it's early, but would you like a glass of wine?" Rachel asked.

"That's very kind of you, but I'm afraid my ancient limbs won't transport me up two flights of stairs."

"Sit down," Rachel indicated to the tub chairs under the windows, "there's wine in the kitchen."

As the wine was poured into glasses Rachel watched as Rosa took the opportunity to look around. "It's looking very nice in here, are you pleased with how it's turned out?"

"I am," Rachel said. "I think Carlino and his men have done an excellent job."

"People will very much like to stay here." Rosa held out her glass for Rachel to touch it with hers and as the rims chinked, she asked about an opening date.

"My heart seems to miss a beat every time I think about welcoming guests and I do want the business to be successful. I will be Marco's legacy and although he's no longer here, I'd like to think he'd be pleased with how things have turned out."

"To Marco," Rosa said and just as they raised their glasses to him the main doors opened and in strode Luca with Massimo, Cosmo and Carlino with Penny bringing up the rear with Mole, Ivan and Sprog.

"We bring lunch," Penny said holding up several foil trays. "Parmigiana melanzane."

"We had a glut in the orto," Mole said. "I hope you like it."

"I love it," Rachel said.

"I bring salmon," Luca said pronouncing it as sal-mon which made the corners of Rachel's mouth rise a little.

"Sprog has dessert but I think she's been in the tub already," laughed Ivan as his daughter protested her innocence with a mouth covered in vanilla ice cream.

The foil trays were all filled with hot food and as Mole went to the kitchen to warm some plates Rachel looked around herself. Memories about how alone she had been at the time of Marco's ashes going missing returned briefly. *How lucky am I?* she thought. As she watched the people that just months ago, she hadn't known and who were now rallying around to make her first night at Sant'Andrea memorable. A moment of well-being flooded her body although a small part of her hoped that Louise had been with her and a large part wished for Marco.

The lunch slipped into an afternoon of conversation until her friends began to leave one by one until only Rosa was left still sitting in the tub chair by the window. "You are a very lucky woman," she said placing her empty glass upon the table. "Good friends and a new life. Many people find it difficult to start again from tragedy." Rachel looked across at the old woman her face seemed to be less lined in the early evening light, almost as if she'd travelled back in time. Her eyes appeared less fluid and clearer. "It is easy to see that you are not yet fully recovered from losing Marco, but days will get better and be less long and you must be open to finding love again."

"What about you Rosa, did you have a special someone in your life?"

"Once. A long time ago. He was –" She stopped speaking and rose from her chair and pointing to the ceiling she continued. "Look to the stars. All of the stories that shall ever be told are already up there, written, just waiting for a new narrator. Now I must go. Thank your friends once again for the dinner. It is late and Rosa has had one too many glasses of wine."

Chapter Twenty-Six

After Rosa had gone, Rachel fixed herself a gin and tonic in the hotel kitchen, pushed open the door and took a stroll along the side of the building through to the front garden enjoying the warm evening air. She wandered slowly along the row of cypress trees, her feet crunching the gravel below. Hidden among the trees, cicadas heard but rarely seen, clicked and whirred and there was a faint whoosh of waves coming up from the sea. A high-pitched screech from an Abruzzo little owl filled the evening air; more animal sounding than a bird – Luca had pointed one out to her previously, no bigger than a grapefruit and a similar shape, however, its voice was somewhat at odds with its fluffy appearance.

After closing up, she went to her room and fastened the bedroom windows back, making sure that the mosquito screens were closed. Pulling back the covers and relishing the cool cotton of the bottom sheet, she slid inside the bed and lay in the dark for a few minutes listening to the new sounds coming in from the open window. Was it the wine from earlier or the whispering breeze that very quickly soothed her to sleep?

The sound of heavy rain woke her. Outside the window the gentle breeze had been replaced by a whistling wind and raindrops hitting against the mosquito screen were split into a fine mist and forced into the room, soaking the dresser below. Rachel crawled out of bed and closed the window before grabbing her dressing gown from the chair and pulling it around herself. Suddenly the room was lit up and the crash of thunder that followed startled her. Looking out over the sea she watched as another flash of lightning hurtled down from the clouds towards the surface of the Adriatic. Remembering her father telling her as a child to count, she did – What was it he'd said, 'Count the number of seconds from the flash to the thunder then divide by five to know how many miles away it was.' But this was Italy and they measured distance here in kilometres, how would the calculation work? She had no time to think about it as another streak of white light arced across the sky before descending into the sea, followed suddenly by thunder that seemed to shake the walls of her bedroom. "No point counting," she said. "I can see that the storm's just metres away."

Climbing back into bed she pulled the sheets up under her chin and sat listening as the storm ranted and railed outside. "What if this is an omen?" she said aloud to herself, "what if the hotel doesn't want me here?" She shook her head and chided herself for such a ridiculous notion. "It's just a thunderstorm."

"Shit and corruption, the kitchen door is still open." She leapt out of bed and raced down the corridor before taking the stairs two at a time. Her naked feet touched the stone floor of the reception area as another flash came. This time it sounded closer as there was hardly a second between the crackle of lightning and the boom of thunder.

Locking the kitchen door, she returned to the reception when a sudden banging came from the main doors, someone was beating their fists against the wood. The sound filled her with dread. Holding her breath, her heart beating loudly in her ears, she didn't know if she wanted to scream or run away, she did know that she needed to pee. She squinted into the gloom and her mind raced. Should she make her way towards the rear of the hotel? Were the shadows in the dining room moving? More irrational thoughts were flooding her senses when the banging started again. "Pull yourself together Rachel," she said.

"Rachel!" Luca shouted from outside and her heart rate began to subside. She turned on the lights and went to unlock the door.

The light spilling out from the reception area lit up the entrance and standing in the rain was a saturated Luca. Still wearing the clothes he'd worn earlier his shirt clung to his body, the white cotton almost transparent and his tan-coloured trousers now a deep brown. Rachel loved the impromptu Mr Darcy moment and found she couldn't take her eyes off his nipples, cold and erect beneath the cotton.

He stepped inside, rainwater pooling at his feet and said, "I was having a drink with friends when the storm started, I came to check that you were okay." Rain trickled from his fringe, running in rivulets down his forehead and into his eyes. He shook his head and his wet hair splayed out, showering Rachel with droplets. Rachel laughed – happy that she hadn't wet herself. A sudden, louder thunderclap sounded, filling the room and reverberating around the walls, Rachel screamed, and Luca stepped forward and took her in his arms. She allowed him to hold her, his dampness seeping through the cotton of her dressing gown, before she said, "Let's go up to the apartment and I'll fetch you a towel."

Half an hour later and looking unsuitably dressed in a coral-coloured robe and yellow pyjama bottoms Luca took the mug of hot chocolate that Rachel offered him. She looked at him, his dried hair mussed up from the towel and his smile made him look younger than his thirty years. In the light from the table lamps his face bore the signs of the stubble that would darken it in a few more hours and Rachel noticed that he was trying his best to stifle a yawn. "Wait here," she said rising from her chair, "I'll make up bed for you."

"I'll be fine to drive," Luca said.

"You can't go outside wearing Louise's pyjamas." Rachel nipped next door to make up the spare bed before returning to find him fast asleep on the sofa. She slid the empty mug dangling from his finger away and walking back into the bedroom, collected a blanket and covered him up before silently padding back to her room.

***

The following morning when she woke Rachel noticed Luca had gone, the pyjamas and dressing gown neatly folded on the sofa. She made herself coffee and sat looking out at the valley. There was no sign of the storm and the sky was cloudless and hyacinth blue. In the distance she saw a man with his dog walking in the olive grove, checking the small green fruits on his trees. Rachel had been told many olive farmers feared storms as the heavy rain pulled the olives from the tree. She hoped he hadn't lost too many.

A knock at the apartment door caught her attention and before she could rise from her seat it opened and Luca walked in carrying a small box and putting it down on the kitchen table he opened it and took out the ornate clock that had been hidden in the plaster fireplace. "I thought I'd return this; it belongs in the hotel."

Rachel remembered the night Marco's ashes had gone missing and how she blamed it on the clock. Looking at the old timepiece she shivered, what if it was worth a lot of money, maybe it's best not to have it on display. She picked it up and inside the rattle of something moving within the case reminded her that they'd been unable to get the mechanism to work. "I'll put it over here," she said walking over to the window and placing it on a low side table beside a chair. "Would you like to stay for breakfast?"

"I'm sorry, I cannot. I have a –" Just then the door opened and Oli came into the room, his entrance interrupting Luca, who continued with, "I'll see myself out. *Buona colazione*."

"This is a surprise," Rachel said and pulled her brother into an embrace.

"I'm visiting a friend in Rome and thought I'd drive over and see the place."

Rachel shared her breakfast with Oli and then gave him a tour of the hotel. She took him down to see the beach and pointed out Rosa's little house before driving him into San Vito for lunch beside the road with the tourists who crowded onto the tables to enjoy fried seafood.

"I want to leave before it gets too late. I don't fancy navigating the giro around Rome in the dark." Oli said when they returned to the hotel. "So let's see this ceiling then."

They lay on the lobby floor looking up, Oli pointing out the constellations to her.

Rachel said, "Rosa told me that this one in the centre is Aquila."

"That's right,"

"It's very interesting," Rachel said moving into a sitting position. "The capital of Abruzzo is *L'Aquila*. The Eagle."

"I'm guessing that's why it was painted in the centre of the ceiling, and see there," Oli said pointing, "That's the star, Altair – the twelfth brightest star in the skies – so I'm guessing that's why it's represented by the largest of the crystals."

Aldo VII

Aldo was unpacking the newly printed brochures and placing them on a shelf inside a cupboard behind the reception desk as instructed when a delivery van pulled up outside. The driver sounded the horn before climbing out of the cab and calling out – his schedule not allowing him time for more than a drop-off and drive away. Aldo appeared at the entrance and was quickly handed a parcel and without so much as a thank-you the van driver reversed and drove away.

"What is it, Aldo?" Rachel asked popping her head around the door.

"A package for you."

"That must be the table lamps I've ordered. I'm busy here helping Silvana, so please can you take it up to my apartment?"

Rachel tossed him her keys and Aldo nodded and made his way up the stairs to the third floor. He knocked softly on the door and getting no response he pushed it open and walked over to the kitchen area, where he placed the box he was carrying on the table. He turned to leave and stopped mid-circle as his eyes fell on the clock sitting on the side table. He could hardly believe it, there was the ornate clock he had discovered weeks before. He walked over and picked it up, the winding key was still tied to a foot and he tilted it to allow whatever was inside to roll. His heart was hammering in his chest. Should he take the clock and run? Should he wait until there's no one else around? Could he hide it? The sound of footsteps in the corridor and a hand on the door handle made it impossible for him to answer his questions and he put the clock down and slid out onto the balcony just as Luca came into the room.

Aldo peered through the crack between the door and the jamb, watching. "As soon as Luca has gone, I shall take the clock and leave," he muttered to himself. "I can no longer be so close but so far away." He was then horrified to see Luca cross the room and pick up the clock. The key was inserted and turned and as usual, nothing happened – Luca shook his head – followed by the sound of it being shaken. Aldo watched as Luca turned the clock over and looked closely at the back of the casing and then his heart plummeted as Luca left the room with it under his arm.

Chapter Twenty-Seven

Luca placed the clock onto a table in the dining room and went off in search of a screwdriver, making his way back with several he'd borrowed from Massimo he almost collided with Aldo who had raced down the stairs, his feet heavy on the wooden treads and disturbing the air of calm the hotel now had.

All the noisy jobs had been completed and the few workmen that came with Carlino were tied up touching up paintwork or making sure screws were tight and cables tucked away. Cosmo was in the corner of the dining room, a brush in hand covering a scratch on a wooden cabinet with fresh stain. He looked up and smiled his hello as Luca came into the room.

Sitting at the table Luca turned the clock over listened to the rattle inside and tried the screwdrivers he'd borrowed but none were small enough to fit into the screw heads. Swearing under his breath he picked up the clock and took it outside to see if there was anything in the orto workshop he could use to open the back. After rummaging through various tools, he gave up and placed the clock in an empty manger on the wall picked up his basket of seeds and went back outside.

He heard Rachel humming softly as she entered the garden. The air was still and butterflies and hoverflies busied themselves among the fragrant flowers of the lavender and rosemary. He watched as she walked through the gap in the jasmine hedge, stopping to breathe in the heady perfume that was almost cloying in the heat. "*Ciao*," she said spotting Luca, "what are you up to today?"

"I'm sowing peas," he replied, "want to give me a hand?"

"Sure," she said rolling up her sleeves to reveal golden arms that upon her arrival, months before had been pasty and white. "What do you want me to do?"

Luca handed her a broom handle and told her to walk along the row making holes in the soil about seven centimetres apart. "Isn't it late to be sowing peas?" she asked as she followed her instructions with Luca closely behind dropping a pea into each hole and covering it over. "Normally I'd make regular sowings throughout the year, but I think there'll be enough good weather to harvest these mid-November." He pointed to a strip of darker-coloured earth that was recently watered, "Over there I've sown some lettuce."

"Lettuce in winter?"

"Our seasons are only a little similar to the ones you are used to, we don't suffer with long cold winters like the English do, but we do get snow."

"Really, I thought it was only up in the mountains and not here on the coast."

"What we do get doesn't last long."

"I'm guessing next year you'll be growing tomatoes?"

"Of course. Growing tomatoes is my birth rite. I am an Italian man, tomato juice flows through my veins." Rachel laughed and at the end of the drill, she handed him the broom handle and walked away, a wide smile fixed upon her face. Luca stood watching until she disappeared through the hedge and turning back to the task in hand he spotted Rosa watching him. "*Ciao Rosa, Come Va?*"

"*Non ci male*," she replied, saying she wasn't too bad. "The orto is shaping up nicely."

"I'm looking forward to working on it next year."

"Ah," Rosa said, "so you will still be here when the builders have all left?"

"I'm hoping Rachel will keep me on as gardener."

"Or something closer to home, maybe." Rosa's smile didn't disguise her implication and shaking his head, Luca rose from his knees.

"We are just friends."

"But do you wish to be more?"

Luca looked at Rosa and for a brief moment, he hesitated, before composing himself and saying, "I am better alone. I have no wish… no, I have no desire to become romantically entangled. I am not looking for a lover, or a partner or even a wife."

"How can someone so young dismiss the need for companionship?"

"That's exactly it, Rosa. I am too young to settle down."

Throwing her arms in the air she exclaimed, "*Mannaggia*. You Italian men waste so much of your lives being single that when you do marry you are already too old to enjoy it." Rosa laughed and Luca joined her, but they both knew that part of what she was saying was true. How many of her friends' sons had waited until they were in their mid-thirties before they had married and when children arrived, they were touching forty when they needed to be taken to school? "*Caro mio*," she said. "Don't wait too long. It is obvious to anyone who has eyes, that you and Rachel are attracted to one another."

Watching Rosa walk away Luca thought about the lie he'd just told her, but how could he say how he felt? Not even a year had passed since Rachel had lost her husband and his ashes were still beside her bed. He knew he must put his feelings aside and just be her friend, to support her in her venture. Wiping his hands on his jeans he returned his tools to the ancient brick building that was his workshop cum store and picking up the clock he locked the door and went back into the hotel.

"Caffè?" Rosa called and he looked up briefly seeing her tinkering with the seal on her coffee flask. Getting closer he noticed she had a small screwdriver in her hand, it looked small enough to fit the screws in the clock. "May I?" he asked and she handed it to him.

Sitting behind the reception desk he began to unscrew the back of the clock, Cosmo and Rosa sauntered over to see what Luca was doing. Aldo walked through and his mouth fell open as he saw the first screw being removed and set aside. "What's going on here?" Rachel said coming down the stairs holding a tray of sandwiches.

"I'm opening up the clock," Luca said without looking up from his endeavour. Rachel placed the tray on the desktop as the final screw was removed. Luca eased the back off the clock and looked inside, his brow furrowed before he removed what looked like a stone wrapped inside a piece of faded newspaper.

"This was inside." Luca held up the object and Aldo held his breath as it was unwrapped. "It's another glass crystal, from the painted ceiling." Luca handed it to Rachel, "It's larger than the others."

"I wonder why it was inside the clock," Rachel said as Aldo breathed again.

"*Un mistero*," Rosa said before ripping the cling film off the tray and helping herself to a sandwich, "*un mistero.*"

Chapter Twenty-Eight

The hotel had been buzzing with activity for days. Carlino's men had packed up and left and Rachel felt a little grief at losing Cosmo and Massimo. However, remembering the wine and flowers Cosmo had left her, she thought it probably best to keep her distance.

Carlino and his workforce had pulled out all the stops and the work had been completed two weeks ahead of schedule – something unheard of in Italy's *'piano piano'* culture. Rachel hoped in the long run that the extra money she had spent asking Carlino to hire more workers would have been worth it. Now all that was left to do was those minor niggling tasks that seemed to keep adding to the daily list of jobs and the final dressing of the rooms.

Luca had started to work at the bottom of the garden and Rachel's workload had meant she had seen very little of him and they'd only spoken to each other in passing. The geometra had arrived earlier in the week with an officious-looking man from the council. They'd walked around the hotel checking off this and that and signing off the work before leaving a certificate stating that the building was now fit for purpose. Which relieved Rachel and sent a frisson of satisfaction up her spine.

Today, Silvana was interviewing for chambermaids, Rachel had pointed out that she was happy to employ male 'room stewards' – as she called the proposed new service staff – but no men had applied. "Italy's gender blurring in employment is still a long way behind other countries," Silvana had told her.

"Well, if possible, can you find some stewards who have some basic knowledge of English? I think my English guests will find it helpful." Silvana had just shrugged, her face telling Rachel that maybe that would also be a stretch in coastal Abruzzo.

Walking into the dining room, Rachel saw Aldo sitting on a dustsheet, he was polishing the fireplace hearth, on the mantle stood the clock and above it, a large oval gilt mirror had been hung. Rachel looked at herself in the mirror, she had changed. Gone was the lingering sadness that had hung around her a few months ago. Seeing herself looking content brought on a new wave of guilt. Once again, she felt that her increased schedule meant that she was ignoring Marco. His ashes remained on the dresser in her bedroom, but she couldn't remember the last time she'd walked around the hotel holding him or even just taken a few minutes to talk to him. She decided that once everyone had left for the day she'd sit down and tell him how things were progressing. Just then a barking dog followed by a familiar voice sounded in the reception.

Walking in from the dining room Rachel saw Penny standing there a briefcase in one hand, lead attached to Sale and a selection of magazines balanced precariously in the crook of her other arm. "Sorry, I had to bring the dog. Bloody thing's getting needy in her old age." She put down the magazines and opened the briefcase, taking out a box of tea bags. "I know I'm early. I'll just make a cuppa and I can wait until you're ready for me."

"I'm free now, let's go up to the apartment," Rachel said moving towards the stairs as Aldo stepped forward and offered to take Sale outside to play in the garden.

"This place is a right hive of activity," Penny said as she began to climb the stairs.

"We're trying to tie up all the loose ends and Silvana is interviewing in the kitchen."

Opening the door to her private space, Rachel showed Penny inside; it was the first time her friend had seen the completed apartment and she looked around with admiring eyes. "You've made this look nice. I particularly like that console table next to the balcony doors." Penny walked over and ran her fingers across the top of the slender table with marquetry flowers decorating the sides. "Where did you find this?"

"One of Carlino's workers found it in an old outbuilding and thought I'd like it. Cosmo cleaned it up and polished it for me."

"I think you've been very lucky with Carlino and his men. This being Italy means the whole restoration could have dragged on for months, but here you are almost complete and on schedule. Have you given any thought to what I suggested?"

"I have." Rachel filled the kettle as Penny placed her teabags on the kitchen table. "A pre-opening event sounds like a good idea."

"I think it could generate lots of interest, we just have to make sure we get the date right."

With the tea made and biscuits on a plate beside the teapot, the two women sat at the table as Penny opened magazines and showed Rachel the articles written by people that she thought would be influential. "This girl," she said pointing to an image of a young woman smiling behind sunglasses, "is one of Italy's most-read tourism bloggers. If she says a place is good you can almost guarantee bookings."

Rachel reached over and slid the magazine towards herself, "How many people are you thinking?"

"Around fifteen. A mix of feature writers, bloggers, Instagram influencers and a couple of TV journalists should do it." Penny reached for a biscuit and dunked it into her drink and after sliding it whole into her mouth she rummaged inside her briefcase and removed her diary. "Okay so we're here now," she mumbled through the half-eaten biscuit pointing at her diary – she swallowed. – "And here's the date I think will be suitable for our preview weekend. October 15th."

Rachel's forehead furrowed "As soon as that?"

"We can do it," Penny continued "Now, I know you wanted to open in January, but I think you're missing an opportunity."

"In what way?" asked Rachel.

"I think you should open in December and catch the late Christmas bookings." Rachel still didn't look convinced, so Penny explained herself.

If we host the event in October, it means the weather will still be short-sleeved and summer dress nice, but not hot enough for us to need to open the pool. The magazines will need around four weeks for articles to be written and okayed by their editor – bloggers will write and post as and when they see fit – this means we'll be in print in time for anyone undecided on where to take a Christmas break.

"Do you think we'll get any bookings so late?"

"In my experience, yes. There won't be a flood of them but enough to make opening earlier worthwhile – besides it'll be great practice for the summer season."

Outside Sale was barking and Rachel looked out of the window to see Aldo throwing a ball. Penny joined her and together they watched as the dog retrieved the ball and dropped it at the man's feet. "She'll have him doing that all day if he lets her," said Penny.

Rachel and Penny resumed their meeting and the dates were finalised. Louise was called and as Penny fired off a few emails they had a brief catch-up where she told Rachel that the hotel's website would be live at midnight, Central European Time. As she disconnected the call there was a knock at the door and Luca stepped inside, he apologised for interrupting them and said he needed Aldo to go into town for some gardening supplies and so was returning Penny's dog. He stayed long enough for pleasantries to be exchanged but said he was busy so excused himself and exited the apartment quickly.

"He seemed in a hurry," Penny said as the door closed.

"Yes, he's got a lot on," Rachel said with little conviction. "I've had an idea," she blurted out, "As Sale is with you, why don't we take her to the beach, I'll open a bottle of wine and to save you a drive later, why don't you stay over, I can easily make up a bed for you."

"You had me at the beach and wine," Penny said, "Very well let's make a day of it."

***

That evening with dinner over, as Sale eagerly lapped up the leftover salmon and pasta, Penny retired to the sofa with a bottle of Montepulciano and a corkscrew. Rachel exhaled noisily as she dropped down onto the sofa, beside her the cork squeaked as it was released and the glasses on the coffee table were filled with the ruby-coloured wine.

The two women sat in silence for a few minutes, each one staring at the red liquid they swilled around the bowls of their glasses. Rachel took a sip before exhaling loudly once again. "This is the life," she said kicking off her flip-flops and tucking her feet beneath her bottom.

"Enjoy it for now because once you're open for business nights like this will be rare."

"Why didn't you tell me this before I started the project?" Penny looked up worried then relaxed when she saw that Rachel was joking with her.

"Have you ever regretted starting this?"

"No," Rachel said leaning across placing her glass down and choosing a chocolate from an opened box on the table. "If anything, I feel it's given me a new purpose and a new lease of life. After Marco died and before I came here, I found it difficult to drag myself out of my pit of grief. I do sometimes wonder what I'd be doing if I was still in England. Probably shuffling from room to room treading the backs of my slippers down and supping wine."

"No change there then," chuckled Penny lifting her glass in the air. Rachel joined in with the merriment picked up her glass and chinked it against Penny's.

"Marco always had a dream that we'd retire to Italy one day. Umbria or Tuscany was his preferred area of choice, and now here I am, in the virtually unknown region of Abruzzo, about to open a hotel and I still trying to catch up with the events that led me here. Maybe it was fate."

"Fate. I'm not sure if I believe in fate," Penny said.

"Well, it was fate that brought us together," Rachel said. "If we hadn't been stood at the same cashier in the supermarket that afternoon, we'd never have met, and there's so much I'd never have achieved without your help."

"Well," Penny said, "our meeting was a chance one that day, but I already knew about you. In fact, I'd spent a couple of weeks looking out for you."

"Really?" Rachel's voice dropped a couple of semitones.

"It's nothing sinister. I'd heard about you and thought it would be nice to meet you. Yes, there was always the opportunity to expand my business through your hotel but that wasn't the driving force. I remember how difficult it was for me as a lone female to set up a business here and I've always thought it useful to pass on my experiences to newcomers. I helped Mole and Ivan set up their little enterprise."

"Fate or not, I'm grateful you took me under your wing." Their glasses chinked again and Rachel took another chocolate and popped it into her mouth.

***

Within days Penny had started to receive acceptances from the journalists and bloggers she'd invited and so the final preparations had to begin in earnest. The kitchen appliances were finally fitted and despite the chef's protestations, Silvana saw fit to organise the layout of the pots, pans and crockery. Two of the newly employed chambermaids were busy on the second floor ironing bedsheets and making up guest beds and Luca and Aldo were outside painting the decking around the swimming pool. Rachel had laid out the reception area methodically and was sitting at the computer looking at the hotel website once more, she'd told herself it was to do a final check for spelling mistakes and typos, but in truth, she couldn't get over how good it felt to have her own business on the digital highway.

A horn sounded and Rachel looked out of the reception windows to see a large van trying to shoehorn itself through the gates. "Must be the television," she said aloud rising and crossing the floor. She'd argued against having a TV in the dining room, but as Penny had explained, a mute TV in the background at restaurants is almost akin to an extra family member joining you for dinner. "But no one ever seems to watch it," Rachel had insisted.

"That's as maybe, but your Italian guests will expect it."

A man in tight blue jeans and white shirt sleeves that strained against his biceps walked up the steps with ease and placed the large cardboard box on the floor. He ran his fingers through his fringe, lifting the dark curls and letting them bounce back onto his forehead before he thrust a delivery note in Rachel's direction. Thanking him, he turned to leave and Rachel found herself watching, as his denim-clad bottom moved away.

Rachel had thought about televisions for the guest bedrooms but keeping a tight rein on the finances she had quashed the idea, telling herself that she'd wait for customer feedback before investing in any. She almost giggled as she contemplated placing an order and requesting the shop send the same delivery driver as today when a ping sounded from the computer. Opening up the business email account Rachel's eyes widened as she saw the hotel had received its first enquiry from the website. Smiling, she looked out of the window again to see Rosa talking to Luca; their conversation was quite animated as most Italian conversations are. Luca pointed and waved his hands as he spoke and Rosa waved and pointed as she replied. Rachel felt a wave of contentment ripple around her, she had found it relatively easy to slip into the relaxed way of life in Sant'Andrea. However, she was under no illusion that it would remain that way when the guests arrived, but for now, she was happy to let it sweep over her at its own pace.

"I've just had a conversation with an independent travel agent in England," said Penny entering the reception, "He'd like to promote the hotel for you. I've asked him to forward his commission rates for your consideration."

"We've had an enquiry from the website today," Rachel said turning the screen around for Penny to see. "Two sisters from Abingdon want a price for a twin room in mid-July."

"Let's see," Penny scanned the mail and then proclaimed, that the hotel was on its way to making its first million, laughing she called to Silvana in the kitchen, asking her to bring them a bottle of prosecco from the fridge.

Aldo VIII

Silvana had informed Aldo that Rachel wanted to see him and with a feeling of dread he made his way through the kitchen to the reception area. He'd seen her talking with Luca earlier and their conversation had looked quite intense and he wondered if he was about to be discharged.

What will I do if I have no job he thought, *go back to Naples?*

Remembering why he'd come here, to discover Giacomo's hidden diamond seemed such a long time ago and maybe he'd given up on ever finding it. Maybe *it was* just the blathering of an old man. As he thought about his uncle he crossed himself and then kissed the emerald on his finger. "*Riposa in pace,*" he muttered beneath his breath before hitching up his trousers and walking into the foyer.

Rachel looked up as he entered the room and her smile told him it wasn't going to be bad news. "Aldo, let's sit over by the window." She stood up and moved around the desk and he followed her over to the tub chairs.

He looked at the view of the garden, framed now by heavy curtains. He recalled nights before hearing a nightjar as he'd helped Luca in his orto. Some Italians still believed in sowing some seeds in the moonlight to get a more fruitful harvest.

"I'm sorry there's no coffee, Rosa's not feeling too well this morning," Rachel said bringing him back from his thoughts.

"*Va bene cosi.*"

"I wanted to speak with you about your position here." Aldo felt a small surge of panic in his gut. "Now that the building work is complete and we are ready for our first guests I wondered if you'd like to stay on with us here at the hotel?"

Aldo's face lit up, "But what can I do, I have no experience in hospitality?"

"Luca thinks you'd make a good assistant gardener. He asked me this morning if he could offer you the job."

"Is Luca leaving?"

"Not at all, he'll become the hotel's groundsman. There's so much work needed to keep the garden..." She paused thinking of the right word to use, slipping into English, "Shipshape."

"Shipshape?" Aldo said, the word sounding more like 'sheep-shape'.

"It means neat and tidy."

"I agree. There's much work needed."

"So?"

Aldo took her hand and shook it enthusiastically, pumping it as he repeated, "*Si, Si.*" Smiling he took his leave before turning and calling across the foyer, *"Grazie mille Signora."*

Chapter Twenty-Nine

The days seemed to speed past like a Formula One driver, there didn't seem to be enough time to get everything prepared for the promotional weekend. Rachel sighed as the email pinged again. She popped her head into the dining room where Luca was fitting the television to the wall.

"*Tutto bene?*" he asked.

"Yes, everything is great." She wanted to tell him she was escaping outside to eat her lunch in peace but didn't want to sound like a moaning Minnie.

She pulled up a garden chair and sat beside the pool, its interior sparkling and clean and ready for the water to fill it.

Away from the reception desk, she felt guilty, everyone else was working hard to get everything organised and all she cared about was having time to eat a salad. She put down her fork, picked up her phone and checked the hotel's inbox.

Three messages: One from a blogger confirming his dietary requirements. An offer for cut-price Viagra, "Didn't take the spammers long to find us," she chuckled as she deleted it and added the sender to the blocked list. The final email was another booking enquiry, this time for a family room in June.

Rachel took a breath, hoping her anxiety would start to melt away. *I've never been this nervous before*, she thought, *what's wrong with me?*

Penny had told Rachel to relax and breathe so many times and that everything would be ready on time. Silvana informed the staff of their expected duties, ending the conversation by saying anyone who didn't turn in for work during the event should return their uniform the following day and leave. Penny ordered the flowers for the bedrooms and dining room from a florist in Casalbordino while Rachel bit her fingernails.

The final few days melted away and it was the night before, Rachel called Penny to tell her about her worries. "I'm so anxious it's unbelievable."

"Take a few deep breaths, have a glass of wine and try to put it out of your mind."

"That's easier said than done. I really don't know what's wrong with me. I managed a demanding job back home without any worries."

"You had your employer to fall back on, now all you have is you. Honestly, everything will be fine and you have a good team around you. Have a milky drink and try to get some sleep. I'll see you first thing in the morning."

Penny rang off leaving and Rachel sat in the kitchen with a mug of hot chocolate with a head filled with doubt and worry.

***

The hotel's promotional weekend began with clear blue skies and sunshine and as the first guests arrived Penny was efficiently milling around answering questions and pointing out interesting facts about the area. Silvana was standing behind reception, smiling and handing over bedroom keys, and Louise, who had arrived that morning, wandered around with a tray of glasses offering people sparkling prosecco.

The guest list had been padded out with some local people; Rosa looked resplendent (if not a tad overdressed) in a charcoal gown with an enormous bow on one shoulder. Carlino was in the corner networking with a local businessman who had just acquired a palazzo that needed restoring. Massimo and Cosmo had turned up in matching blue suits and Rachel did her best to contain her surprise as Cosmo introduced his wife.

"Pleased to meet you," she said accepting air kisses from the stunning woman who wouldn't look out of place on the cover of a glossy magazine.

Standing in a corner Rachel looked around her, happy to see so many people milling around inside the reception area. She glanced across at Cosmo as he introduced his wife to another guest; he was beaming, obviously proud of the wife who stood several inches taller than himself.

Mole and Ivan had arrived minus Sprog and were chatting animatedly with a woman Rachel had been told was a respected holiday blogger. Several of the suppliers who had been involved with the hotel's restoration had also been invited to answer any questions about the work that had taken place: Penny had thought it good for background details.

Handing her tray to a girl in a starched white blouse Louise sauntered over to Rachel and nodded her head towards two people standing in the hotel entrance. "Who is that?"

Rachel looked over and her eyes widened. "It's the TV delivery man."

"He can tune my channels any day," Louise said placing a hand on Rachel's shoulder and giving it a congratulatory squeeze. "I think the weekend is going rather well so far. I'm so proud of you Rachel."

"I wish you'd been here last night to say that."

"Good job I wasn't. We'd have drunk too much and looked like death now."

A lump began to form in her throat as she thought about Marco and how he'd have enjoyed all the fuss of the opening event. The moment was fleeting as Silvana called for silence to tell everyone that a buffet lunch had been laid out and was now ready in the dining room. "I'll just go outside to tell Luca lunch is ready," Louise said and exited out through the main doors into the garden.

The dining room looked spectacular, the curtains had been drawn and the wall lights twinkled, their light illuminating the gilt frames of the pictures on the walls. In the centre had been placed a long table that contained everything from plates of antipasti to caprese salad and cloche-covered bowls of pasta dishes. At the end of the table stood a man in a scarlet waistcoat, he was holding a long knife with a blade that looked as thin as paper and as each guest approached him, he sliced off wafer-thin slivers of prosciutto crudo from the ham-leg mounted on a silver stand.

Rachel looked over as Luca entered the room giving her a thumbs up before picking up a plate and loading it with slices of salami and cheese. "All these people," she said as Penny joined her. "It all seemed an impossible dream a few months ago."

"The hard work starts now," Penny said with a smile.

"I don't doubt it."

"As I said last night, you have a good support network in place and you know I'm always available for any advice."

Rachel hugged Penny. *I know how lucky I am*, she thought. *Many people could have failed before they started but I seemed to be in the right place at the right time and gathered around me so many knowledgeable people and also good friends.* Her thoughts were interrupted by a tinkle of laughter over at the drinks table. She glanced across and saw Luca chatting with a girl as she topped up his glass. The girl was amused by something he'd said and before walking away his hand stroked her arm.

"Who's that girl?"

"I'm not sure, I think she's named Mirella, one of the room stewards drafted in to be a waitress for the weekend."

Luca had moved away and was now standing talking to Carlino, but even as she took a plate and began to serve herself, Rachel's gaze kept drifting over to Mirella.

After lunch, many of the guests followed Luca outside into the garden where he had planned a brief tour to point out the pool, and the views and of course, to make sure each of the guests/reporters was aware that the hotel would be producing most of its own produce. Rachel and Penny remained to entertain the guests who preferred to stay inside close to the bar. "He's looking at you," Louise whispered in her ear as she handed out a brochure to a man in a linen suit. "Don't look!"

"Who?" hissed Rachel.

"The television man." Rachel looked across the room and smiling, he lifted a glass in her direction, feeling a flush rise in her cheeks she looked away in an instant.

"What's wrong?" Louise whispered, "He's fit as…"

"I don't know. It just feels strange."

"Well, do you fancy him?"

"It's not a case of fancying him," Rachel said, "is it appropriate."

"Appropriate," sniggered Louise taking her friend by the elbow and leading her away to a corner of the room.

"But what about Marco?"

"No one is asking you to have a love affair, just flirt a little, enjoy his company."

Rachel looked up and saw that he was still looking across at her, this time she smiled back and tiny shards of colour from the wall lights seemed to catch in his eyes. "He is handsome," she told herself, "and would it hurt to spend some time with him?" He placed his glass down and made his way across the room towards her. She found herself looking at his impossibly tight trousers, his hips swaying with each stride and was embarrassed when he reached her side that she was still looking down.

"Hello again," he said, his English accented by a deep, rich timbre. "Can I get you a drink?"

"A glass of wine would be nice," she replied before adding, "red."

He walked back across the room and she found herself watching his rear as he made his way over to the bar. Mirella was serving and Rachel watched as she opened a fresh bottle of Montepulciano and poured the wine into glasses, finishing with that same earlier tinkle of laughter as she handed them to him.

"Would you like to take a stroll in the garden?" he asked as he returned with her drink. She accepted his offer and together they left the reception area and stepped outside. Rosa called out to say goodbye as she left the party, "I hope it all goes well for you," she waved. Rachel watched her head off down the lane, her gown swishing around her ankles revealing white training shoes.

"This is a nice view," her companion said moving closer to her and pointing to the strip of sea that could be seen from the gates.

"I like it," Rachel replied, a little uncomfortable with his closeness. She stepped back and he filled the space she'd vacated. His eyes were the colour of chocolate spread and above them were neatly trimmed brows. His nose was narrow and sat above a perfect set of plump pink lips. He smiled revealing straight white teeth and reaching out his hand stroked her arm. She knew she'd need strength to resist his advances, should he make any. "So, tell me where are you from?"

"Pescara," he answered before taking a sip of his wine. "I live near the stadium, so it's often noisy." Rachel lifted her glass to her lips but stopped midway as he said, "I'm Marco, by the way."

"Marco?"

"Yes."

Panic began to rise inside her, she felt a strangeness rise from her waist, up her torso to spread across her shoulders. She tried to speak but nothing came out of her mouth, then as the tears began to roll from her eyes she dropped the wine glass, turned and ran down the lane.

She was on the steps sobbing and looking down at the beach when Rosa approached her. The old woman said nothing, she draped a shawl across her shoulders and led her away.

Sitting at her kitchen table Rosa listened as Rachel spoke. "Of all the names he could have had. It must be a sign."

"A sign for what?" Rosa opened a small bottle of Genziana and poured them both a measure. Rachel grimaced as the brownish liquid slipped across her tongue before continuing to explain that she believed that her husband was sending her a message. "And what is that message?"

"That it's too early to meet someone else. Maybe."

"And to do this he sends you someone with the same name?"

"Yes… I don't know… It's just –"

"Coincidence. That's all." Rosa laid her hand on top of Rachel's, "Marco is quite a common name after all."

"But –"

"Maybe it's not the name. Maybe he was just not the right man. Maybe it just didn't feel natural." Rachel sniffed and nodded, she remembered how uncomfortable she'd felt when he'd stood too close. In her mind she could see him, he was handsome, perfect in every way but how could she let herself fall for another Marco?

"I'd better get back to the hotel, people will wonder where I am."

"They'll cope for a while longer," Rosa said pouring another glass. "Silvana is more than capable of running things." She tipped her glass up and swallowed her drink, "

"How do you drink this stuff," Rachel held up her glass, "It's so bitter."

"Sometimes we need to be reminded that not everything is sweet and sometimes to grow strong we must taste the bitter herb."

"Is that an old Italian proverb?" Rachel drank the remnants of her drink and shuddered.

"No. I just thought it up. It felt like the right thing to say," and the two of them started laughing as Rosa secured the cork back in the bottle and spooned coffee into the pot on the stove.

Chapter Thirty

Louise looked concerned as Rachel entered the reception and mouthed, "Are you okay?" across the room to be repaid with a nod of the head.

Penny was organising guests into a snake-like line for a trip down the lane to see the private beach and Rachel peered into the dining room and saw Silvana overseeing the clearing of the table with two girls gathering up the tablecloths and unused cutlery. On the console table stood a tray of glasses that had been washed and returned and Mirella was buffing each one with a cotton cloth. Rachel noticed that as Luca entered the room the glass polishing stopped and he received a smile.

"Penny has taken everyone down the lane," he said joining Rachel. "Where did you get to?"

"There's was something I had to deal with," Rachel said as Mole joined them.

"All the guests have checked in and their luggage is in their rooms. Ivan is with Penny on the walk to the beach, so is there anything else you'd like me to do?"

Rachel moved in and hugged Mole, "No, you've done more than enough. Thank you for coming, why don't I fix us both a drink."

"I'll make your drinks," Luca said interrupting. "It's still quite warm outside so why don't you two take a seat by the pool."

Dropping onto a sun lounger Mole let out a satisfied sigh, "I think everyone has enjoyed it so far."

"The weather has helped." Rachel looked up as she heard her name spoken and stood in the kitchen doorway was Cosmo. He thanked her for the invite, saying that his wife had enjoyed the lunch. He was about to leave when she called out his name. "Cosmo?"

"Yes?"

"Thank you for everything, especially the ceiling, it looks magnificent."

"*Grazie mille*," he said and with a rosy hue peppering his cheeks he turned and left.

"I think he's smitten," Mole said lowering her voice.

"No," Rachel replied. "You saw his wife; she's stunning, a real Italian beauty."

"Compared to you, an English rose."

"English rose. Are you planning more flowers for the garden?" questioned Luca as he carried out two tall glasses of pink-coloured liquid. "Rosato spritz for you." They accepted the drinks and as he walked away Rachel's eyes followed him until he was out of sight.

Mole and Rachel enjoyed the tail-end of the afternoon, their faces turned upwards to take in the last of the sunshine. They sat in companionable silence as the sounds of people working in the kitchen drifted outside. In the sky above her Rachel spotted what looked like a large hawk and pointing it out to Mole was told it was a red kite, "You can tell them apart from the buzzards by the triangular cut out in their tail feathers. There's quite a lot of them now. When we first came you hardly saw any," she said.

Louise wandered over to tell them that the guests were all making their way back up the lane and with a sigh Rachel eased herself out of her lounger and smoothed down her skirt. "I guess I'd better meet them at the door." Louise slipped her arm through her friend's and together they walked around the outside of the hotel towards the front door.

"Where have you been?" Louise asked.

"I'll tell you later." Rachel welcomed her guests back and apologised for disappearing saying she had to attend to something but was now able to give them her undivided attention.

"Penny has looked after us so well," a woman with her spectacles perched on top of her head said. "The hotel looks amazing considering how it first looked when you took it on." Rachel must have looked confused as the woman added, "I saw the images on your website."

"Of course," Rachel said remembering the photos that Louise had uploaded to the hotel's blog. It all seemed such a long time ago now.

The guests began to disperse, most going up to their rooms to take some time out before changing for dinner. A woman with hair the colour of burnt caramel was interested in the ceiling at the reception and listened intently as Rachel explained the layout and pointed out the constellations painted above their heads. "The glass balls are interesting," she said.

"Yes, at night when the lights are turned down, we use uplighters to make the crystals shimmer like stars."

"How clever of you to have thought of that."

"Oh, I didn't, it was already in place. One of the builders' Cosmo restored it."

"I'll look forward to seeing it later."

Rachel continued to field questions as Mirella over at the bar continued to serve drinks to the handful of guests who had decided to sit in the chairs beside the tall windows and talk. Rachel hoped the discussions were positive ones. She grinned as she looked across at Louise who was chatting to a man standing behind a seated guest. She guessed her friend was eavesdropping on the hushed conversations. How like Louise, she thought, she has no fear.

That evening dinner was a more formal affair, the chef had prepared a prawn and langoustine terrine for the first course and for the vegan guests he'd done a confit of sweet peppers with roasted pine nuts. As the second course arrived Rachel began to feel more relaxed, the 'Marco' debacle from earlier had not been forgotten but now it seemed less significant to her. Luca was sat at the other end of the table and he chatted animatedly to the woman sitting next to him. Rachel imagined his friendly smile winning over his companion.

After dinner most of the guests retired to their rooms; probably to write up their notes Rachel assumed. The dining room had been cleared and Penny who was staying overnight was chatting in the bar area with a couple of guests who lingered over a bottle of brandy. Luca strolled over and looking past him Rachel saw Mirella hanging back in the doorway. "Good night," he said leaning in and giving both Louise and Rachel an air kiss. "I shall return tomorrow after breakfast." He walked over to Mirella and Rachel caught her laughter as they left the hotel together. Looking out of the window she watched as Mirella got into Luca's car and as it drove away, she watched the red taillights until they disappeared around the corner past Rosa's cottage.

"Is everything okay?" Louise said bringing her back from her thoughts.

"Sure," she replied a little too quickly as she looked over to see Silvana turning off the dining room lights and closing the door. "Shall we go up to the apartment, I think Silvana has everything in hand?"

Louise kicked off her shoes and sprawled across Rachel's sofa as she was handed a glass of Montepulciano. "I'm shattered," she said. "I don't think I've sat down all day for more than five minutes."

"You've been a star," Rachel said dropping into the chair opposite. "Let's hope it's all been worth it."

"Oh, I think it has been. Everyone seemed to enjoy the day, the food was excellent and the weather gave lots of perfect photo opportunities."

Coincidentally, Rachel's phone pinged and looking at the screen she saw Penny had sent her a link to one of the blogger's Instagram accounts. The screen opened up to reveal a picture of a hotel bedroom. The duck-egg walls and pale yellow paper meant it was one of her rooms. Beneath the image, the poster had written, '*A little slice of heaven in Abruzzo – my room for the night.*' Excited she held out her phone for Louise to see.

"Hopefully over the coming few days, there'll be lots more posts to drive interest to your door."

"I hope so," Rachel said, "I know I wasn't sure at the start but now, I want this to work."

"If today is anything to go by, I think you'll make it." Louise emptied her glass and holding it out to Rachel for a refill said, "So, tell me what happened with you and the handsome TV delivery man?"

"It started out well. I was flattered that he wanted to spend some time with me and then he told me his name."

"And?"

"It's Marco."

Louise's nose wrinkled and she said "Urgh, awkward."

"Tell me about it. I got freaked out that it was an omen and ran off. I ended up drinking coffee with Rosa in her kitchen until I'd pulled myself together."

"I can see how you'd feel at odds with someone with Marco's name."

"Maybe I'm not ready to move on yet."

"I'm not so sure," Louise chuckled and held up her glass as if blaming her statement on too much wine.

"Meaning?" Rachel said.

"Luca. You can't deny he'd be a great catch."

"He's not interested in me romantically. Besides he seems to be getting on very well with Mirella."

"So, you noticed that too?" Louise said and Rachel nodded, "I thought they looked very friendly today."

"She left with him."

"Maybe we're jumping to conclusions."

"Don't be daft Lou. She's a pretty, young thing, how could he not be flattered when she bats her eyelashes at him."

"So, what are you going to do about it?"

"What can I do? A while back, I overheard him in the garden telling Rosa he wasn't looking for a lover."

"You'll have to work on changing his mind." There was an impish glint in Louise's eyes. *Could it be the wine or the lighting*, Rachel thought.

"I won't have time. I'm flying back to England to put the house on the market, then I'll be coming back here to get everything ready for the official opening before Christmas."

"Is it still okay for Ben and me to come and stay over Christmas?"

"Yes, It'll be lovely having you both here and I'll also get two extra members of staff who won't be on the payroll." Rachel started to laugh and Louise rolled her eyes before lifting her glass to salute her friend.

Chapter Thirty-One

Rachel stood at the end of the driveway looking at the red-brick house that had once been her home. The modern semi-detached on a modern open-plan estate had been her and Marco's first house together. How different it looked after months of living in Italy, where her new home was surrounded by bamboo and rocky outcrops, here the flat squares of lawn and flower borders looked ordered and sterile.

Pushing open the front door there was no woosh of post sitting below the letterbox; Louise had been taking care of postal deliveries and on the hall table was a small pile of unimportant circulars and sales brochures. The scent of vanilla hung in the air and looking at the wall socket she saw the electric air freshener that she assumed Louise had plugged in.

Leaving her cabin case in the hallway she walked into the sitting room. Everything was as she'd left it months ago, and she could tell that the surfaces had been given a once over with some furniture polish. Like the outside the interior looked very different to what she had got used to lately. Here there were carpets and gas fires whereas in Abruzzo she'd become accustomed to air-conditioning and tiled floors. She wandered from room to room but oddly didn't feel sad, she remembered meals at the dining table with Marco and the sofa still had a small indent where he'd often sit engrossed in his PlayStation. This had been a happy home, filled with love and laughter and that's how she wanted to remember it.

On the kitchen worktop was a brochure from an estate agency and on the front cover was stapled a business card from the agent who would be visiting the following day with the appointment time scribbled in biro. Propped up against a bottle of wine was a note from Louise telling her that the boiler was turned on and there was milk and butter in the fridge.

In the bedroom, she unpacked her case and hung up the few garments she'd bought with her in the wardrobe. It looked alien to her now seeing a space populated by naked coat hangers. She remembered the day she had packed away Marco's shirts, the desperate sadness she had felt, the pain she thought would never leave her that now registered sorrow but not grief.

Having spent many months taking showers, she looked longingly at the bathtub and added some fragrant essence to the running taps. After placing a glass of wine on the side she stepped out of her robe and slid beneath the bubbles and closed her eyes.

Rachel was surprised by how soundly she had slept, maybe it was the hot bath and the wine; *maybe the familiarity of her old bed,* she thought as she pulled the duvet over her shoulders, *probably the flight and drive from Stansted.* She closed her eyes again and allowed herself a few more minutes before she got up and pulled on her robe.

In the kitchen, she made herself some toast and scrambled eggs before she dressed and prepared for the agent. She was listening to the news when her phone buzzed and seeing it was Louise, she picked up quickly. "Hi… yes everything is fine… thanks for getting me some basic groceries… yes let's go out for dinner tonight."

The doorbell rang and she quickly ended the call explaining it must be the agent and promised to call back afterwards.

Opening the front door Rachel was greeted by a woman in a charcoal suit who held out her hand. "Rachel Balducci?" Rachel nodded, "I'm from the Marks and Webber Estate Agency, we have an appointment for this morning."

"Yes, of course, come in." As the door closed behind the agent Rachel said, "Sorry I didn't catch your name."

"I'm Glenn, as in Close not Hoddle."

"Oh."

"I'm not offended if you expected me to be a male, most of my clients do."

"No, not at all, would you like a coffee?"

"Do you mind if I take a quick look around first?" Rachel switched on the kettle as Glenn set about walking from room to room with her muted vocalisations giving nothing away. "It's a tidy little property," Glenn said rejoining Rachel in the kitchen, "In the current climate, I think it should sell quickly if the price is right."

Rachel placed a mug of coffee down for Glenn and then apologised for not having any biscuits. "I only flew in from Italy yesterday."

"Yes, your friend…" she looked at her iPad, "Louise said you were living out there. I've always wanted to go to Italy." Not missing a trick Rachel opened her purse and slid a business card across the worktop.

After a quick chat, Glenn set about recording the room sizes with a laser measure and jotted down answers to questions she was asking. "So will all the furniture be removed before the completion of the sale?"

"Yes, unless the buyer wants to negotiate for any pieces."

"We'd rather not go down that route. It can get messy."

"Okay." Rachel blushed.

At the door Glenn held out her hand once more and told Rachel the agency photographer would call later that day and with a brisk, professional 'goodbye' she walked towards her silver Porsche parked at the end of the drive.

***

"I've missed a curry," Rachel said spooning some lime pickle onto a popadom. "I love Italian food but there's only so much pasta a girl can eat."

"You have some great seafood restaurants nearby though."

"I know but here in the UK there are all kinds of restaurants and cuisines on offer whereas in Italy everywhere is similar. I went to the supermarket earlier and it's so different from Italian shops where everyone sells the same products…" she paused as the waiter placed their main course down on the table. "…I reckon that's the difference between a holiday and living there, you start to see differences more acutely."

Louise tore off a piece of naan bread and dipped it into her jalfrezi and with little refinement she folded it and stuffed it into her mouth, smiling as orange sauce coated her lips. "So, what's the feedback like from the promotional weekend?" she said after swallowing.

"The bloggers are all speaking about it favourably and one magazine has already published a two-page review that sang the hotel's praises. Enquiries are coming in and we've already had some firm bookings."

"I checked the website and traffic is up and the hotel is moving up the search rankings, so that should increase business."

"Penny thinks I should apply for a licence to host weddings."

"Sounds like a good idea, but it will mean more work."

"I know, flowers, photographers the whole kit and caboodle."

"Yes, but it's a service that other hotels in the area don't offer. Would you like me to do some research?"

"You do enough unpaid work as it is," Rachel said.

"I'll find a way for you to recompense me another time." Louise's smile was wide and full of love even if there was some spinach stuck to her teeth."

Back home, Rachel checked her emails, there was a selection of photographs from the estate agency including Glenn's observations. Mole had sent a quick message to say everything was ticking over at the hotel – she had volunteered to look after Rachel's apartment while she was away. – *Rosa said she'd like to plant some roses outside the gates*, she wrote, *I told her to discuss it with you when you get back*. Then she spotted an email from an address she'd not seen before.

Opening it up she saw it was from Luca. He said he hoped she had a safe flight and that she didn't feel too cold away from the Abruzzese sunshine and he was looking forward to seeing her upon her return home.

Home. One word, four letters.

"She hadn't thought of the hotel in that way. It was a business. Yes, she had her apartment upstairs but until now she'd always thought of the modern semi where she now sat cradling a glass of wine as home.

"I'm guessing it's not any longer and *Le Stelle* is now home," she said aloud before picking up the bottle and topping up her glass.

Chapter Thirty-Two

Rachel stepped through the doorway onto the steps at the rear of the aircraft and the hot air outside washed over her. She crossed the strap of her shoulder bag across her chest and carrying her cabin bag she descended the steps and followed her fellow travellers into the arrivals building.

The international airport at Pescara was small in comparison to many others she'd flown into and its small size gave it a welcoming feel. There was the usual wait as the customs officers verified everyone's passports and eventually, she entered the main part of the building to find Luca waiting for her.

As she reached him, he embraced her and placed the customary two kisses across her cheeks. "Welcome home," he said and took her cabin bag. "It takes too long to leave the airport car park so I'm parked across the road at the supermarket."

As Luca led the way, the plastic wheels of the cabin bag rattling on the concrete, Rachel found she was watching the ripple of his hips as he walked, there was something feminine about his gait but his carriage was still obviously masculine. After crossing the road and dropping the case into the boot of his car they headed out of the town of Sambuceto, Luca saying he'd prefer to drive back along the coast road rather than the autostrada.

"Sambuceto looks a bit depressing I always think," Rachel said as the car passed apartment blocks and shabby-looking shop fronts. "It's such a shame arriving for a holiday and this is the first place you get to see."

"It is what it is, but if you take time to look around, you'll discover it has so much to offer."

"Such as?"

The car slowed and Luca pointed across the road. "There, see that little gelateria, it's been run by the same family for years and they make the best ice cream you are ever likely to taste. There," he pointed out a drab-looking shop front, "Signora La Malfa and her family have been making wedding dresses for over sixty years. Brides-to-be have travelled from as far as Sicily to have a dress made here.

As the car slipped between the narrow streets flanked by shops on the Francavilla road, Rachel found herself looking at Luca's hands on the steering wheel. She stared at the half-moons of his fingernails topping his slender fingers, she smiled as she took in the dark hairs on his forearm that wrapped around the strap of his wristwatch like blades of grass creeping into a border. Glancing across at her he asked if she was okay and she replied that she was just a little tired.

For most of the journey, they sat in companionable silence, Luca occasionally muttering under his breath when he was exasperated by another road user, and Rachel hummed, almost silently as she watched the now familiar coastline slide past.

Thirty minutes later they arrived outside *Le Stelle* and Rachel sat looking through the windscreen at the hotel's entrance. Mole burst onto the steps welcoming her back. Rosa was sitting at a table in the reception area, a bottle of prosecco on the table in front of her and Ivan offered to carry her bags up to the apartment. "I didn't expect a welcoming committee," Rachel said, her hand on her throat and a wide smile across her face.

"Come. Sit," Rosa said patting the seat beside her and picking up the bottle she handed it to Mole to open. "We have a surprise for you."

Mole poured prosecco into glasses and Luca pulled the curtains over the windows as Ivan returned from upstairs. "What's going on?" Rachel asked as the wall lights dimmed, above each of the sconces pinpoints of cool blue light shone upwards and moved slowly.

"*Guarda*," Rosa said pointing upwards to the ceiling that sparkled as the LED lights picked out the facets of the crystals sending a wealth of colours across the ceiling that glittered brightly.

Once again Rachel's hand clutched her throat and she was lost for words.

"It was Cosmo's idea to install them," Luca said sliding his arm across her shoulders. "He saw them in a shop window and knew they'd make the whole room look extra special."

"They do." Taking her glass Rachel raised it aloft, proposed a toast to Cosmo and wished everyone well, thanking them for their welcome.

***

A gentle breeze moved the curtains and through the mosquito screen, the heady perfume of jasmine drifted into the room. Rachel opened her eyes and stretched her arms above her head, she'd slept well, a result of air travel and prosecco. Pushing back the duvet she swung her legs out of the bed and padded into the kitchen where she filled the coffee pot and lit the gas beneath it. As she waited for the water to boil, she opened her shoulder bag, took out a notebook and looked through the notes she'd made during a conversation with Louise about advertising the Christmas vacancies and the official opening. As she flicked the pages over, scanning her writing she stopped when in the corner of a page she saw that inadvertently she'd written Luca's name. He seemed to be entering her thoughts more randomly than before and she was at odds with her feelings for him. She liked him; He was a good friend but she knew that her friendship had started to melt into attraction. The coffee pot bubbled and she put her thoughts aside as she poured steaming liquid into a mug and carried it over to the balcony.

Opening the screens, she stepped out and her attention was taken by a pair of red kites circling above the olive grove in the distance. She watched the birds as they rode on the thermals before the sound of voices below distracted her. Looking down she spotted Luca as he placed a tray of seedlings onto the ground, his companion however was obscured by the balcony floor and even leaning forward Rachel wasn't able to see who he was talking to. She took a step back, concealing herself and watched as Luca pulled apart young plants ready for transplanting in the ground, he said something she couldn't distinguish and the orto was filled with familiar tinkling laughter.

"Mirella," Rachel said aloud before returning to her kitchen, putting down her mug and making her way to the bathroom.

As she descended the stairs into the reception area Rachel saw Mirella clearing the prosecco glasses from the previous evening and seeing her boss, she turned and said, "Good morning, Rachel. Welcome back."

"Thank you, Mirella," Rachel said, trying to keep a small sneer out of her voice. Just then Silvana entered through the kitchen doors and ignoring Rachel she handed a list of groceries to Mirella, telling her to go to the local supermarket when she'd finished clearing the tables.

"Morning Silvana."

"*Buongiorno Signora*," Silvana replied, "There's post behind the reception desk for you."

Rachel slid behind the desk and saw several large brown envelopes alongside the electricity and the council tax bills. "These must be the hard copies from the magazine articles about our promotional weekend." Tearing the envelopes open she flicked through the magazines until she found the articles written about their marketing venture.

"Anything interesting?" Rachel looked up as Penny entered the reception.

"Listen to this, Rachel read from the magazine she was holding – "*Le Stelle is perfect for anyone hoping to have a break away from the hustle and bustle of the tourist trap. The private beach makes it perfect for both romantic getaways and family holidays.*"

"I've already seen them," Penny said, it seemed that everyone who stayed had a great time. We've not received a single negative comment from any of the journalists or bloggers. In fact." Penny dropped her bag on the reception desk and removed her iPad. "I've been waiting for you to return so I could show you this in person."

Rachel took the offered tablet and her eyes widened as she looked at the screen. "Are all of these booking enquiries?"

"Yes. And forty per cent are asking about the Christmas season, I've even provisionally booked a party of young people for New Year."

"Oh." Rachel's mouth formed a straight line to match her misgiving at Penny's comment. "I'm not sure about the hotel being taken over by young people."

"I understand your fear but in Italy, it's traditional for parties of young people to go away together for New Year, but unlike in the UK, they have a strict code of conduct. It's a celebration, yes, but there's no overt drunkenness and they'll even clear up after themselves." Penny could see that Rachel wasn't convinced and so said she'd introduce her to some holiday homeowners who've had experience renting to youth groups. "I think we have a lot of work ahead of us today."

"I'm ready for it," Rachel said and she stepped aside to allow Penny to move into the chair behind the computer.

Chapter Thirty-Three

The weeks leading up to the official opening were slipping by and Rachel found herself tied to the computer most days answering emails. There was so much administration that she'd hardly had a chance to talk with Luca who was still beavering away in the orto. She'd walked around it the night before after everyone had left and was impressed by the raised beds filled with winter greens. "Who'd have thought you could grow lettuce and fennel outside in November," she had said to herself.

The pool was covered over and the decking had been power washed, its chairs and loungers locked away, walking through the jasmine hedges she'd wandered down to the bottom of the garden and stood at the fence looking over the valley. The town below was lit up orange against the amethyst-coloured sky and in the distance, a fox shrieked. Rachel hugged herself, she felt good about being here, any worries she'd had had dissolved away and with the enquiries that had followed the positive reviews she was looking forward to the opening in December.

She'd sauntered back to the hotel; the darkness and the sounds of the countryside held no fear for her. The moon was high over the sea and she imagined it casting a silver glow across the surface of the Adriatic. She decided to take a walk down the lane to the beach and as she passed Rosa's house, she looked in through the tiny kitchen window, the inside was illuminated by the standard lamp beside the fireplace and the old woman was sleeping in her armchair.

Taking care to walk down the steps she reached the beach and walked towards the sea. The waves were sluggish and barely made a sound as they moved back and forth. With water rising and falling over her feet she stood looking out at the expanse of water before her. "Marco would have loved it here," she said, talking to the sea. "Maybe this should be his resting place."

In the distance a ship glided across the horizon, its lights bright and advertising that inside, the decks were filled with holidaymakers enjoying a cruise. Rachel imagined the people inside looking out to sea, maybe they could see her, maybe they'd choose to stay with her at *Le Stelle*. Despite the ship being so far away she waved to it before turning to leave the beach. "I'm truly lucky to live here. Thank you, Marco."

Passing Rosa's house again, she was startled when the front door opened and the light from inside bled into the lane. "*Sera*," Rosa said "*Nocino?*" Between her fingers hung two small glasses with long slender glass stems.

Rosa stepped aside and Rachel entered her kitchen and sat at the dining table. "*Fatti in casa*," Rosa said pulling a cork from the top of a bottle and pouring the homemade brown spirit into the glasses.

"*Grazie*," Rachel said before taking a sip of the bitter-sweet walnut liqueur.

"It's good?"

"Yes, very good."

"You've been to the beach?"

"Yes, I wanted to see the moon on the water so took a walk. It's very calming at night."

"Let's hope it stays that way once your guests arrive."

Rachel suddenly thought about the increased traffic in the lane and said, "I hope they don't disturb you too much. You must tell me if they do."

"It'll be good to see people coming to enjoy our treasures." Rosa topped up their glasses and as Rachel took a sip added, "Besides I'm as deaf as a dead cat." Spluttering Rachel placed her glass down and Rosa laughed as she handed her a handkerchief to wipe her mouth.

"Thank you for the drink," Rachel said rising from her seat, "but I think it's time I made my way to my bed. I have the *comune* and mayor arriving tomorrow to tell me about the application to host weddings."

At Rosa's door, the old woman took Rachel's hand and said, "It's not in our stars to hold our destiny but in ourselves... *buona notte*."

With the bedsheets pulled up to her chin, Rachel sat up in bed with Rosa's words moving around her head. Where had she heard that phrase before? She guessed the reference to stars was because of the hotel's name but what had the old woman meant?

Grabbing her iPad, she Googled the quote and screwed her eyes up. "What's an old woman in Abruzzo doing quoting Shakespeare?"

***

Silvana had already welcomed the visitors and had organised drinks when Rachel entered the dining room. She apologised for being a few minutes late and shook hands with the three men assembled around the table. "I hope you've been looked after," she said as the door opened and in walked Mirella with a tray of coffees.

"Silvana has been looking after us," a tall, thin man with spectacles that magnified his eyes said. "She has always been most efficient."

"Do you know each other already?"

"Yes. We've worked together on previous hotel events." The man removed his spectacles and instantly his eyes became pinheads in his face as he took a handkerchief from his pocket and began polishing the thick lenses.

"That's nice," muttered Rachel as the mayor removed some papers from inside the folder in front of him. Everyone listened as he explained that the licence for weddings had been granted and must be displayed in the foyer.

"As you are aware *Signora Balducci*, the ceremonies are not religious ones and therefore are not governed by the church." Rachel nodded, thinking that most of the weddings she'd host would be from overseas couples wanting to seal their union under the Italian sun.

As the meeting wound up Rachel shook hands with the men around the table and as they left the hotel, the man in spectacles lingered to chat with Silvana at the entrance, she filed away the paperwork and then fired off a text to Louise telling her that she had the wedding licence.

Her friend's reply buzzed in her pocket as she saw Silvana walking back through the reception area, her determined gait indicating that she wanted to talk. "Rachel? Do you have a few minutes to discuss another issue?"

"I'm a bit busy at the moment, will it wait until later? I need to speak with Luca first."

"It is Luca I wanted to discuss." Intrigued Rachel indicated towards the old chair and Silvana sat down. "The hotel is ready for guests, there is no more work required. Therefore, I was thinking it may not be prudent to retain Luca as a project manager any longer."

Oops! The thought bounced around her head like a ball against a wall, *There it is, the awkward conversation I've been avoiding.* "I understand what you're saying Silvana, and I have already given this some thought."

"So would you like me to tell him the position has expired?"

"No," Rachel replied immediately, "I'll speak with him."

Silvana rose from the seat and left, leaving Rachel groaning through gritted teeth.

At that moment, Luca popped his head around the doorframe and said, "Silvana said you wanted to speak with me." Rachel shook her head, *The audacity of the woman. How dare she.* The groan became a growl and she made a mental note to speak with Silvana about boundaries.

Thinking on her feet Rachel said, "I was wondering if you were free this evening. I could cook for us?"

"Sorry, no. I'm going to watch a basketball game with Mirella." Luca said, then added, "Why don't you come along?"

"Not my thing, but thanks," Rachel replied with a small stab of jealousy in her chest.

"I'm free tomorrow. I'll bring wine." Luca smiled before turning and heading back to his orto.

Chapter Thirty-Four

Rachel and Penny had chosen to sit outside for their lunchtime meeting. The lavender hedge was covered with small black bees that looked like musical notes as they went about their business singing and humming. Rosa had already been over to deliver their daily coffees and as Penny took off her sunglasses and pulled her sun hat down level with her eyebrows, she closed her journal and dabbed her finger in the pastry crumbs on a plate. "Well, that's another two bookings confirmed for next year."

"Summer is starting to fill up quite nicely," Rachel said, "It's exciting but also scary."

"You'll soon get into the swing of things, and then you won't need my help."

"I'm so thankful, you've gone over and above what I could have expected."

"Don't forget the Aspire Abruzzo bookings attract commission." Penny gave a small laugh before saying, "Shall I call Silvana over and ask her to bring us more coffee?"

"Best not, she's in a foul mood since I spoke to her this morning about overstepping the mark. It's an uphill struggle to get her to realise that she isn't the hotel manager."

"Interesting."

Just then Mirella walked past and Penny asked her if she could bring them a bottle of chilled rosé and a couple of glasses. "Now tell me more." Penny listened as Rachel told her about Silvana's interference regarding Luca's job and how she'd sent him to speak with her. "Cheeky mare." The women stopped chatting as Mirella delivered the wine and as she walked back into the kitchen Penny asked, "So what are you going to do about Luca?"

"I don't know. Silvana is right, there is no need for him to carry on as project manager."

"There hasn't been for several weeks, to be honest."

"I know. I just kept putting it off."

"Why not offer him a job as a gardener?" Penny poured the wine as Rachel shrugged her shoulders.

"He's coming over for dinner later so I'll try to broach the subject then."

"*Signora Balducci*!" Rachel turned to see Aldo standing in the kitchen doorway, "*Il sindaco*." Rachel looked up and saw that standing behind Aldo was the local mayor. She beckoned him over and he declined the drink she offered saying he had a lot of business to attend to but as he was passing, he wanted to deliver a letter personally.

"Thank you," Rachel said taking the envelope and with a small bow the mayor made his excuses and left.

"Special delivery from the mayor?" Penny said with raised eyebrows.

"I hope it's what I'm waiting for." Rachel tore open the envelope took out the single page and scanned the text. "Yes! I'm so pleased they've granted me permission."

"Permission?" Penny asked picking up the bottle and filling their glasses.

"Yes. When he delivered the marriage licence yesterday, I asked him about obtaining permission to scatter Marco's ashes on the beach." There was a moment of silence as Penny watched as Rachel read the letter. "I didn't think it would have come through so quickly."

"The mayor must like you." Penny joked and Rachel laughed before telling Penny about the late-night stroll across the beach when the idea had come to her.

"I've been so busy lately that I feel like I've neglected Marco, I can't remember the last time I sat down and talked to him. It feels wrong to say this, but as each week passes, I seem to miss him less than the one before." Penny's forehead creased a little but she didn't reply. "Don't get me wrong, I do still miss him but that aching pain in my heart has become nothing more than a dull throb when I do get a few minutes to reflect."

"We humans are strange creatures. We think we'll grieve forever, but when the grief subsides and life begins to take over we blame ourselves for not caring enough." Rachel opened her mouth to speak but Penny held up her hand. "I'm not saying you care any less, but a part of loss is acceptance and maybe that's where you are now. Maybe you feel that the time is right for you to move on."

"It certainly feels like I'm ready, hence my thoughts about where to scatter Marco's ashes."

"The beach is a perfect place, and near enough for you to visit when you need to feel close to him." Penny's phone buzzed and she excused herself saying she had an appointment with a couple who'd restored a property and were thinking of doing holiday lets.

***

The smell of roasting lamb filled the kitchen and Rachel opened the window to let out the steam before draining and adding the par-boiled potatoes to the roasting tin. Knowing Luca's taste, she tossed in a few extra garlic cloves and another sprig of rosemary she had picked from the garden earlier. On the chopping board lay broccoli florets ready to be steamed and beside them sat a shop-bought cheesecake defrosting beneath a netting cloche.

Rachel opened the fridge and checked that the wine she put in the door was suitably chilled; maybe a glass to calm her nerves would help. She'd enjoyed dinner with Luca many times before but knowing that this one was to discuss his job she was apprehensive.

The gravel drive crunched as a car drove over it and she looked below and saw Luca climb out of his Alfa. He walked around to the passenger side and opened the door, for a moment her heart stopped, had he brought Mirella with him? Her fear was assuaged when he lifted out a potted plant and a carrier bag that clinked with bottles.

The main entrance was open, so she didn't need to go downstairs to let him inside. In readiness she reopened the fridge and removed the cork from the chilled *Trebbiano*, pouring two glasses. A knock sounded at her door and she opened it to find Luca and Rosa standing outside. "Look who I found outside," Luca said as he stepped inside after kissing Rachel on both cheeks, his eyes dipping in an apology.

Huffing and puffing, Rosa walked into the apartment and picked up a glass of wine from the counter before saying, "We'll need another glass. It's such a struggle for an old woman to climb so many steps." Rachel shrugged and let out a long sigh remembering the old woman had told her once she couldn't climb the stairs. She removed another glass from the cupboard and turning around she saw that Rosa had opened the oven and looked inside. "*Arrosto di agnello.*"

"Yes," Rachel said, "I thought a roast would be nice now that the evenings are cooling down."

"*Con patate?*"

"Yes, with potatoes."

"Perfetto," Rosa said as she dropped into a chair beside the balcony doors where the voile curtains moved in the breeze.

Luca mouthed, "I'm sorry," as he put the wine he'd brought with him inside the fridge. "I got this for you," he slid the potted succulent across the worktop. "It's a money plant, it'll bring you wealth." Rachel picked up the pot and after thanking him she walked across to the bookcase and placed it on a shelf before returning to her cooking.

As they ate dinner Luca complimented Rachel on the lamb with Rosa adding that it needed a little longer in the oven. Rachel wanted to say that the English didn't like their lamb cremated but she held her counsel and just smiled. As the plates were cleared away and the cheesecake was placed on the table Rosa sniffed loudly but didn't refuse a slice. Luca poured more drinks for everyone and after, as they pushed back their chairs, they drank wine and nibbled on biscotti.

"I never thought I'd see myself sitting here again," Rosa said, her words slightly slurring. "I had come to believe the hotel would remain empty."

"Would you like a coffee?" Rachel asked.

"No." Rosa drank her wine in one mouthful and held out the empty glass for Luca to refill. "Getting old is a curse," she said before taking another gulp of wine. "All you are left with are those memories that you are fortunate enough to remember, but age steals so many others. Sometimes, something I thought I'd forgotten makes itself known and I'm transported back to my previous life."

"When the hotel closed, did you never think of moving away?" Rachel asked.

"I couldn't, I was waiting."

"Waiting? What for?" Luca topped up Rachel's glass and before he put the bottle back Rosa's was thrust out towards him again.

"My love. One day I prayed he would return." Rosa's words were now merging and as she slipped into dialect Rachel found it hard to understand what the old woman was saying, and Luca's eyes widened as Rosa began to ramble.

"We loved each other but when my father discovered our love, he sent him away. My mother did the same with our baby. Gave it away, sent to live with an aunt in Tollo so that no shame came to our door."

Rachel leaned forward and patted Rosa's hand, the old woman looked into her face and beaming said, "Now that his stars have been repaired, I can imagine he's here again." Rosa's head slumped and a tear squeezed itself out and upon reaching her chin it dropped into her wine. "I don't know why he never returned. Maybe he tried but –" A loud snore followed and Luca and Rachel looked at each other and chuckled. Luca took the glass from her as Rachel went into the bedroom to fetch a blanket.

"I think I should be going," Luca said standing up and nodding towards Rosa he said. "Do you think she'll be okay?"

"Yes," Rachel said, "I'll let her sleep it off, and in the morning, I'll be on hand to dole out the paracetamol."

Rachel escorted Luca down to the lobby and standing in the open doorway she watched as he pressed his key fob and in an instant, the driveway was illuminated by the flashing amber lights as the car unlocked. His hair shone in the moonlight, giving it a blueish hue beneath the plum-coloured sky, she wondered how it would feel running her fingers through it, mussing up his carefully styled locks.

The clicking call of a nightjar made her put her thoughts aside and Luca pointed towards the cypress trees, showing her where the birdsong was coming from.

Before he drove away the driver's window slid down and he said, "Sleep well, Rachel. Tomorrow we shall talk about my job."

Chapter Thirty-Five

As usual, the view from the roof terrace took her breath away. The early morning sky was streaked with oranges and reds and the rolling of the sea made it look like it was vibrating with colour. In the distance, the trabocco was in shadow, a sleeping black and spindly dragon. *We must book dinner on one soon, Luca will know a good one*, she thought and then stopped and asked herself, "When did 'I' become 'we'?"

She'd been thinking about Luca more since their conversation about the project manager position. He'd been very understanding and told her he realised the job would only last as long as the building work. With the orto completed she'd worried he might decide to move on, but as he'd pointed out, the gardens needed tending daily and there was also the wedding gazebo to build. She knew she wanted him to stay and had spent the night before in bed dreaming up new positions and job titles to offer him. He had suggested that he remain as the gardener, she'd suggested 'groundsman' and he'd laughed saying a fancy title was still the same job when pulling out weeds and adding ointment to wasp stings.

She locked the door to the roof and carried her empty coffee mug into the kitchen, dropping it inside the sink. Looking at the clock she calculated that she had three hours before her solitary ceremony on the beach. She glanced across at the dress hanging from the top of the bookcase. A lemon off-the-shoulder midi with lacy puff sleeves to show off her tan. "Marco's day will not be a day for wearing sombre colours," she'd told Louise during one of their late-night phone calls. "It'll be a celebration and I plan to look fabulous for him."

After showering she pulled on a bathrobe and with wet feet leaving prints on the stairs she walked downstairs and switched on the computer behind the reception desk. Marco's ashes were placed on top of the desk; Rachel had moved him there the night before so he could have a final night alone in his hotel foyer.

As the screen blinked into life she walked into the kitchen and opening the fridge took out a small bottle of *succo di pera*. She shook the bottle of pear juice pulled the ring pull off and drank straight from the bottle as she made her way back to the desk. Opening the email folder, the PC pinged telling her she had new messages and she quickly scanned them noticing two were booking confirmations for the following summer. "More bookings, my darling," she told him, "I think *Le Stelle* is on track for a successful first year."

The sound of a car made her look up; she wasn't expecting anyone, she'd given the staff the day off. Without time to run upstairs to dress as the knocker sounded on the wooden door, she called out, "Who is it?"

"It's me," came the reply.

Rachel half-ran, half-slid across the floor and flung open the door to see Louise standing on the steps. "How When Why?" she blurted out, happy to see her best friend standing there.

"How, by aeroplane. When, yesterday and why, because I can't let you go through today unsupported and alone." Rachel stood with her mouth open, overwhelmed by the kindness of her best friend. "Well, can I come inside?"

"Of course." Rachel stepped aside and then noticed Luca standing at the side of his car. "Luca picked you up?"

"Yes, I was on the evening flight, he met me at the airport and let me stay at his place last night so I could surprise you today."

"You've certainly done that." Rachel turned to Luca and mouthed a thank you and after he'd delivered Louise's cabin bag into the foyer, he said his goodbyes and drove away.

"You look stunning," Louise said as Rachel spun around to show her the dress she'd chosen. "I could fancy you in that – if I was of that persuasion."

"I got it in Lanciano. There's a nice little boutique opposite the bank."

"Then we shall pay it a visit while I'm here."

"I'm so glad you're here. I was going to ask if you'd come, but you've already been out twice this year."

"I couldn't let you do this alone."

"But what about work, were they okay with you taking more time off?"

"I quit a week ago, I'm taking a leaf out of your book and going solo." Rachel stood open-mouthed again. "I'm now freelance, working remotely."

"Good for you." Rachel stepped forward and hugged Louise. "So, you can stay for more than a couple of days?"

"Try and stop me."

Rachel was making toast and scrambling eggs while Louise unpacked her things and as she re-entered the sitting room handed her a plate. The two friends sat on the balcony, both with napkins tucked into the front of their dresses and ate their breakfasts. From below them, in the groves came the buzz of petrol-powered olive harvesting machines, around the men wielding these tools that looked like a grass strimmer with a comb attached were other friends and family either using handheld olive combs or laying nets beneath the next tree to be picked from. A tractor stood idle for now, plastic crates balanced precariously on its trailer. Louise and Rachel sat watching the harvest; marvelling at the workers' efficiency until it was time to leave for the beach.

The walk down to the beach was taken in silence. Rachel glanced across at Rosa's as they walked past and saw no signs of life inside the little white house. A breeze sent the perfume from Rosa's rose garden spiralling across the lane delivering smiles to the faces of the women walking in silence. Ahead of them a cat lying on the top step down to the beach yawned, stretched and then went back to sleep. It didn't move as they reached it and they stepped over the sleeping feline, that deigned to open one eye and look at them questioningly.

As they descended the steps Rachel noticed a small group of people gathered below. "I hope you don't mind, but they all wanted to be here to support you," Louise said. Rachel just shook her head. As they stepped onto the beach, she saw Rosa standing beside Luca. Penny was talking with Mole and Ivan, and Sprog was sitting on the sand arranging shells into a picture.

Rosa stepped forward and took one of Rachel's hands in both of hers. "We can leave if you wish," she said.

"No, I'm glad you're all here," Rachel replied before leaning forward and placing a kiss on the old woman's wrinkled cheek. Letting go of Rosa, Rachel cleared her throat and said, "I'm not going to make any speeches, but I would like to say. It has made me enormously happy to find you all here today to support me and help me to say goodbye to Marco." There followed a mumble of voices from the group but no one spoke up.

Rachel opened the tube and handed the lid to Louise, who squeezed her shoulder in support. Slowly walking to the edge of the shore Rachel said a final goodbye to her husband in her head and then stood for a few seconds looking out to sea.

As the wash from a tide ebbed away, she scattered the contents of Marco's tube in a straight line, completing the task just as a new wave rolled towards her, picking up his ashes before retreating with them back out to the open water.

Aldo IX

Aldo closed the gate behind himself, walked up to Rosa's front door and knocked. As the door opened, he could hear the old lady muttering to herself, "Who is calling on me at this hour?" Surprised to see Aldo standing there she asked him what he wanted, he told her he needed to speak with her about a potentially important issue.

"Potentially important, I'm intrigued. You'd better come inside then." Rosa stepped aside and Aldo walked into the small kitchen and sitting room.

The room reminded him of his mother's kitchen back in Naples. White plastered walls with dark framed pictures hanging from them, the large open fireplace that gave off very little heat to the room but was good for slow-cooked recipes. Above the sink was a wire rack where a handful of plates and several glasses were stored. Rosa held up a bottle of grappa and Aldo nodded, watching her as she removed two shot glasses before sitting down and pouring a measure.

"What can I do for you..." Rosa paused trying to recall his name.

"Aldo."

"Yes, Aldo."

He took his phone out of his pocket and placed it on the table before taking a sip of his drink. "*Buono*," he said putting the glass down. He took a deep breath and said, "Rosa, I may have got confused and what I think I know, may be wrong."

"What do you think you know, Aldo?"

"Maybe it will be easier to show you and if I'm wrong the conversation can then end and I shall leave you in peace." He picked up his phone and with a few stabs at the screen he turned it around so she could see the photograph he'd asked his brother to send him.

Rosa's mouth fell open and her eyes bulged as she looked at the image on the screen. She grabbed at her glass and tipped the fiery liquid into her mouth, coughed a little and then refilled her glass and drank again. "How do you know this man?" she said, her voice almost a whisper.

"Giacomo was –"

"Was?"

"My uncle passed away six months ago." Aldo looked away as Rosa's face crumpled a little and she dabbed at her eyes with a tea towel that was lying on the table.

"Uncle?" she said, and Aldo nodded.

He reached inside his pocket and removed the ring that Giacomo had worn. He placed it on the table and slid it over towards Rosa, who tentatively picked it up,

"I remember this," she said as Aldo topped up his glass. Rosa left the table and stepped inside her bedroom. Aldo could hear her searching for something. Coming back to the table, she said, "I am shocked by this revelation. Your suspicions may prove true Aldo, I need to show you something."

She placed a photograph on the table and picking it up Aldo saw a couple smiling for the camera. One of those people was Giacomo and he assumed the other was Rosa.

"You are the woman in the photo frame. Ever since he came home my uncle had your photograph on the wall beside his bed. But we had no idea who the woman in the frame was. Sadly since the accident, poor Giacomo couldn't remember either."

"Accident?" Rosa sat upright. "Accident, what accident?"

"Many years ago, he was driving back to Naples and his car collided with a lorry just outside Caserta and he suffered a head injury and –"

"When was this?" Rosa asked interrupting him.

"It was back in 1970, I remember as it was the year that Emilio Colombo became Prime Minister." Aldo looked across at Rosa, she swallowed hard and tears filled her eyes before he continued. "He was hospitalised for many weeks before we brought him home. Because of this head injury, his memory was lost and over the years only fragments returned, until this last year when he developed dementia and he said, excerpts from his memories would return to him in his dreams."

Rosa's fingers raked through her white hair. "I always knew something had happened. He'd promised faithfully to return, and I believed him." Dipping a biscotti into her grappa she sucked the spirit from the hard almond biscuit before continuing. "My parents were wary of him, that age-old suspicion of Neapolitans, but. Giacomo was unlike any man I'd ever met." Rosa hesitated and cried silently, tears rolling down her cheeks to drop onto the table.

"Tell me about him," Aldo said after she had composed herself again.

"He came to the hotel to paint a fresco in the dining room and we all marvelled at his talents." She paused as her recollections caught up with her words. "Along with his passion for art, he was also a lover of great literature."

"His bookcase was filled with classics," said Aldo, "works by Sophocles, Manzoni and many others."

"Giacomo would tell me stories from the Iliad. He had brought a copy of Shakespeare's *Julius Caesar* with him and he had read me passages from it. Aldo put his hand over his glass as Rosa went to refill it. "You're driving?" he nodded.

Rosa picked up the ring and examined the stone as if she remembered every inclusion in the emerald. "I'm glad my father was wrong when he said Giacomo was a typical Neapolitan who'd leave a broken heart in his wake."

"The family always hoped he'd remember, my mother, his sister, said she knew the woman in the frame was her brother's great love, she could see it behind his eyes and prayed they'd be reunited one day. If only things had been different."

"If only. Two small words that cannot change history." She tilted her head back and looked up as if searching for stars.

"If only, the accident hadn't happened." She looked back directly at Aldo.

"If only, I'd been strong enough to stand up to my parents."

Aldo gave Rosa a quizzical look and she told him that she had been pregnant when Giacomo had returned to Naples.

"He was going home to tell his family, he promised he'd be away from me no longer than a week. When he didn't return my parents waited for the birth of our daughter and within days, she was passed over to an aunt in Tollo to save the shame I was bringing to the family."

"Tollo." Aldo questioned then softly said, "Silvana?"

Rosa nodded before adding, "She doesn't know and I'd like it to stay that way."

She handed him back the ring, which he took, looked at briefly and then pressed into the palm of her hand, before saying goodnight and taking his leave.

Chapter Thirty-Six

With just 48 hours until the first guests arrived, the hotel was a chaotic mix of raised voices and neglected tasks. Silvana had double-checked all the bedrooms had been dressed to her high standard, re-instructing room stewards where necessary. Penny had dropped by and was sitting at the computer checking emails and making sure deposit payments for the summer season had cleared at the bank.

Rachel took a letter from the *casetta* beside the main doors and tore open the envelope. "Oh bugger," she said under her breath, then called Luca over. "Aldo's gone," she handed the letter to Luca, "he says he's grateful for the work and kindness he's received but he's going back to Naples to be with his family."

"I wish he'd given more notice," Luca said. There's still much work to complete before guests start to arrive. The oleander hedges still need to be pruned."

"I can help you," Rachel said.

"You are too busy inside the hotel. I'll ask Mirella to help me… if that's okay?"

"Sure," Rachel said with little enthusiasm.

Rachel watched as Luca handed Mirella a pair of gardening gloves and secateurs and began to show her how to prune the oleander bushes. They looked good together Rachel thought despite the stab of jealousy she had begun to feel whenever she saw them together. The familiar tinkle of laughter made her wonder what Luca had said to make her laugh.

Lunchtime arrived and the chef had created a taster menu for the staff, Rachel looked out of the window and saw Mirella and Luca standing beside the jasmine hedge that had been trimmed earlier that morning. They looked to be having some sort of disagreement and Rachel unable to curb her curiosity opened the window to listen.

"If you don't tell Rachel, I shall," Mirella said.

"You can't," Luca said. "It will change everything between us. Rachel has become a great friend and I don't want to jeopardise that." Mirella huffed and having heard enough Rachel gently closed the window.

***

Rachel was sitting at the kitchen table checking her handwritten card index against the spreadsheet on her laptop. "Why do you do that, isn't it just making more work for yourself?" Louise said as she drained pasta in the sink.

"Italy has yet to embrace the digital age with most accountants and the tax offices preferring old-fashioned hard copies," Rachel replied, "the broadband isn't so reliable here at the coast."

Louise poured the contents from a jar of pesto over the spaghetti before taking a bottle of wine from the fridge.

"It's such a shame about Aldo leaving, I thought he got on so well with Luca," Rachel said, almost as if she were thinking aloud.

"Are you pleased that Luca has agreed to stay on?" Louise placed two bowls of pasta on the table. "Eat up while it's still hot," she said before opening the wine.

"You sound just like my mother. Yes mum, I won't let it go cold."

"You haven't answered my question."

"Yes, I am glad Luca has agreed to stay on, albeit in a lesser role. I was thrilled that he said, he was happier now with just the responsibility of the garden."

Picking up a remote she pressed play and a tenor began to sing an accompaniment to their dinner.

"I knew there was something I'd forgotten to tell you," Louise said. "When I stayed at Luca's I saw two tickets on his sideboard."

"Tickets?"

"To see *Il Volo* in concert in Rome."

"He must be taking Mirella. I hope she enjoys it."

"Now you know you don't mean that." Louise was right.

"I do," protested Rachel, her eyes moving upwards in their sockets as she remembered watching Mirella as she left for the day. She'd half-skipped, half-danced towards Luca's car, happiness in her every step. She hated herself for being jealous.

"Have you asked him if they're involved?"

"It's obvious, isn't it? They arrive together every day, she's always talking to him and there's that annoying little laugh she has whenever he says anything to her."

Louise twisted the spaghetti around her fork and mumbled as she chewed, "Do you think you're ready for another relationship?"

Rachel nodded her head, "I think so. Saying goodbye to Marco at the beach was a turning point."

"And it made you realise how you felt about Luca?"

Another nod, "Yes, but know that he's only ever seen me as a friend."

Louise collected up the empty bowls and Rachel refilled their glasses as her phone pinged. Louise shouted at her from the kitchen to leave it, saying she needed a night off and whatever it was could wait until tomorrow.

"But what if it's a booking enquiry?"

"It'll still be there in the morning. You need to set aside some time to relax, no one expects you to be working 24 hours a day." Louise placed another bottle of wine on the table reached across and pulled Rachel's phone away from her. Using her teeth she tore into a box of chocolates and soon the two friends were relaxed and ready to drink wine and talk into the depths of the night.

***

Still feeling a little fragile the following afternoon, Rachel heard raised voices coming from the reception and halfway down the stairs she saw Silvana talking to a young couple with suitcases at their feet. "*Non è possibile, siete in anticipo di un Giorno,*" she heard Silvana say.

"Can I help?" Rachel said stepping behind the desk.

"We've made a real blunder," the woman said. "Or rather my husband *here* has."

"What seems to be the problem?"

"We've arrived a day too early. I know it's an inconvenience but is there any chance we can add it to our stay?"

"We don't officially open until tomorrow; the rooms are ready but I'm afraid we have no kitchen staff or room stewards in today."

"We can eat out," the man said, "but if you could accommodate us, it would save us having to look elsewhere for one night."

"Of course, I can't see it being a problem." Rachel took their names, added the extra day onto their account and asked Silvana to show them up to their room.

The remainder of the day went by without further incidents.

Silvana stomped around for much of it with a peevish look on her face. Rosa popped in for a glass of wine after dinner and sat beside the tall windows, the lavender lights illuminating her face as she chatted with Luca. They both looked up as the guests returned and as the husband went to the bar his wife stood looking up at the painted ceiling. "This is magnificent," the woman said. "Very apt for a hotel called, The Stars."

"It was already here when I came," Rachel told her, "and a friend restored it."

"*Vedi quella stella al centro*," Rosa said to the confused guests who looked at her quizzically. "*È Altair*."

Luca quickly translated telling them that the central star was the brightest one in the Aquila constellation. "L'Aquila means eagle and the town is the capital of Abruzzo."

Rachel wondered how many times they would say that to guests over the course of a year as these new ones thanked him for the information.

"Is everything okay with your room, do you need anything?" said Rachel shaking herself from her thoughts.

"Everything is perfect," the man said. "Thank you for being so accommodating earlier."

"Why don't you take a seat and I'll fetch a couple of bottles of prosecco, we can all celebrate the hotel's opening together."

Luca followed Rachel into the kitchen and closed the door behind him, as she opened the fridge he said. "There's something I must tell you."

"Is it about taking Mirella to Rome to see *Il Volo*?" Rachel asked choosing two bottles of prosecco."

"What do you mean?" Luca said his brow knotted in confusion.

"Louise told me she'd seen the tickets when she stayed over, I thought you must be taking Mirella."

At that moment Louise popped her head around the door and said that Penny was on the telephone. "I'll have to talk to her," Rachel said handing the bottles to Louise, "I hope it's not bad news," and she scuttled out of the kitchen.

Rachel replaced the receiver and sighed. "Bad news?" Luca said looking at her over the desk.

"No Penny just wanted me to know when she comes tomorrow, to help me check in the guests, she needs to bring Sale with her."

"I can look after the dog. Now you can tell me why you think I take Mirella to Rome?"

"Because she's your girlfriend."

Luca began to laugh loudly and everyone stopped talking and looked across at him. Louise called him over, asking him to open the prosecco.

"I'll fetch the glasses," Rachel said. With the dining room door closed behind her she groaned, why did I mention the tickets and why did he laugh at me? she thought. "I wish I hadn't said anything now, he'll think I'm an idiot."

"You think Mirella is my girlfriend?" Rachel turned around and saw Luca had entered the room, "Mirella is my cousin, not my girlfriend."

"I'm sorry I just assumed because I overheard you both talking and Mirella was saying you had to tell me that –"

"Yes," Luca said, "That I think I shall have to stop working here." Rachel's heart lurched and she painted a fake smile across her face.

"Let's get these glasses to everyone otherwise the prosecco will be flat by the time it's served." Rachel pushed open the door and returned to her guests. She looked across at Luca as he entered the room and she felt incipient tears beginning to prick her eyes. How would she cope without him, she'd already lost one man she loved and now it looked like she was going to lose another before she'd had the chance to find out if she could truly love him.

She escaped to the kitchen and was wiping away tears when the door opened and Luca entered. He asked if she was okay and she gave him a weak smile. "Why do you want to leave? Are you not happy?"

"I'm perfectly happy."

"It's just that it's getting harder for me to be around you."

The door opened and Rosa stepped inside and Rachel hoped her irritation at being disturbed again didn't show on her face. The old woman said she was leaving and thanked her for a lovely evening.

"I'll walk you down the lane," said Luca.

Left alone Rachel wondered what he meant by 'harder for me to be around you,' Had she offended him in some way? She searched her mind but couldn't recall any time she might have said something that would have upset him. Minutes later the door opened again and Louise told her the guests had retired for the night and she was going up to the apartment.

Seeing something was wrong she asked, "Are you all right?"

Rachel nodded, holding back the tears that now threatened to burst forth, "It's Luca, he wants to leave the hotel."

"Why?"

"I don't know."

"It's dark outside," Luca said as he returned. "*Le nuvole autunnali nascondono la luna* – the autumn clouds are hiding the moon," he repeated in English for Louise, who said goodnight and left the kitchen.

Rachel stood looking at him the tears now rolling down her cheeks, Luca took the tissue she had scrunched up and wiped them away.

He asked what was wrong, "*Cosa c'è che non va?*"

"What have I done to make you want to leave?" she sniffed. "Have I upset you?"

He took her hand and led her out of the kitchen and into the reception area. The wall lights illuminated the stars on the ceiling making them sparkle.

Luca handed her a glass of prosecco. "I am not upset with you, maybe a little with myself." She sipped her wine as she looked at him, her eyes questioning. "I am finding it hard to control the feelings I have."

"Feelings?"

"Yes, I want us to be more than friends, but I know you don't see me in that way."

"I do," she blurted out and choked on her wine resulting in much coughing and back slapping.

Suitably recovered she said nervously, changing the subject, "The ceiling looks beautiful. Cosmo has done such a good job of the restoration. Have you noticed that when the light catches the Altair crystal it sparkles with a yellow glow."

"I hadn't noticed," Luca said pulling her into him. "I see only you, not the stars," and beneath the twinkling lights on the ceiling, they shared their first kiss.

THE END

Acknowledgements

There are so many people to acknowledge for the creation of this book, so I'll break it down into two groups.

Gli Italiani - The Italians
Thanks go to Piero Nasuti for his kindness and support during my time in Abruzzo, for helping me not only with the language and finding me a job, but for allowing me to become a part of his family, so I also have to thank, tutta la famiglia Nasuti e anche tutti della famiglia Crognale. Anche e miei amici, Massimo, Nicoletta e Matilde. (I have fond memories of Nicoletta telling me that the Italian for scissors is forbici.) Without these people, I would never have learned about the culture, the lifestyle and those subtle nuances of what it means to be Italian.

Also, thanks go to Faye, Steve, Amanda and Alberico – let's do a Chinese buffet in Lanciano again soon.

The English – L'Inglese
Thanks as always, go to the Renegade Writers', whose words of wisdom and sometimes brutal feedback have enabled me to be the author I am slowly becoming.

Once again, my heartfelt thanks go to my excellent beta readers, Jan Edwards and Misha Herwin and also to Faye Wilson who gave this book a test drive in Abruzzo, Italy for me.

Thanks also go to Kerry Parsons and Bowen's Book Publicity for their support and Flatfield Books for putting up with some of my more madcap ideas for a book before delivering a resounding, no.

Where is Abruzzo? The region is situated in central Italy, east of Rome on the Adriatic Coast. Made up of four provinces, this book is set in the Chieti (key-ett-ee) province. Sant'Andrea is a fictional village set outside the marina town of San Vito Chietino, which like all other towns and locations in the book is real and well worthy of a summer visit to indulge in the seafood and gelati.

Under Italian Stars, has had many guises throughout its 14-year history. Originally, I wanted to write a comedy based on the story behind the Medici Diamond. This then morphed into a thriller, but thrillers take up a lot of headspace in creation, so it was shelved. My job at Italy Magazine as a features and travel writer took over, along with the restoration of a farmhouse in the hills that was to become my home. Other books were written and The Hotel in Italy (working title) was resurrected in 2022 and in 2023 after another final edit, it was ready for publication.

Printed in Great Britain
by Amazon